Lie Lie Lullaby

Katherine Black

Best Book Editions

BBE Best Book Editions

1 3 5 7 9 10 8 6 4 2

Copyright © Katherine Black, 2023

The right of Katherine Black to be identified as the author of this Work has been asserted by her in accordance with the Copyright, Designs and Patents Act 1988

All rights reserved

First published in 2023 by Best Book Editions, bestbookeditors.com

Paperback ISBN 9798397615419

This publication may not be used, reproduced, stored or transmitted in any way, in whole or in part, without the express written permission of the author. Nor may it be otherwise circulated in any form of binding or cover other than that in which it has been published and without a similar condition imposed on subsequent users or purchasers

All characters in this publication are fictitious, and any similarity to real persons, alive or dead, is coincidental

Cover by Best Book Editions

A CIP catalogue record of this book is available from the British Library

Contents

Dedication	VI
Message from Katherine	VII
1. Chapter One	1
2. Chapter Two	12
3. Chapter Three	30
4. Chapter Four	36
5. Chapter Five.	48
6. Chapter Six	57
7. Chapter Seven	67
8. Chapter Eight	77
9. Chapter Nine	89
10. Chapter Ten	96
11. Chapter Eleven	108
12. Chapter Twelve	116

13.	Chapter Thirteen	125
14.	Chapter Fourteen	136
15.	Chapter Fifteen	148
16.	Chapter Sixteen	169
17.	Chapter Seventeen	179
18.	Chapter Eighteen	192
19.	Chapter Nineteen	200
20.	Chapter Twenty	206
21.	Chapter Twenty-one	219
22.	Chapter Twenty-two	232
23.	Chapter Twenty-three	239
24.	Chapter Twenty-four	249
25.	Chapter Twenty-five	258
26.	Chapter Twenty-six	270
27.	Chapter Twenty-seven	281
28.	Chapter Twenty-eight	290
29.	Chapter Twenty-nine	293
30.	Chapter Thirty	302
31.	Chapter Thirty-one	315
32.	Chapter Thirty-Two	325

33. Chapter Thirty-three   332

To "Robin Hill"

The Silas Nash series has some character evolution throughout the books. However, each novel is a contained story that stands alone and the books can be read in or out of sequence.
I hope you enjoy my books.

To get in touch you can email me at katherine@bestbookeditors.com

I'd love to chat to you in my reader group. **Katherine Black Reader Group https://www.facebook.com/groups/1229439867780291**

If you enjoy my book, I'd appreciate it if you would leave me a review on Amazon/Goodreads

While I don't consider there are any major triggers in this book, I suggest reader discretion.

Chapter One

DCI Silas Nash felt the familiar rush of blood to his brain as his boss, Bronwyn Lewis, handed him a new case file.

They were the Cumbria Homicide Division, and they were ready to put a bad guy to bed. Lewis was a great boss, at times a dragon, sometimes a friend, and occasionally a mother to the younger members of the team.

It was one of the toughest jobs imaginable, and when it got overwhelming for one of them, she'd slide open her desk drawer and quietly pull out a box of tissues and a bar of Galaxy.

She was only a couple of inches shorter than Nash, who was six feet. Lewis was fire and ice, with flaming red hair, scarlet lipstick, and the coolest green eyes of a typical Irish girl—she had the temper to boot if you got the wrong side of her, which Nash liked to do at least three times a week. But there was nothing typical about Bronwyn Lewis, and, in return for her loyalty, she expected the best from her team. She trusted Nash, and he got results. God help him if he didn't.

Nash was meticulous. Brown, his DI, always joked that he looked like a mature Catalogue Model. 'David Beckham's dad,' was a favourite jibe. So he liked to dress well and keep his goatee trimmed, what was wrong with good tailoring? Nash took a lot of ribbing from his team, and he wouldn't have it any other way. When they worked, they worked to the bone, they sweated blood and went all out to get justice for their victims. Every dead face pinned to their whiteboard was still a person. They had mothers and fathers, children, and friends. And they were loved. Nash tuned into them and took time to get to know them—and then he tuned into their killer.

He liked a relaxed atmosphere and made sure he was approachable to his team, but they never doubted who was in charge.

The incident room was bright, sunlight danced on the floor, and they had the standard set up of tables and chairs for forty people, though most of them sat on the tables, and ignored the chairs. The initial team was made up of twelve people, with room for more officers if they needed drafting in. It was a tradition that every first team brief was a celebration. They were celebrating another family getting justice for their loved one.

Their attitude was positive, and they didn't harbour the possibility of failure. Coffee was served in hot urns, and trays of pastries were laid out on the top table.

This was often a happy room, but sometimes it was filled with untold sadness and sorrow, and for that reason, they had purposefully chosen the room that had the most sunshine. Shirt-sleeves were the order of the day in hot weather and industrial-sized fans. Lewis signed a standing order for fresh flowers once a week to commemorate the victims and brighten the room and the artwork had been chosen with care to be upbeat and mood-lifting. The incident room was where the officers started most days.

The team was assembled, and Nash looked around the incident room at his people. 'Listen up, team.'

'What we got, sir?' PC Jay Bowes asked. 'If it includes any jollies to Greece, I hope it's my turn.'

'No such luck, Bowes. We've got an interesting one, a bit different, but it's going to be a lot of legwork and paper-chasing.'

The whole team groaned.

'Interesting, how?' Sergeant DS Phillip Renshaw asked.

'I'm glad you asked. Cold case.'

They groaned again.

'How cold?' Renshaw asked.

'Could be worse, still cold enough to cause frostbite, though. But this story is going to blow your mind.' That got them. 'A woman is duped by a bloke on a dating site. A professional con man and he took her for an idiot. Happens all the time, nothing new there. But and this is where it gets interesting, eight years later, the same bloke pops up in her email using a different name. She was hurt and filled with hatred. She decides to play him. But this guy is good—with a capital G. She's no match for him, and he rises to the challenge. Get this. On their very first date, he convinces her to marry him.'

The team reacted with shock and then laughed. 'What an absolute tool she is,' Bowes said.

'You'd think, wouldn't you? And she was stupid when it came to him, but this woman was no idiot.'

Nash took his marker and added initial intel to the whiteboard. 'The case is three years old. The woman, Clara Watts, was found suffocated and dumped in woods in the middle of nowhere. Take a left off the A590 at Gilpin Bridge, drive into the wild for a couple of miles, and you'll be surrounded by wood and marshland. That's where her body was found. There are less scenic places to die.'

'Remind me to order a place for when my time comes. I wouldn't want it to be booked out,' Renshaw said. 'What else have we got on her?'

'She was seeing our suspect, a much older man, at the time of her death. We know he's conned a lot of other vulnerable women. He's a bad one, by all accounts. He conned her twice, eight years apart, and the night she was murdered, she took ten thousand pounds with her for them to start a business. The poor cow thought they were getting married. She'd bought the wedding dress, booked the venue, the lot.'

'Didn't she learn her lesson after the first time?'

'He told her he was a reformed character, apparently. She found out he was a married man the first time, but that was after he'd dropped her like yesterday's crap. The second time, he told her he'd left his wife to track her down and be with her it was heady stuff. But if you believe that—players rarely leave their wives for a bit of fluff on the side.'

Nash saw the look pass between DCI Brown and Renshaw and ignored it. 'He couldn't live without her, blah, blah, blah. But believe me, this story gets weirder the more you delve into it. That's just the pocket version.'

The word weird went down a treat, and he saw his team sit up straighter and pay attention. Better. He had their focus again.

'As you all know by now. We've had some dealings, for want of a better word, with a renowned psychic called Conrad Snow.' Nash waited for the jokes and spooky noises to die down. 'You'll also know that I've always been sceptical about these things and was, let's just say, reluctant for Mr Snow to have any involvement with us. However, I can't deny that he was very helpful in the Greece case.'

Lawson had his hand up to speak.

'Lawson?'

'I heard you're bringing this bloke in to work with us. You took a pretty hard stance against him. What changed your mind?'

'He was instrumental in saving at least one young man's life. That's something I can't ignore.'

He picked up a book from the desk he was sitting on the edge of and handed it to Molly Brown. 'Here you go, Brown, some bedtime reading for you.'

'What is it, sir?'

'The woman's diary. This is the first, and there's another one when you've finished. Sign the second one out when you sign this one back in. Enjoy.'

'And here we go again. You do it every time we have a briefing, sir.'

'Christ. What have I done now, Brown?'

'Sexism. Again, sir. Why do you assume that because I'm a female, I'm the best officer to read this woman's crappy diary?'

Nash was up late the night before. He hadn't had much sleep, and he didn't function well when he was tired. He stormed across the room and tore the book out of Brown's hands, handing it to Renshaw.

'You don't do yourself any favours, Brown. It had nothing to do with your gender, and everything to do with the fact that you're next in rank to me—and, as I've already read it, I wanted to clue you in. But, no worries. I'm sure Renshaw is man enough to read it.' He handed the diary to Renshaw, who was next in the pecking order. 'Brown, you're on numberplate tracing this morning.'

'That's not fair. That's the PC's job.'

'Very true, but you've declined your job because I offended your delicate circuitry. In which case, I've got nothing else for you. Right, I'm too busy for nonsense this morning. Chances are this man may have already killed other victims before he got to Clara Watts, and there's even more likelihood that once he got the taste for it, he did it again.'

'You reckon we've got another serial killer, sir?' PC Paul Lawson asked.

'That's what we're going to find out. There isn't a shred of evidence to support it, so far. So I think probably not, but we have to keep in mind that if he's killed once, there may be others. However, in a county this size, if unclaimed bodies were popping up, we'd know about it. He was never sent down for Clara Watt's murder, and she's a lady who's screaming for justice from her grave. It's our job to get it for her.'

'That's not like you, sir. It sounds as if you've hung, drawn and quartered this bloke before we've even spoken to him. What if he's innocent?' Renshaw said.

'He's guilty. He put a bag over our victim's head, and when that didn't kill her fast enough for him, he strangled her and left her for the worms. The only damned reason he didn't go down for Clara Watt's murder was insufficient evidence.'

'Nothing else?' Lewis asked. She'd read the intel and was up to date on the case.

'That, and the fact that the rat went to ground and nobody had a clue who he was.'

'Cold cases are tough, sir. What makes you think we can turn up anything new after three years?' Lawson asked.

'Thanks for that dazzling appraisal of our abilities, Lawson, you little ray of sunshine, you. We'll turn over every blade of grass and pick up every used fag-butt in a five-mile radius of those woods. And, Lawson, we read every report, witness statement, and test result until it talks to us. If there's anything to find, we're going to bloody well find it.'

'Five miles.'

'Not literally, you idiot.'

'What about the murderer? Who is it?'

'That, we have to find out.'

'I thought they had him at the time, sir?' Bowes said.

'They did. And then they let him go. He'd given false info and went straight to ground. It must have been a busy day in the office that day.'

They laughed. Checking info before releasing a suspect was basic policing. It came immediately after colouring books at the age of five and remembering your warrant number.

'Why haven't we got a name, then?' Lawson asked.

'Because he used an alias—two of them actually—and they didn't dig deep enough to find his real name.'

'What were his aliases?' Brown hadn't spoken for a few minutes but was coming out of her sulk, one skinny leg at a time, like a butterfly from a dirty grey chrysalis.

'He's used both Mike Thornton and Steve Thornley. And there may be others.'

'Do you mean Michael and Stephen, sir?'

'If I'd meant that, Brown, I'd have said so. No, the names he used were Mike and Steve. He had a passport and driving licence in the name of Mike Thornton. It's in the file with a fake picture, close enough to the real thing to pass muster. We didn't find any documentation in the name Mike Thornton, but that doesn't mean there wasn't any. He seemed to drop that name a couple of years before he killed Clara Watts.'

Brown was getting to him, but it wasn't her fault he'd had no sleep. He gave her a smile—and got a glare back. He made a mental note to buy cake and then put a red mental line through his mental note because he wouldn't buy a chocolate fancy, or a fairy cake for one of the boys. She was right, he was a misogynistic old bastard.

'So, let that be a lesson to us. This bugger's clever, team. He tricked the system and left them with egg on their faces last time—he's not doing that to us. Because we're the new team, and we're better than the last lot—and we're better than him. Got it?'

'Sir,' they all parroted.

'Another thing to note is that this bloke is charming.' He wrote the word in capital letters on the whiteboard, under the heading MO. 'This isn't just a slimy personality trait. It seems to be his sole Modus Operandi. Without exception, everybody that dealt with him back then said they liked him and bought into his innocence. Right Bowes, Lawson, Patel, and Brown, you're on records. Pull every legal certificate, every illegal document, and anything else you can find. I want the names and stories of other women he catfished—what he got from them, and how they're doing now. This man is, first and foremost, a conman—or he was back then. He may have evolved since. But at the time of the first investigation, he left a lot of broken women in his wake. They are alive and well, and they're the best chance we have of nailing him. I want you to shake them down until their teeth rattle—get every sordid detail. Find out if they'll make credible witnesses. This man destroys lives. I want you guys on the computers and doing the initial legwork. Get new statements. Time has a habit of kicking up dirt they may have forgotten at the time.'

'Sir.'

The four officers were resigned to their lot in life, and Brown didn't look happy. Nash did it to remind her who was boss. Brown had played the role of his daughter during their undercover case in Greece. They were thrown together and it built a strong bond. They were close, and the lines between rank, and more so, between work and friendship, were blurred. Now they were back on home soil, Nash needed to pull her in line and re-establish the professionalism of being part of the bigger team. He was harsh with her, but Brown was career-driven and ambitious. She'd use her position against the younger officers if she thought she had special privileges over them outside of her higher rank. But he didn't want to break her. 'Don't work too hard, Brown. When we track this joker down, I've got a job lined up for you that I think you'll enjoy.'

'That's more like it, What?'

'All in good time. For now, just find him. Let's get this boxed off and put to bed fast. Thanks, everyone.'

As they filed out of the incident room, Nash saw Renshaw nudge Brown in the back. Policing—and particularly working the night shift on surveillance could build strong bonds between patrol partners. He knew Brown and Renshaw had crossed professional lines—but she'd promised Nash it was over.

They'd been having an affair for two years, and it caused a scandal when their personal lives leaked into the department.

He followed them into the custody suite corridor and saw Renshaw grab Brown by the arm and pull her to one side. Nash coughed as he passed them and went into the kitchen to get a cup of tea to take to his desk. It wasn't long before he heard raised voices, and he longed for a radio in the kitchen so he didn't have to hear.

'Leave me alone, Phil.'

'I can't. Why haven't you answered my messages?'

'You know why.'

'I can't stop thinking about you. We need to talk.'

'Not here.'

'Where?'

'Nowhere, Phil. I can't do this.'

'Let me come to yours tonight. Purely professional, I'll bring this sodding diary, and we can go through it together.'

'No.' She walked away, swinging her hips and her ponytail at him as if the tail was a phallus.

'See you at eight. Don't eat,' he shouted.

'Eat my finger, Renshaw.'

Damn.

Nash was furious. He wouldn't approve of any relationship between his officers, but this one was toxic. Phil was married with two kids. His eldest, Dylan, was disabled and his care put a strain on the marriage. Dylan had Asperger's Syndrome and swung between being a joy, and a handful. Phil found his home life hard—but then so did his wife, Sal.

Nash went to his office and poured over the old case files to build a personal timeline of his weekly meetings and interviews, but he couldn't get the problem of Renshaw and Brown out of his head. Instinctively, he knew it was unfinished business, and he had to decide whether to intervene.

Falling in love wasn't illegal. But it was against company policy, and strictly frowned upon to have an inter-departmental relationship. One of them should transfer. However, technically, it was still an advisory caution, not a hard rule that relationships weren't allowed. He only had two roads to go down, he could warn them off as their superior officer. Though their personal lives were down to them as long as it didn't interfere with the department. Or, he could come down on Renshaw. As the lower-ranking officer, he was the most expendable, and Nash could demand that he be transferred to another division.

He could even give him a more official reprimand and suspend him, as he was misappropriating case files by taking the diary assigned as his work to Brown's house. It was petty, but he had his department, and two officers he cared about, to protect. The safety and well-being of the department were his responsibility.

Renshaw was going to Brown's at eight. It left Nash with little choice but to pull him into the office for an informal chat before then. But, when he went to find him, Renshaw had already left the building to conduct his interviews. He'd put in the diary that he was going straight home after his last appointment.

Damn.

Chapter Two

She'd said no. She'd said it hard, and she'd said it clearly, but the man was infuriating. He'd be here, which meant getting her and her house ready for him. She wouldn't change the bedding. That's something she refused to do because he'd be going nowhere near her bedroom, and that was a fact. She kept the place clean, so there wasn't much to do.

Her career meant that she didn't have hours to spend on household tasks and living alone she found that she could keep her small house tidy with half an hour's attention a day. She didn't have much in the way of things. She liked to be uncluttered, but she did appreciate colour in her life. Her living room was a vibrant red, her furniture was good and she had some local artwork on her walls by the same artist who provided the canvases for the station.

At thirty-three she had to work that little bit harder to keep in shape these days. Molly loved yoga, and if she didn't get a session in before work, the world knew about it. She found that it calmed her mind and made way for clear thought. Her body was near-perfect, her skin glowed and her waist-length chestnut hair shone with nutrients and vibrancy. She put a lot of this down to her healthy diet and plenty of yoga. Never enough sex, though, she mused.

The bell rang at ten to eight. To hell with that bloody man. Molly flung the door open. 'I said no. Yet here you are.'

'And if you didn't want to see me, you wouldn't have opened the door,' Phil said.

'And you'd have taken curry for two back to your wife with your tail between your legs.'

'Probably, something like that. Yes. Don't start, Molly. Bloody hell woman, I come in peace.' He held up both hands, one with a takeaway bag and a bottle of red, and the other holding the book.

'You look like the Statue of Liberty. You'd better come in before somebody sees and starts taking selfies with you.'

It was a fast battle quickly won in a long-drawn-out war. She was defeated, and they both knew it. Phil moved in and tried to take her in his arms, but she sidestepped him and busied herself getting plates and glasses. 'You can open the wine. Where does Sal think you are?'

'Overtime.'

'Of course.'

He went to the cutlery drawer where Molly kept her corkscrew. He knew where everything lived. 'It's not a lie. I'm here to work. Unless you want to stop playing games, and I'll forego the pretence. I've missed you, babe.'

'We'll work while we eat.' She was determined not to give an inch.

'I can leave this horrendous diary of somebody bleeding their unimportant life onto the pages until tomorrow? I'd rather talk about us.'

She carried the plates through and left him to bring the uncorked bottle and glasses. 'Bring the diary with you. You've already looked at it, then?'

'Have I hell. "Today, I'm wearing my biggest knickers that come up to my titties." Not a chance.'

She sat beside him on the sofa so they could both see the diary, but she made a point of ramming two fat cushions between them.

'You smell good.'

'That's the curry.' She spooned the food onto their plates and ate hers as she took the book from him. It still had traces of dusting powder on the cover, but it was well smudged in and wouldn't come off on their hands. She'd never admit it, but she was curious to read about this murdered woman's life. She sat back and was aware of Phil's shoulder touching hers. She opened the diary to the first page and held the book between them with one hand while her plate rested on the arm of the sofa.

'I'd rather be watching a movie.'

'Read,' Molly said.

~~~

1st January 2011.

Hello, Diary. It's me again. Clara. I always begin a new year with a wish. It's tradition. I'm not allowed to be greedy and can only wish for one thing. But I have two biggies.

I want to do well in my career, and when it comes down to it, that's the one I've got to wish for because if it goes tits up, I'm doomed.

I've put on weight again, and my other big wish would be to lose it, but that has to take a back burner in the genie stakes. If my plans go well, I'll lose weight anyway, with my job taking on a more physical aspect.

It's the same old story, the weight creeps up when I'm not looking. It's not critical yet.

I eat too much for the amount I move. Simple physics dictates that I need to eat less and move more. That's so unfair. My diet is boring. I either have a ham salad sandwich or a cheese-savoury sandwich. Bread is my demon seed, and I live on the stuff. I don't bother eating properly and just grab picky bits on the go. I live on junk. I'm such a bad role model for my daughter, who does eat properly, and never tires of lecturing me.

So, this year's wish. By this time next year, all I ask is to be turning a financial profit, even if it's only twenty quid a week over the break-even point. More would be nice, because money's tight, and I'd love to give Emily more of the nice things in life. My zoology degree cost me five grand this year and I want to pay it off to be out of debt fast.

I'm a zookeeper, and I'm in line for a promotion to one of the six head keeper positions. Juggling work and a ten-year-old, who has discovered the shallow world of fashion, isn't easy.

~~~

Molly looked up after the end of the first entry. 'Okay. Not much to go on there.'

'Fatty wants to be skinny, so what? It's just waffle. Doesn't every woman want to lose weight, apart from the underweight ones, and they want to gain it?'

'It shows she's vulnerable and open to being taken advantage of. We know from the file that she was a single mother. Look at the ambition in her words. She wanted to better herself and had everything to live for. And now she's dead. It's sad.'

'You're right, it is. Go on. Let's see what the next entry says,' Phil said.

~~~

9 March 2011

I use my diary as a free therapist. Sometimes it's my best friend — and other times it's my only one.

I'm eight years in, and it'd be a shame to let it go when I've got so much to say. Let's see how long it lasts before I slip again, and it's something else to beat myself up about.

How often have I used the old excuse — I haven't got time? Make time, woman. My diary is important, and it's life-defining for one whole person — Me.

I'm evolving into somebody different. I want Emily to have the things I didn't. I've been promoted to Zone-six zookeeper. The hours are long, and I work fifty-two of them in my shortest week. Being the control freak I am, worrying about paying the bills is killing me.

Every few years, I have a destructive urge to re-invent. Training late for my zoology degree left me at the mercy of the state for three years. But nothing ventured. It paid off, and now I've got my dream job and avoided going down the student loan route — I've just got a big credit card bill to pay for the things my grant didn't cover. I want everything to be better for Emily and me from now on.

I'm talking to a guy online, not my usual type. That's got to be a good thing. Right? But that's another story.

~~~

'I'm feeling her,' Molly said.

'And I could be feeling you. Come on, let's talk things through.'

She turned the page to the next entry and moved his hand onto his own leg.

~~~

20 June 2011

I let my diary slip again. This is irregular and contrary to the terms and conditions of my O.C.D contract. Despite empty promises, things went astray. I've been working a lot of overtime and feeling like the mother from hell for not being here as much as I should for Emily. At ten, she's growing too independent by far.

I've been talking to a man called Mike. He works with animals too, though not so much the ones that can kill him. I don't suppose he smells of lemur crap as often as I do, and I doubt he's ever cleaned a tiger pool. He's a gamekeeper, of all things. I didn't know they even have them anymore. He's talking about meeting in person, but I don't know. We're chalk and cheese.

~~~

The hairs on the back of Molly's neck rose at the word gamekeeper. The term chalk and cheese resonated. Nash had used it to describe the man he was talking to.

The boss had been talking to somebody from a country estate near Kendal, on an online dating app a couple of weeks before.

It'd be worth mentioning. If gamekeepers socialised like Young Farmers, Nash's friend might know this Mike, even if that was eight years earlier.

'What's up?' Phil asked.

'Nothing. Read on.'

~~~

28th August 2011.

Right, let's see how far I get with this one. Fasten your seatbelts.

I had a brilliant day on Friday. It took a lot of persuading because I don't think he's my type, but I agreed to a date with Mike, the gamekeeper. We've been talking online for a few months and I couldn't keep putting him off. He was an absolute arsehole, but at the same time, one of the most interesting people I've seen in a long time.

We met at Grange-over-Sands, a retirement town where, they say, people go to die. My first thought was what the hell is that? He wore a trench coat down to his ankles and looked like something out of The Matrix. He was leaning against a Land Rover when I pulled up, and when he moved it was as though he peeled himself off the vehicle. He walked towards me and his coat fanned out at the sides. And then I saw his face. It was weathered and he looked so old. He had a shock of dark hair that dropped in waves to his collar.

And then he was next to me, and he smiled. His eyes crinkled at the corners and came to life and when he looked at me, I felt that he was cold reading me and gleaning every spec of information there was to know. He looked at me with such a long stare that I felt naked in front of him and blushed. His eyes were brown and I couldn't meet them because of the intensity. He was like nobody I'd ever seen before, and he fascinated me from the first second.

'So it's you then?'

They were the first words he spoke to me. What a stupid thing to say. I thought he was a pretentious prat. But then there were those eyes that took me prisoner and held me captive. It was far from love at first sight—but his allure was more powerful than any man I've known.

The date was sweet and lowkey because all we did was walk, and after the prom ran out, we just kept going, but then he had to get back to work. A couple of times his hand brushed mine, and I wanted to hold it, which was ridiculous because he was an opinionated oaf.

He's a typical countryman, and I enjoyed listening to him and learning about the game. He talked about his geese a lot. He's a wealth of history and knowledge, but I found his dialect irritating. He's Westmorland, and it's all thee and thines. It was like talking to Moses.

He's blunt to the point of rudeness, but there's something in his delivery that stopped me from taking offence. But even when he covered his comments with his killer smile, half a dozen times I came close to slapping his face and walking away.

We were walking alongside the bay. The tide was out, and the marshes had an unpleasant, sulphurous smell. He said to me, 'Jesus bloody Christ, thine stinks.'

I thought he was mistaking me for the marsh smell coming from low tide, but he wasn't done and felt the need to hammer his point home.

His language was full of words particular to his accent, but I'm writing it straight, otherwise, it'll drive me mad.

'At least you didn't come in fancy dress. I expected you to turn up in a skirt and those spiky heel things, but hell, you'd benefit from being held underwater and scrubbed until you come out smelling more natural. You didn't say you were coming via Boots the Chemist.'

The penny dropped. He was objecting to my perfume. 'I'm not taking you on a shoot with me, lass. The game would smell you from five miles downwind, and we'd come home with nowt for the pot.'

We'd already spent hours online arguing our opposing stances on hunting. 'What makes you think I'd ever agree to shoot with you?'

'You will — but you'll get in the bloody bath first.'

He tells it straight. I found out that he doesn't like people, especially women. He doesn't like politics, drinking, pubs, litter, and broken countryside law.

This year he's shot four dogs. I found the conversation hard to stomach, especially as he shot three of them in front of their owners. I tried to change it to something else and thought about calling a halt to the date and leaving. It made me feel sick, and I told him how I felt, and he said that if we were going to get on, it had to be starting from an open place and agreeing to tolerate the other's lifestyle.

'Look lass, you can have your views, and wrinkle up your cute nose, but pet dogs are killers. They're responsible for taking thirty of my flock a year. When it comes to shooting dogs on the estate, I have a rule. I tell folk to get their animals on a lead and off the land. I give them two minutes to do it. Then I shoot to kill.'

I hated the way he was speaking.

'There are huge *Private Property* signs all over the estate. The notices say that dogs found on the land — worrying or not — will be shot on sight.'

And all the time that he was saying these horrible things, his eyes were twinkling, and his lips were full. I kept having the fleeting curiosity of what it would be like to kiss him. I felt as though his strength would engulf me, and I wanted to feel it.

I didn't know whether to believe that he'd actually do it.

'Some people might not be able to read your signs.'

This man loved to shock. He confided that he couldn't read and write very well, either. 'It doesn't bother me though because I don't have to read my gamebirds a bedtime story. I just sing them a nice lullaby.'

'Can we talk about something else, now, please? I don't like this talk of murdering people's pets. Sorry.'

'I'm not sorry. And you need to understand. After all, a big red sign on a gatepost isn't likely to say; Come in. Ravage the land and leave your litter all over the place. Poison our game with your human food. Let your dog kill the animals. And please, before you leave, be sure to strangle a few geese with discarded plastic from your lager cans, is it?'

'Would it make any difference if the dog owners had children with them?'

'Not a bit. My job is to protect my game so that some yuppy solicitor on a team-building exercise can come along and kill them. And I'm damned good at my job.'

I couldn't get my head around him killing a family pet. I have no idea why I didn't leave. The only way I can explain it is that he's hypnotic. Mike has a magnetism that keeps you there when common sense says you are polar opposites, and will never agree. I've never intentionally killed so much as an insect.

He's a strange mix of personalities. He's uneducated and ignorant. Then, in his next sentence, he holds you captive with insightful and interesting conversation.

And then he floored me. We'd stopped at a wall. He was leaning against it rolling a cigarette. I'm not a smoker, but I wanted to taste the smoke on his breath. He was leaning, and I was standing in front of him as we talked. His eyes only left mine to put tobacco in his cigarette paper and it was as though it was an effort for him to drop his gaze. And then they were back on me. And he licked his paper. There was nothing suggestive or lewd about it, that would have been the biggest turn-off in the world, but he gave it a quick lick and stuck it together before lighting it. He looked so relaxed that he gave off vibes of being way too cool, like an actor in a Western. It was one of the sexiest things I've ever seen, and I had to look away.

And then he did it. There was a light breeze blowing my hair around. He lifted his hand and tucked a piece of hair behind my ear. The back of his thumb scraped across my cheek and his touch was feather-light but it affected me like a force field of electricity. The jolt of physical attraction was so strong that it hurt. I resisted grabbing his hand and holding it against my face before kissing the palm. We were surrounded by fresh air, but I couldn't get any of it. He stole the air from my body and must have seen the way he'd affected me, just by moving my hair into place. Christ, I dreaded to think what a kiss would do.

~~~

'Bloody hell. Is this woman for real? He's on about killing pet dogs in front of kids, and she's getting horny, The guy's nuts, and she's as mad as a box of frogs,' Phil said.

'I know. Why didn't she run like hell? Surely the alarm bells indicated the kind of man she was getting involved with. And he brags about killing people's pet dogs. What kind of monster is he?'

'He's a regular psychopath. I get him, loud and clear. He started by killing insects and worked his way up. It's classic psychological profiling, you know that. He's a textbook case. Watts is the one I don't get. Why do so many women lack common sense? This loser's walking around like Rambo with a bloody big gun killing things, and against all her so-called principles, she's going along with it.'

'No, I don't get it either, Phil. But I know how easy it is to turn a blind eye to things you don't agree with and to turn your back on your morals. Okay, don't look at me like that. I admit, I was having a dig. What time is it? We've got work in the morning, and won't Sal be wondering where you are?'

Phil reached over for the bottle and poured them another glass of wine. 'It's still early, and I can't leave now. Not a chance. I want to know what happens with the crazy woman and Psycho Mike.'

She laughed and turned the page.

~~~

Mike was passionate when he told me about the shoots. Businessmen and Hooray Henry types pay extortionate amounts to attend the geese shooting. 'Game should be killed for the table, If they're sick, or to cull them for protection of the species. Nothing else.'

'I agree.'

'You're not against killing then? There might be a hunter in you, yet.'

'I wouldn't bank on it. I'm very much pro-life and against killing under any circumstances, but I'm a zookeeper, so I understand the need.'

'I raise my poults, and I get to know them. I spend time with them and have my favourites. Then I have to release them to the scree for somebody to kill. They pay their shoot fee of two hundred a head, seventeen pounds fifty each for ammunition, and a sixty-pound head keeper's tip. Sometimes on a big shoot, my tip is per dead head of birds — Pappa's blood money. I rear my kids and then fly them out to die. The bastards tear my game to pieces for sport.'

Mike hates it and respects the birds. He loves them. His words and his passion for what he does humbled me. I felt unworthy next to him. When he talked, he was a giant, and I was an ant.

'It's my job, and it's what I do. Do you know, I have to doff my bloody cap to them like a prick and call them, Sir. I hate the city shooters with a vengeance, and I'd love to take a gun to them all.'

~~~

'He killed her,' Phil said.

'No shit, Sherlock. But, don't forget this is day one, and she wasn't murdered until eight years later.'

'True. But this man's angry. He talks openly about shooting people as well as dogs. I think he's probably taking out the posh people, too. I don't like him.'

'Nor me, but she seems to, and that's just insane. Read on,' Molly said.

~~~

I wanted to dislike Mike. He's not bright in most respects, talks like a farm hand, and has no finesse, but I didn't want to leave him. He loves what he does, and killing animals is a minor part of his job. He's funny without meaning to be. He talks with honesty and without a filter. I don't think it would occur to him to tell a lie. He's a nice man.

He has some strange ideas, though. He told me about his divorce. They'd been happily married for over twenty years. He met his wife when they were kids in school, and she's the only woman he's ever had sex with, and until now, he's had no dealings with women since they split. He said I'm the first woman he's had any interest in, other than his wife. Wow.

She's an NHS nurse and worked in a well-woman's clinic. Her work involved conducting mammograms and cervical smears. He thinks it turned her.

'One night, she went out drinking and had a one-night stand with a woman. After that, Mike said she was eaten with self-disgust, and couldn't be faithful. She turned into a slut, clubbing, and sleeping with any man or woman who'd have her. She came home with love bites and stinking of booze and men. One day she dropped the kids off at her mother's and ran off with a younger man. Mike was left bringing up two young children on his own. He's said women were the root of all evil.'

~~~

Phil was flabbergasted and spluttered, trying to get his words out. 'Lady. Wake up. He's just said that all women are evil, and you're going, "Oh, okay then, Mr. Psychopath. Shall we shag now?" Get the hell away from him. You idiot.'

Molly laughed. 'I wish she'd written the wife's name to give us something to chase. And he says he's only ever been with one woman in his life? That's weird enough by itself. He's a consummate liar and she's lapping up every word. This Mike must be the best-looking bloke on earth for her not to hear alarm bells and run.'

'Or he has the biggest dick. Come on, next one. This is the biggest pile of shite I've ever read, but it's addictive. I want to see how many levels of stupid this woman can descend to.'

'Stop being mean.'

~~~

'I'll tell you, lass, never be a nurse. It'll turn you into a lesbian.'

I had to laugh. 'That's ridiculous.'

'It's true. You can't be touching another woman in her special place like that, and not turn.'

'Mike. Change the subject, please. This one's offensive. And you're scaring me. Some of your opinions are very extreme.'

He wouldn't let it drop, so I explained that his wife must have had confused feelings all along. It had no relevance to her job. But it was an opinion that he'd clung to for a long time, and he wasn't going to see anything else.

'When was the last time you had sex with a goose?' I said.

'What?' He jigged about like an indignant Rumpelstiltskin.

'Admit it, you have a thing for your geese. If a job can turn you, it's the same principle. When was the last time you looked at a plump goose and thought, that's a fine-looking goose, wouldn't mind a bit of that?'

He calmed down, laughed, and told me I was a feisty filly. We left the prom and kept walking. In all, we walked nine miles, and I enjoyed it. He said he hadn't spent time in a woman's company for years, and that I'd cracked his head. Whatever that means.

As I was leaving, he leaned in to give me a kiss and a hug. It was odd because he didn't seem like a hugging, goodbye-kiss type of man. I leaned in to give him a friendly peck and he kissed me.

I mean, he really kissed me.

I blushed crimson, mumbled something incoherent and jumped in my car. He blushed crimson, mumbled something incoherent and asked if he could ring me.

I said yes because I didn't know what else to say and flew.

And I cursed myself all the way home. I couldn't have picked a less suitable man as a potential boyfriend. I don't like chauvinism. I don't like his 'nursing makes you a lesbian' chip on his shoulder, and I don't like killing innocent animals. But that kiss, wow. I get butterflies every time I think about it. As I set off, the radio came on and I could have danced on air. He kissed me. I was effervescent and bubbling over. I thought about him, his touch, and the kiss all the way home.

There's more about this man that I don't like. He's rough, he's a bully, and he's as tight as a bear's arse. He wouldn't let me stop at a cafe to buy us a coffee with my own money. He said there's no way he'd let me pay two pounds fifty for a cup of coffee when he's got a perfectly good flask in the car.

And although he's a year younger than me, he looks as though he's been left out in the rain for too long, and he's dried out like an old boot.

He looks at least ten years older than me, and that's being generous. But his eyes are electric. His smile, and the wrinkles at the corner of his eyes, I don't know how, but he makes me want him. He's not even good-looking in a classic way, but he's extra manly if that makes any sense at all. When he talks, he makes you want to listen.

He's a real man. He's strong and bossy. He doesn't mince his words, not that I can understand most of them, but what he's got to say, he says straight. And whether I like it or not, when he rang me that night, I agreed to go out with him again.

Don't I ever learn?

~~~

'I feel sorry for her and, at the same time, I want to shake her until her teeth rattle,' Molly said.

'She's so gullible.'

'She wants to be loved, and when you have your sights set that hard, it can blind you to anything.'

'Molly.'

'What?'

'What's with the nasty digs?'

'I was talking about the victim—but if the cap fits.'

Chapter Three

Molly had nodded off in his arms. She woke to Phil sitting on the edge of the bed, putting his socks on. When he realised, she was awake, he swore softly.

'I wasn't going to wake you,' he said.

'Obviously. It's much easier for you to sneak away. What time is it?'

'Eleven.'

'Twenty-three hundred hours. Shift changeover at the office. Bang on time. Your work here is done, Officer Renshaw.'

'Don't be like that, Molly. You know I have to go.'

'Go. Don't keep your wife waiting.'

'Listen up, team,' Nash said. What have we got? Renshaw, talk to me.'

'Nothing much to report. The man's a psychopath and the woman's nuts. Nothing jumping out as evidence, but I haven't got very far.'

The meeting progressed with Nash going around each officer to see what they had to offer up.

'Team. Leave anything important on my desk, and you're dismissed. Get back on your jobs from yesterday.' He waited while they filed out of the room. 'Not you two,' he said, holding Renshaw and Brown back.

'I knew I should have given the diary to Brown. And I suppose she's read as much as you have, has she?'

'Sir,' Brown said.

'Sir, what?'

'Sir, I've read as far as Renshaw.'

'I see.'

Silence filled the room, and the air he sucked in was replaced with the physical weight of Nash's disappointment in them. Molly hung her head and tapped one of the table's legs with her foot. The heat from her cheeks could have warmed a small country. Nash let the silence play out until it felt as though nobody had spoken for an hour. Renshaw's head dropped, but he raised it and met Nash's stare as he put his point across.

'The diary should have gone to Brown in the first place, Nash. I thought it was a bad call, and I felt bad about you giving it to me. So I took it to her so we could both read it.'

'And that's the biggest crock of shit I've ever heard. I wasn't born yesterday, Renshaw, and I know a feeble excuse for a booty call when I see it. Don't take me for a fool, eh? So, you think my judgement was poor?'

'I just thought we could discuss it together, and she'd have a different interpretation and viewpoint to me. Two heads being better than one.'

'And were they?'

'What?'

'Better than one.'

'As it happens, yes.' Molly answered this time and was on firmer ground now that she had justification for their breach of protocol. 'The reason we didn't get very far is that the woman wrote thousands of words some days, and we had to filter through all the entries to get to the relevant parts.'

'Go on.'

'I've put an asterisk before and after the relevant articles and initialled them. I'd suggest getting one of the staff to transcribe it electronically and separate anything irrelevant to the case so that we lose the white noise around it. Nash, this woman is unbelievable. Even though she's no longer with us, she's the most credible witness we've ever had. She spills her guts into every word, and if she farts, she writes about it. She's met up with this Mike guy, and he's screaming danger from every sentence. He's shot family pets, hates women, and openly threatens to murder people.'

'Has he threatened her?'

'Not yet. I thought you'd read it.'

'I skimmed it. Right. I don't want this going to one of the secretaries. It stays in the immediate office. Is the diary in a fit state to have the pages scanned?'

'I doubt it,' Renshaw said. The handwriting's a scrawl, and it's difficult to read in real copy. I don't think we'd get it clear enough.'

'Okay, clarity is key. I want Bowes typing up the notes. God help us. His typing is worse than a cat on a keyboard, but I can't spare anybody else.'

'I think it's the best idea, but it's a lot of work. Is there anybody else that could be sworn in to do it, sir?'

'No.'

'I'll get him on it,' Renshaw said.

'Good. Next. I want you to pull Clara Watt's account from the dating site. Get the orders. Judge Bradbury is sitting this morning. I want every conversation she's ever had on that dating thing, and we need Mike's surname, account information and contact details.'

'Sir.'

'Try and get an order to pull his conversation history as well. I want it from the day he opened his account. William Bradbury's a stickler. He'll scream GDPR breach at you and he'll dig his heels in. Use the tack that there may be other victims in the online profiles. You'll get the Watt's account released, he can't refuse that, but I don't fancy your chances of getting the gamekeepers until we have more to work with.'

'I'll sweettalk Bradbury,' Brown said.

'You'll be lucky. He eats officers for breakfast and then snacks on criminals throughout the day. And, Renshaw?'

'Yes.'

'You're bloody useless. Hand the diary back to Brown. And, going forward, she's the only person authorised to read it. I want this mess contained.'

'I think that would be a big mistake, sir.'

'Why? It doesn't take two of you to read a bloody book.'

'I think you're wrong. We found that we had differing viewpoints. If you check the report, we've made three pages of observation and notes of how we think we can nail this guy.'

Molly said. 'It's true. And, with both of us on it, we can catch him faster, and before anybody else gets hurt.'

Nash went as far as the tilt position in his chair would let him and scrutinised them. He saw the pulsing twitch at the corner of Phil's eye. Renshaw wanted this case, and Brown was champing at the bit. Nash had kept them apart as much as possible since things got messy, but they'd produced some great work together before muddying the waters with their affair. They'd been shift partners for a long time, and sometimes that was closer than a marriage. He took his time responding and left them squirming.

'Okay, if you feel you can input more as a team, I trust you. You can both stay on it but don't give it too much time. I can't have you tied up with it for long. Phil, you can oversee Lawson for the rest of your time. You need to go to the judge, but Lawson can do the rest of the donkey work to free you up. Keep an eye on him. I want results—and fast.'

'Thanks, Nash. You won't regret it.'

'Just one more thing.'

'Yes?'

'The book doesn't leave the station. You will not go to Brown's house under the guise of working. You work on this when you're on duty and during your shift only. What you do in your private life is up to you. But I will not watch two good officers tear themselves apart if I can do something to stop it.'

'Sir,' they both said again.

'Come to your senses before it's too late. I don't want to see anybody getting hurt—least of all your family, Renshaw. This can only end in tears. Now get out of here. Dismissed.'

He waited for the door to close and released his chair to the up position. He wanted to kick Renshaw's arse from one side of Barrow to the other. They should be kept apart, but the case was bigger than the individuals working it, and that took precedence. And what good would it do? It would only drive them together after hours. The more time they spent together, the sooner it would blow up, and reach some kind of resolution. Nash knew it was going to hit the fan. They'd been having an affair for two years. Time had proved it wasn't going to blow itself out naturally, and things had to come to a head for any kind of resolution. So far, they'd been lucky, but Nash listened to the gossip and heard people saying that Renshaw's wife was ringing the station to speak to him and seemed suspicious.

They'd tried to stay apart, but gravity always pulled them back together. He saw what it had done to Phil and the heavy burden of guilt he carried.

Nash feared for them.

Chapter Four

Renshaw and Brown sat at the long desk in an empty interview room with jotting pads and a laptop. Brown opened the diary, and after they'd skim-read the next entries, she put asterisks around the three of them. They were about Clara's work and home life with her daughter and bore no relevance to the case.

Phil said, 'This is bloody ridiculous. This stupid, lonely woman's telling us about her day as a zookeeper, and I can't get enough of it.'

'Mad, isn't it? I never realised there was so much to do. I swear, my heart's in my mouth when she describes the tiger tunnels they have to use. Especially after that girl was killed in that very run by one of the tigers. Here we go, next entry,' Molly said. 'Bingo, she's back onto Mike.'

~~~

11th September 2011.

Mike came to see me yesterday. When we arranged it, I thought I had everything boxed off. Emily was going to tea with her friend and was having a sleepover. The best-laid plans and all that. Kayla's mum forgot she had an after-school club, so Emily didn't go. That threw me into a panic. I didn't want Emily meeting Mike. She's seen too many men coming into my life in the last couple of years. I can't get past three months in a relationship, and I didn't want Emily to know anything about him. Not yet. Maybe not ever.

I went on the computer to cancel, but Mike had already set off. The bloody idiot hasn't got a phone. He says he's a countryman and doesn't see the need for one. 'I don't need to ring my geese, lass,' he said. The man's impossible.

After our first date, I didn't know how I felt about him. When he kissed me, it came out of the blue, and I didn't expect it. A woman can tell when a man's gearing up to lay one on her, but not this time. And that's what I like about him. He's different from anybody I've met, and his unpredictability is exciting. I haven't got time for a boyfriend. I work fifty hours a day. He could've had the decency to come along before I got my promotion. In the last three weeks, we've had a lot of animal births, and that means going in through the night sometimes. Childcare's hell to arrange, and I've been so stressed and tired that I don't know my own name. If I had a boyfriend, something else would have to give — and there isn't anything. I'm committed to my job. I love the zoo, which takes up most of every damned day. I need more family time. I just haven't got anything to spare to give to somebody else. I don't go out for fun anymore because I never seem to be at home as it is.

Mike is an inconvenience I can do without.

But things happen when it's inconvenient. Everybody said to stop looking for a partner, and one will come along.

Please, God, don't make me retract this next week or the week after, but I think Mike is what I've been looking for.

We are complete opposites. We couldn't be more different. He kills things. I hate killing. He's quiet and reserved. I'm an extrovert. He's a pain in the arse, and I'm wonderful. We disagree on almost everything we've talked about. He won't eat foreign food, but Emily and I live on pasta dishes. Salad is for rabbits. I love salad. He loathes women who drink. I like vodka. He doesn't own a telly and having one on annoys him. He doesn't like music. How can you not like music?

He's country. I'm town.

And yet.

He walked through the door, and I wanted him to kiss me again.

He's intense and talks about forever.

Forever terrifies me. Hell, if we're together next week, it's a major achievement for me.

He wants security and to settle down again. He's a nest builder and admits that he's looking for wife number two to end his days with.

What?

To hell with that. I've told him I never want to marry again. Marriage terrifies me. I'm a nomad. I can't do it.

'Will you still be roaming the country with your guitar in hand in a year's time, in five, or in ten?'

'I expect to be nomadic all my life.'

'Do you like it?'

'Sometimes.'

'I have a chance of taming you, then?'

'Probably not.'

He was holding my hand and his felt like leather. Every time his thumb stroked my wrist at the pulse point, a jolt of electricity ran through me. His words sounded worried when they came.'I should run away now and not look back. I don't want to be hurt again. And you're one hell of a gamble, lass.'

'It'd be the best for both of us if you did,' I said.

He told me he didn't want to stop.

I don't want him to, either.

This man will stick by me, and he'll take my shit. I know that much of him already. We've only met three times, and he says he's mad about me. In time, I think I can make him love me. His parents want to meet me. Men don't take me to meet their parents. He's even told his kids about me. Hell, we've only known each other for five minutes.

He turned up, and I made the awkward introductions to Emily who didn't look impressed, and thankfully she didn't stay downstairs long before escaping to her room.

She was sitting on the floor playing with the dog, and Mike asked, 'Now then, what do you think of your mother having a boyfriend around?'

And my mind was screaming at him to slow down. Just stop, will you? Apply the brakes and set off again slowly.

A boyfriend.

But he's what I want, a man who's straight as an arrow. He knows what he wants. He won't let me down. He won't lie to me. He won't cheat on me. He'll be as loyal and faithful as his two black Labradors. And for the first time in my life, I know I can have somebody who will love me.

He doesn't want to sleep with me.

He wants to court me.

He says he won't take me to bed until he can tell me that he loves me. And then he'll only sleep with me if I feel the same.

He's different and refreshing and new.

He's the blueprint of what I've been looking for.

But our lifestyles are so different. I want to go out and have fun sometimes. I'd like him to come and have fun with me, but it wouldn't be fun for him. It'd be hell. I like karaoke bars and live bands. I love dancing. He'd rather slit his throat.

I don't know where this road is leading, but we had our chance to turn off at the crossroads and didn't.

I've got a boyfriend, and I'm reluctant to roll with it.

We had our first fight today.

I have no means of contacting him. He lives in the gamekeeper's cottage on a big country estate. His home phone is tapped through from the main office, and he's not allowed to make personal calls unless it's an emergency because the company pays his phone bill. He doesn't want me to ring him on that because he's a very private man, and all calls go through the office before they come to him. He's never had a mobile and doesn't know how to use one.

We are going out with each other and he's my boyfriend. I want to be able to contact him. So last night I bought him a phone. I told him I needed his address because I was sending it to him today, along with a card with ten quid's worth of credit on it, and he hit the roof. He'd said yesterday that he'd get into town when he could and buy himself one of those new-fangled phones that you keep in your pocket, so I thought I'd surprise him with one. It's nothing fancy, just a bog standard forty-quid Nokia.

'You know I'll have to pay you for it?'

'No. It's a gift, and I won't hear another word about it.'

Yesterday he was rambling on about being unsure if I was for real. 'I don't know, lass. You hear so many stories about people being taken for a ride, and I don't know if you're just stringing me along. How can I know if you're real?'

'I am. I promise you.'

'I'm terrified that you're playing me, Clara. I don't want to be hurt again.'

I wanted to do something nice for him and thought buying him the phone would show some commitment to getting to know him and it would make him feel more secure. But he threw it back in my face. He says he won't accept it without paying for it, and it's not up for discussion.

I was angry and told him to forget about the phone. I refuse to take money for something that was bought as a gift. 'If you won't take it, that's fine. I'll keep it as a spare, and we won't mention it again.'

I'm annoyed because he was going on about wanting to trust me. I did something to show I'm trustworthy. And he was furious with me.

And I'm annoyed with myself. He told me he'd sort it in his own time. But, as usual, I jumped in with all horns blaring, like a hippopotamus in a glass-blowing factory. I couldn't be cool if I tried. I interfered. I should have left well alone. Now I've embarrassed him and made him feel awkward. I only thought about myself, and how I'd feel when I bought him a gift. I'd have done the same thing if the situation was reversed. I'm proud too, and hate being bought things for no reason. It's too early for buying random gifts. It makes me uncomfortable, and I can't accept it. I'm proud and independent, and Mike's the same. I overstepped the mark.

Now there's tension between us. My feelings were hurt, and it was a stupid thing to do. I wanted to please him, and I've done the opposite.

~~~

They sat up to ease their backs and take in what they'd read. Neither of them spoke for a minute.

'Christ,' Phil said.

'She's so vulnerable.'

'You think? I just see her as weak and stupid. What kind of person has no contact with the outside world, and isn't allowed to make calls on his house phone? He hasn't got a phone? Everybody has a phone, but she can't see that he's lying to her?'

'At least he refused to take the phone.'

Phil laughed. 'Come on. Tell me you didn't buy that act. He's going to take it, and he'll have it sold to Cash Converters ten minutes later. He'll tell her he lost it, or something equally feeble, and she'll suck it up. What a fool.'

'He seemed pretty adamant,' Brown said.

'Bet you a tenner he takes it.'

'You're on.' She asterisked another couple of entries in the diary, and they leaned forward to the next section about Mike.

~~~

18th September 2011.

Why do stars suddenly appear every time you are near? Sorry to be so sickly, but I'm falling in love.

~~~

'Puke,' Phil said.

'Shoot me now. I'm with you this time. Clara Watt gives womanhood a bad name.'

~~~

If things don't work out with Mike, I'll have my lady bits surgically removed and something useful, like a toastie maker, installed in their place. My friend, Meg, looks at me in disgust, or like I'm some alien sub-species. 'How can you possibly have feelings for somebody you've only known for a few weeks?'

'I don't know. I get that it's mad.'

It isn't for want of fighting it. Mike lives too far away, he works seven hundred hours a week, and he's so far removed from the ideal boyfriend that I've always had in my head, that he's unrecognisable. But I carry him with me every second of every day.

He says he wants to be with me forever.

I just want to be with him next Wednesday on my day off.

I don't know if I can be with him long-term, or if he's enough to keep me grounded and working for us at the first hint of trouble.

Words that describe me are frivolous, flighty, nomadic, changeable, fickle, lightweight, impossible, and high maintenance.

Words that describe him are steady, reliable, strong, sedate, home-loving, unchangeable, unmoveable, grounded, and dependable.

He's everything I've wanted in a man and the epitome of what I've always run a mile from.

I know he's a bit older than me at forty-two. I'm only thirty-three. He admitted he lied on his profile about his age. I hate liars, but I suppose I can forgive him for that vanity. I hope he never finds this diary and reads it because I've got to say he looks much older than his age. The more I look at him, the more I find his face interesting. And the more it interests me, the better it looks, until I can't take my eyes off him and think he's the most attractive—lived-in—man I've ever seen. It must be with being out in all weathers. He's only been with one woman, his wife, and she's turned him against women and made him bitter. That's a problem because he's very angry about the breakup of his marriage and how he was treated. It turns out he only went on the dating app to shut his friend up, and it was his friend who chose me for him as the first person to meet. He didn't want to fall for me any more than I did him, but he trusts me, and that's a responsibility.

I've given him my oath that I'll never be unfaithful. It was an easy promise to make. I've never been unfaithful in my life. But I do run when things get tough. I'm glad he didn't make me swear that I wouldn't get bored and want something different after six months.

Today I want him more than I can describe. I can see myself living with him and raising his geese and pheasant. I've said, 'This is the one,' dozens of times before, but I've never considered moving in with any of them.

I'm not packing my boxes as we speak. I have several grand's worth of debt to clear before I'm clean enough to give my life to anybody. But I'm giving thought to the future. He doesn't want a lightweight relationship. He wants a full-blown commitment with all the trimmings. Marriage one day? No chance — well, not much of a chance anyway.

Last month he didn't exist. Today I have the ability to break his heart and send him back into a semi-reclusive existence, where women are the scourge of the earth. If he doesn't work out, next month or the month after, I'd be writing to my diary and saying that I've met this wonderful new, life-changing man.

He probably wouldn't move on so fast. But he'd have another break-up behind him to be even more bitter about.

When I walked into his life last month, he dreaded our date. He begrudged donating his time to a woman. He'd been grouchy with his employees the day before, and told me, he'd intended to meet me for half an hour to get his friend off his back. He wanted to despatch me at the earliest chance. Women are all self-serving, money-grabbing, duplicitous wenches, who should be lined up and shot. His words.

And somewhere between yelling at me for wearing perfume, and deciding he wanted to kiss me, some bloody great momentous brick fell out of the sky and cracked his head.

'All sensibility went out of the window, Clara. You asked me questions about how the estate was run, and I was flattered that you were interested. But I was struggling to tell you because every time I formulated a sentence, I had an almighty urge to kiss you and forgot what I was going to say.'

And I thought he was just a big, arrogant, surly git.

He's coming for lunch tomorrow. I'm pushing the boat out and cooking up a storm. He's bringing his best friend, Simon, and I've invited Meg—who's also single—to make up the numbers. Simon and Mike have been friends forever. I think Simon wants to vet me. He's already called me a witch. Mike told me he's never seen him like this and wants to know what I've done to him. He said he could understand it if I was a shotgun.

I know this is over the top, and I should know better after all the dropkicks I've met. I'm acting inappropriately. It's too much too soon, but he feels the same, and it's infectious.

This morning I got home from work, and I could see forever. It's not such a scary place. I've thought about the things I could find out about him that would kill the way things are going, but there isn't much that would put me off.

He's married and living happily with his wife and sixteen kids.

He's the real Yorkshire ripper.

He has a goose fetish that goes beyond feathers.

Being serious for a second, is he just like all the rest and playing with me because I'm easy to string along? He seems too good to be true.

~~~

Chapter Five

Nash was frustrated, and it made him fractious. 'Brown, Renshaw, have you got anything concrete?'

Brown spoke up. Nothing much to go on. A couple of new first names to trace and a line of enquiry with Labrador breeders. Other than that. Nothing.'

'Two days and you've got bugger all? Before we get onto the names Brown has for us this morning, Renshaw, what's happening with the dating site?'

'As you know, we've hit a brick wall. The company liquidated in 2016. We've tracked down the CEO, but he's as good as useless. He knew very little about the technical side of the business, but we got a list of his key workers. I found the guy who can pull the chat history, A Kris Cherry. He's a nice bloke and wanted to help us, but the website was folded and destroyed. It's not like a modern App where everything backs up. In those days, it was just a website, and when the plug was pulled, the heart stopped beating. There's nothing left.'

'And you've checked with phone people and ethernets and internet providers that there's nothing to bring it back?'

'Not a thing, sir.'

'Lawson, talk to me.'

Lawson sat up and consulted his pad. 'We've concentrated all our search efforts in a 50-mile radius. Logistically, given his timeline, it can't be more than that. Though if he was really covering his tracks, and travelling inter-country, we can extend it later if need be.'

'Jesus, basically what you're saying is we're looking for somebody called Michael from somewhere in England?'

'That hits the nail on the head. But fingers crossed that we're lucky, and he's in Cumbria. We started with the country estates. We've pulled the employee records for every large estate in our catchment. From what Molly's read so far, our best bet was always going to be either Lowther or Holker, with my money on Holker all day long. Unfortunately, they've both come up blank. Lowther's more of a zoo than a country estate and is run as such. Holker's had the same reliable gamekeeper and estate managers for years. Some of the lower staff have changed, but they've all checked out. None of them is our guy.'

'The bastard.' Nash scored a line through Holker Hall and Lowther Wildlife Park. 'All you're giving me is what we haven't got. What else?'

'We didn't stop at proper estates. We figured this bloke might have been bigging his role up, so we've checked any large country house that employs anything from gardeners to maintenance technicians. We looked at men called Mike, who were aged 42 in 2011, and we took it five years in either direction to be sure. There's no long list, I'm afraid. Just one man. Michael Collins, a gardener, and groundsman at a place in Westmorland around that time. He's so clean, he squeaks. Clara Watts described Mike as being a big man. This bloke is small and wiry. It's not him. When we checked every Mike in his forties, there was nothing.'

'Extend the search.'

'Sir. And I wondered if it's worth looking at hotels in the area as well?'

Nash sat one buttock on the edge of his desk as he thought about it but stood up to deliver his answer. 'No. He says he works as a gamekeeper. I like the way you're thinking. Good work, Lawson, but if we're going to pull every employee from all the hundreds of hotels, where do we stop? Guesthouses and B&Bs? If we're going to do that, we might as well do schools and then corner shops. It's too much of a long shot.'

Nash turned to the whiteboard and wrote in big red letters, Mike. Says he lives and works on an estate, but no record of him. Underneath his heading, he listed two bullet points. He lied. And, he gave a false name. Under gave a false name, he bullet-pointed, Dating site. Why lie? Protecting his career? Married? Social Stigma?

'That site's folded, but try all the others, and find somebody who can check out every male in his forties.'

'Already done it. I had the same thought, that with it being a dating site, he'd given a false name. There were a couple of guys that fit the bill. We're still doing background checks on them. One in particular that we knew was using dating sites back then. He's married now and reluctant to talk about it. I think there may have been an overlap in the wife coming on the scene, and the dating game flying off it. A man by the name of Daniel Mason. In all honesty, I don't think it's him. He's cagey, but I doubt he's our guy. He's of average build, a bit of a gut on him these days, but he couldn't be called big either.'

'Keep on it, Lawson. Good work. Bowes, wake up. Are we keeping you up, son?'

'No. I was listening.'

'What have you got? Come on. We haven't got all day. Where's your pad?'

'In the workroom.'

'You must bring it to every team meeting. I bet you haven't even written any notes, have you?'

'I don't need to. Got it all up here.' He tapped his forehead.

'Give me strength? Come on, then. Spin us a yarn.'

Bowes grinned. 'Okay, so, a gamekeeper without a shotgun licence is like a builder without a hod.'

'Get on with it, Bowes.'

'Sir. We pulled records for the ten years preceding 2011. 15 licences were issued to males called Michael. One of them is now Michelle and he lives on the Norfolk Broads with his girlfriend in a houseboat. He's got tits and everything.'

Nash raised his hand to stop Brown from opening her mouth. 'I've got this one, Brown. Bowes, write yourself up for an inclusion refresher course. I want it in your diary by the close of play.'

'What? No way. What did I do?'

'You know damned well it's her girlfriend, or theirs—not his. I don't mind you playing for the laughs. The team can use it, but I won't accept homophobia in this station, latent or otherwise.'

'I'm sorry, sir. I'm up to date. Can my apology be enough?'

'On this occasion but be aware that anybody in this room could have gender issues, never mind in the field. People are people, Bowes. And we love everybody equally and all that shit. Back to it. What else?'

'Like Lawson, we're still checking records and interviewing, but so far, they all check out. Not our man.'

'And you checked this, Michelle, out? Just because she's living a different life from the one she had back then, doesn't mean it couldn't be her. Leave no stone unturned?'

'We've already cleared her. Again, working within a fifty-mile radius, we've been to every outlet selling rifles and shotgun paraphernalia. The law states that they only have to keep purchase records for five consecutive years, so historical records are often obsolete. But this might be something. We did speak to a bloke from a shop in Lancaster. It's a shop selling firearms and fishing stuff called *Cock and Tackle.*' He grinned and waited for the laughter to die down.

'The owner's a man called Simon Shaw. He said there was someone that used to come in who gave him the creeps. As well as buying boxes of ammunition, he used to take gunpower to make his own rounds. The owner said this geezer had a machine for it at the estate where he worked. His licence and ID were in order, so he had no reason to refuse him.'

'What was his problem with the customer,' Nash asked.

'When pressed, he couldn't put his finger on it, but he said there was something off about the man. He didn't ring true, and Shaw said that if he was in charge of handing out the licences, he wouldn't be happy about signing one for him. He said the man used to go in regularly, but he hasn't seen him for a couple of years now. He assumed the bloke had either died or moved away—but said he hoped that his licence had been revoked because he should never have had one. He had a look in his eye, apparently.'

'You've spent hours looking for a bloke, who seemed a bit off?' Good God. What do we pay you for?'

'It's all we've got, and you said not to leave any stone unturned and miss something.'

'Thanks, Bowes. Right, let's wrap this up. Renshaw, Brown what fairy stories have you got?'

Renshaw stood up. 'We've been looking at the old interviews and going over ancient ground. Clara Watt's ex-husband, Billy, has re-married. Watts reverted to her maiden name. Apparently, there was a row in the Crystal Palace a couple of weeks before she died. Things got heated and the two women got into it. The new wife had told Emily, Clara's daughter off, and Clara didn't like it. Alcohol fuelled. The new wife, Jill Richmond, said she'd rip Clara's head off. All hot air.'

'From what I can gather, trouble between them was an ongoing thing. And Billy wasn't great at keeping up his CSA payments, either. It caused bad feelings. He argued that with Clara meeting different men, they should be taking up the baton of responsibility and being the new baby daddy, even though the kid's ten. He's a right charmer.'

'Do we think there's any life in it?'

'No. They were interviewed at the time, and we've hauled them in again. Their stories are airtight. And dumping her miles away like that. It doesn't fit the profile.'

'Alibi's?'

'No. With the body not being found for weeks and having such a wide window of opportunity, it was impossible to tie them down to any timescale. Same with other suspects. Watts had been seeing a local nightclub owner a couple of months before she went missing and dropped him when this country bloke came back on the scene. We've interviewed Nat Focus, the nightclub owner, but he reckons it had already pretty much fizzled out months before. It wasn't amicable, but not murderous, either.' Renshaw said.

Nash had his back to the room updating the whiteboard with the current information. 'Okay, let's get back to our mystery gamekeeper, then.'

Brown was on more solid ground having read the diaries. 'First up we have some new names to throw into the mix. Somebody called Simon was his best friend. Now, going by what we know about this man, he doesn't like pubs, or anything remotely modern. We thought fishing might be a good route to go down. Every fishing club has in-season competitions. Ulverston Canal, for instance, has one every week. I'd like to contact all the clubs, working within a fifty-mile radius, and of course, checking for men in their forties called Mike, but I thought we could go for the duo. I bet these guys went fishing together. Can we get some of the PCs asking around to see if any of the fishing waters had two blokes called Simon and Mike attending?'

'If he works on a big country estate, do you think they would be part of a fishing club? Wouldn't they have their own stretch of fishing?' Nash said.

'At this stage, everything's a long shot. We thought about looking at the fox-hunting crowd as well. It may be illegal now, but it wasn't back then.'

'Check it out by all means, but don't spend too long on it. And the other name?'

'Clara Watt's friend. It's a woman called Meg. She's interesting because she disappeared around that time, too. Though we've no reason to believe anything untoward happened to her. We think she lived nearby. She'd met Mike and Simon, and initial searches show, she dropped off the face of the earth. Watt's lived on Queen

Street, and we found a Margaret Hartley living on Prince Street at the time. It could be her.'

'Have you traced her and brought her in?'

'No. She moved away. We know she went to live down south with her daughter for a while. Then she moved to London, but it didn't last long. She showed up on the next census, using her maiden name, and had a flat in Epping. And there were some tax and domestic trails for a few months. She was on benefits for a while. But from the end of that year, she was gone without a trace.'

'She could have moved in with somebody and took their name,' Brown said.

'Why would she take somebody else's name?' Nash asked. 'It seems a bit stupid when she'd gone back to her maiden name.'

'It happens a lot with divorcees. She's been married three times and probably thinks it's a farce. Then there's divorce and the trouble of getting one. Women of a certain age, jaded with marriage, often shack up with somebody and use the partner's name. It's not illegal, and it's a thing.'

'A thing? Have you got anything more solid than a thing?'

'We know Mike has kids, once we have more to go on, we can check out schools. We don't know how many kids, what sex, or how old they were at the time. The other thing is these two black Labradors. He got them from somewhere, and they probably came from either a registered breeder or a similar countryman who uses them for pheasant hunting and the like.'

'Has anybody got anything on this joker, except puppies, playmates, and things? I'm losing the will to live here.'

'No, sir.' The team parroted.

'Get me something by tomorrow. If this fella exists somebody, somewhere knows him.'

'Sir.'

'Dismissed.'

Chapter Six

Brown cleared their dirty coffee cups. 'Come on, we need something solid for Nash before he blows a bloody gasket.'

Renshaw opened the diary on the next page. There were no dud entries, and it got straight down to business. Within seconds they were enthralled in Clara Watt's life again.

~~~

20th September 2011.

Mike came for lunch yesterday. I have no contact with him between dates, so I didn't have a clue what time they were arriving—or even if they were. By eleven o'clock it was bedlam, with pans boiling, and the floor covered in a skating rink of splattered fat from the turkey tin that I'd taken out of the oven and tilted. There were dishes, concoctions, peeled things, sliced things, soup things, dinner things and crumble things. The giblets looked like something somebody had slaughtered and were waiting to be made into gravy.

I was a limp bedraggled mess. I was in my knickers and a long sloppy T-shirt. I'd got up and hadn't even washed properly. I stank of onions. My hair was all over the place, and I was red-faced and flustered from cooking.

There was a knock at the door. Good, bang on cue, Meg to the rescue. I didn't know what time they were coming and needed any help I could get.

Emily shouted, 'Mum, Mike's here.' She was laughing.

'Oh, God. Don't even joke about it,' I screamed, doing battle with ten pounds of steaming gobbler.

'Hello, my darling.'

There was nowhere to crawl away and die. Where was my new skirt and blouse that made my tits look great, the makeup and straightened hair? What about my damned stilettos, for God's sake? I was standing in my knickers surrounded by chaos, and a total lack of order—and this wasn't cricket.

'You said you'd be here this afternoon.'

'Thought I'd surprise you,' Mike said.

'You're insufferable.'

He's never seen me anything but respectable, and worse he'd brought his best mate for lunch. The only way out of the kitchen and to blessed escape upstairs, was through the lounge where Emily was killing herself laughing and beckoning to Simon to, 'Come and look at this.'

Mike was leaning against the door. He gave me a long wolf whistle and said, 'Wow. You look beautiful.'

He held me, told me he'd missed me, kissed me, and didn't seem keen to let go. The kitchen looked like something out of a St Trinian's cooking lesson. I flew through the living room, said a hasty 'Hello, pleased to meet you' to Simon and ran to the calm of the bathroom for a thirty-second shower and hair wash.

From that moment, the meal was doomed. I flung my new clothes on, didn't bother with make-up, and only had time to drag a brush through my soaking hair before going downstairs. I had tons of things to do in the kitchen, but I just wanted to sit and talk to Mike.

Simon's nice. I like him. I hope he thinks I'm good enough for his friend. I'd been ambitious with lunch. 'Keep it simple,' Meg said. Not a chance. I was out to impress.

Now they were here, the kitchen lost its appeal. I muddled on and the meal was good but not my best. Meg said she'd have done better. Of course, she would. Then she criticised what I was wearing, 'Clara, my friend, I have to say that skirt does nothing for you.' Fine, but did she have to say it in front of Mike and Simon? Why would she do that? She said the crumble wasn't a pleasant mix of tastes. I like strawberry and pear crumble. She didn't, but still managed to put away two bowls of the stuff.

Mike was defensive of me and when she commented on my skirt, he said she ought to grow herself a backside to fill her saggy jeans.

After the meal, we were chatting, and Mike asked me to sit on his knee. I was comfy on the sofa but he asked three times. I was embarrassed, it felt awkward with having company, but our time is precious, and we weren't going to get any time alone. I'm overweight and was worried about squashing him.

Time is a big problem. He's on call twenty-four hours a day for ten-day stretches. He's been skiving work to see me, and that means giving up his days off to make the ground up.

I'm worried about him. He doesn't eat properly, doesn't get enough sleep, and has been married to his work for years. Now he has me and he's not giving the same attention to his job, and that's a concern. I don't want him getting into trouble for skiving to come and see me. The job is his life, and what pulled him through his marriage break-up. If he loses it, he'll resent me. But he says he wants to spend as much time as we can together. I want that too.

I nearly died of shock when he asked me to move in with him when he goes into business for himself next year. He's bought fifteen acres of forestry to raise his own game, and he's building his own house on it and says he'll take me to see it next week. It's scary stuff.

They couldn't stay long because they had to get back for a night shoot with the Hooray Henry brigade. They'd caused a stir in Dalton, though. After parking in the car park, they'd jumped out of the car, and stripped to their boxers to change into decent clothes. They'd washed and shaved from a plastic water bottle with a pack of Bics. The idiots could have sorted all that out here.

Mike bought me a beautiful bouquet of flowers.

I didn't want him to go and had the impression he didn't want to leave.

~~~

25th September 2011.

I worked late last night, one of the giraffes birthed, and two of the six head keepers had to be on hand. And

Scarlet, the red panda, was off-colour so we were waiting to see what the vet said. I'm worried about her.

It was my day off today, so I didn't get up until nine, and I had an hour before a ten o'clock Skype date with my boyfriend. I couldn't wait to speak to him. It wasn't a real date, the best we could manage was a couple of hours chatting online, but it was the best he could get, and it would have to do.

I had a coffee and waited for Mike to come online. I was doing chores in between bits of conversation with him. And as usual, he was late. He must have been busy with work—always his bloody work. I would have waited for him on that computer all day.

When the knock came at the door, I was shocked.

I couldn't believe my eyes when Mike was standing on the doorstep. Mixed feelings shot through my mind. Delight at seeing him, and horror at the state of the house and the state of me. I'd done one load of washing but hadn't even started the rest of my morning routine of housework. That was twice on the bounce, that he'd caught me when I was unprepared for him. This time, I hadn't brushed my hair since the night before. I hadn't washed or brushed my teeth. I was still wearing my night-shirt. This was awful and wonderful, and shameful. I didn't want to invite him in, but I had no choice, and I couldn't wait to get him in to kiss him, but I couldn't kiss him because I hadn't brushed my teeth.

He saw me dithering and was uncomfortable. 'Is this a bad time? Have I done something wrong? I wanted to surprise you, but you don't look happy.' He was looking over my shoulder and into the living room as though he expected another man to be sitting there.

Happy? I could have bawled with happiness. Everything was awful, I want to be the perfect girlfriend, but I was so happy to see him when I wasn't expecting it.

'I can't kiss you on Skype, lass, and rather than spend hours struggling through my dyslexia and battering a keyboard, I can be here, kissing you in person.'

I asked him to sit, wouldn't let him near me, and begged him not to follow me to the kitchen.

'Something is wrong, isn't it? You don't want to see me anymore.' In his panic, he ignored my request and followed me through, I didn't want him to see Emily's mountain of pots from the day before, or the pile of her washing she'd brought down and dumped on the floor in front of the washing machine.

He looked distraught.

'I'm so happy to see you — but look.' I spread my hands and blurted out the truth. I was embarrassed by the state of the place and me.

He laughed. 'Any room you're in is wonderful. And, as for you, you look tired and vulnerable, and here, and I just want to hold you.'

As he'd seen the Happy Hovel at its all-time worst, I told him to make a brew and I'd grab a shower. 'When I come down, you'd better have that cuddle on standby.'

I was in the shower, and it crossed my mind that he might have run for the hills by the time I came down.

We had a lovely morning. He couldn't stay long because he'd skived work to be with me again. He'd parked the

Land Rover in the top wood with the door open so that the Lord would think he was in the woods if he came looking—that's not Our Lord, God Almighty, by the way. It's the Lord of the manor—The Duke of Westmorland, no less. Risky. I don't want him getting into trouble. And it means he's got to give up his precious days off again to make up the time he's abused with me. So we gained two hours and lost two days, but he says it was worth it to see me.

I'd rather have waited and done things properly. We'd made plans to spend two whole days together, and he'd swapped it for two hours. I felt cheated. We cuddled on the settee and talked rubbish, and then he had to go. I ignored three urgent calls asking me to go to work, and it was chaotic bliss.

~~~

Brown made notes on her pad. 'Stop turning pages. We have to glean every clue this bugger drops. We've got two valuable things there.'

'Don't see how you work that out. Her house is a mess, her daughter needs a slap for not clearing up her rubbish, and the mother's a doormat who likes kissing.'

'Don't we all,' Brown said and could've kicked herself. She covered her awkwardness with words. 'The estate is in Westmorland. So from that, we know it's around the Kendal area. It has a top wood, which presumably means it has at least one other wood. This says it's a big hunk of land. And his boss is the Lord of Westmorland. This is great.'

'I was so engrossed in how stupid this woman is, that I missed most of that. The stupid cow's life is a running soap opera.'

'Get your head in the game, Renshaw.'

Brown fired up her laptop and did a search for the Lord of Westmorland. She made some initial notes to follow up later. 'This is great. It's our first strong lead.'

~~~

As soon as Mike left yesterday, I blitzed the house. Horses and doors and all that. Today I've been alone. I couldn't wait to get Emily off to school and talked to Mike most of the morning. The house is spotless, and he isn't here to see it.

But he's hoping to come tomorrow.

He asked if I'd go away with him for a weekend in Wales near Christmas.

'No funny business. All above board, Clara. I'll book two rooms in the hotel.'

Bloody hell. Christmas is three months away. Surely, we'll have moved things on by then. 'Won't that be a waste of money, if one's going to be wasted?'

'I don't want to put you under any pressure. I'll wait for you for as long as it takes.'

I'm ready now but didn't know how to tell him that. With his ex-wife being promiscuous, he has some funny ideas about sex. The way it's going, It'll take us until then to find time to get it on.

'I won't make love to you until we can spend the whole night together. You're worth more than that, lass.'

I'm in no rush. It's nice being courted the old-fashioned way. I fancy him though. More every time I see him. When we go to Wales, I'll drive, and he can relax and catch up on some sleep. He wouldn't hear of us going halves on the expenses, so it's my way of contributing to the cost.

'You can drive my car.'

Thank God he's dropped the stupid thee and thines as he's come to relax with me.

'You'd be mad to let me drive your posh car. With my navigational skills, I admit, your Sat Nav is a bonus, but I'd be terrified of hitting something.'

'You'd better get used to it fast, then. I'm putting you on my insurance so you can drive the Land Rovers too. I need you to help me get the animals in at night.'

He's too trusting.

We fought again today. I've got myself in trouble with my credit cards. It's only a bit of overspending since I've been seeing Mike and nothing I can't handle. I'm buggered if I'd let him buy me out of it. He said he'd give me the money to clear my debts because he wants to be with me always.

How can he respect me if he thinks I'd fleece him like that? We've only known each other a month. I don't want his money. I won't take it. And I won't live with him, in his place, or mine, until I'm debt free. I owe about five and a half grand, it's not massive, but it's a millstone. Things will stay as they are until I can pay my way.

Mike isn't a fool. He's careful with money, and as level-headed and sensible as they come. I don't think he's trying to buy my affection rather than being alone. He just wants to help and sees it as a means to a future together. I'm touched, but furious with him for making idiotic suggestions, and sticking his nose in. I don't want his handouts. I didn't even want to tell him I'm in debt, but I had to be honest. No secrets, but I want him to mind his own business and let me do things my way and on my own.

If I asked him for the ocean, he'd try and get it for me.

I'm crazy about him.

Hopefully, he's coming tomorrow. I can't wait.

~~~

'That changes everything,' Renshaw said. 'We've got him down as a conman out to fleece lonely women, but this stupid cow's up to her eyes in debt. What's in it for him?'

'Five grand's nothing. She's hardly drowning in money worries.'

'What about her house? Could that be the ultimate prize?'

'Rented,' Brown said. 'And she's only on a couple of grand a year above minimum wage as a zookeeper. She has three credit cards, and she uses one to make the minimum payment on the others every month. She hasn't got a pot to pee in—but her credit score's good, she has access to more credit, and he wouldn't care if he left her in a mess.'

'What's his game? I'm not buying this St Mike routine. Read on.'

Chapter Seven

10th October 2011

Here we go, it's all going wrong. I've written six emails to Mike and deleted them all. The letters ranged from, *Are you okay, Mike?* to, *this isn't enough for me, let's call it off* as I got more annoyed. But no harm was done because I didn't send them.

I haven't heard from him since Tuesday morning when we talked on Skype. He said, 'I'm coming to see you tomorrow, darling.' But he didn't turn up and there wasn't a word from him to say why.

It was my day off, I could have caught up on some sleep, but I put my life on hold to sit by the computer waiting for him to come online.

He didn't.

I have a dial-up network that overrides the phone line. So if I make a phone call, or answer one, it cuts the internet off. I watched for him coming online and worried that he might be trying to ring me on the landline. When I came offline three hundred times to check for messages on my phone, I worried that he'd chosen that thirty seconds to use his computer, saw that I wasn't there, and logged off again. He won't ever ring me on my mobile because it costs too much. He's so frugal that it's ridiculous. And he hasn't got a phone of his own to text me. I've never known a man like him. He said that sometimes he turns all his lights off and has a candle to save electricity, but if the company are paying for his phone, wouldn't they be paying for his amenities as well? He asks so many questions and knows everything about me, but he doesn't like talking about himself. If I ask him anything personal, he changes the subject. I know so little about him.

I needed to draw my wages from the bank but didn't dare leave the house in case I missed him. The dog hasn't had her run for two days because I might miss Mike coming online if I take her. He couldn't even take the time to drop me a single sentence in an email to say everything was okay. He could be dead for all I know. It isn't fair.

The last time we spoke online, we left it on an argument over the stupid phone. Maybe he's decided I'm too much to take on. He must be too busy to get on the computer this week. The shoots are every Thursday. It's one of his busiest days. This morning I set my alarm for seven again and repeated yesterday's and Wednesday's schedule. I'm still watching his offline status and looking out of the window every time a car drives past. But I know he's not coming.

Mike lives at work. His home is his work, and his garden is the scree. He has thousands of birds and wildlife to take care of and needs to be on hand all night to guard against poachers and foxes. He's literally on patrol all night five nights a week, and on-call the other two. He sleeps in snatches through the day after the animals have been seen to. Because he lives on-site and doesn't trust his staff to do the job without him, he works his days off as well. His job is his life.

I've come into the picture, and it's gone to hell. I make demands on his time, and he has to try and make a box to fit me into. But I'm expanding the box and trying to stretch its dimensions and extract more time than he can spare.

I said, 'Don't worry if you can't make it. It doesn't matter.' But that was a lie, it does matter. His two-hour visits aren't enough. I want him to make more time for me. It's the same old story and the reason men get sick of me.

I told him on date two that I'm high maintenance. He didn't understand what I meant and assumed I was talking about money and wanting material things.

These last two days are what I was talking about. When I don't hear from him, I assume his feelings have changed. Then I get resentful. Why hasn't he rung? He tells me he can't use the phone because the boss pays the bill, surely that can't be right. I know there aren't any phone boxes in the forest, but why can't he nip to the nearest one, and give me a two-minute call to tell me everything's okay? He lives on caffeine and must fill his flask a million times a day. He could drop me a couple of lines while the kettle's boiling. I don't get it.

I think about him all the time. But I seem to be out of sight out of mind. He was the one that came onto me. I didn't want him. He did all the running. He tells me he's in love with me after a few weeks. He's supposed to be my boyfriend. So, why can't he keep in touch?

I don't need much reassurance, but I do need some form of daily contact. Is that unreasonable? I'm too clingy, it's horrible. I hate it in other people and yet subscribe to it myself. For all I know he could have been shot. We've sworn that we'll always be honest with each other, and I'm really pissed off with him.

I don't know how I'll be when I speak to him. I feel neglected. I know I'll be cool with him, and the poor sod won't have a clue what's wrong.

He's had three days of thinking time after he said he loves me. He says I can only do one thing to get rid of him, and that's being unfaithful. Why the hell can't I just trust in that, and know he's busy?

I had these exact feelings with Rick. He was always too busy mowing his lawns and doing his ironing to spend time with me. I was right about him. He was seeing other women. He confessed to three, and one was his next-door neighbour, a famous Coronation Street actress who I used to make supper for after the pub. And all the time she was sleeping with my boyfriend.

I had the same with Sam. He was always packing his bloody boxes, whatever that meant, I never did find out. And he was having sex with other women in posh hotels.

Men lie to me. They always have. They say they don't have time for me when what they mean is, they don't want me. Mike won't give me any means of contacting him. He only checks his email once a week because he struggles to read and finds it a chore to work through what's important and what's crap. He wouldn't take the phone I bought him. He says it's down to money. But I think it's because he doesn't know how to use one and feels stupid admitting it. I'd show him how it works. Or, the other reason is that he doesn't want me to contact him. Which means he's hiding something, and I'm not as important as he'd have me believe.

I turned down an overtime shift yesterday on the assumption that he was coming. I've turned down more work today. It's more money that I could've spent on one of my credit cards to get my debts down. And from tomorrow, I'm on seven long day shifts, so there's no opportunity to see him for at least a week.

When I get a new man, he becomes the centre of my world. I'm back at work tomorrow and hate that I've wasted my three days off. I haven't caught up on sleep, I haven't done a damned thing with my time. I can't concentrate. If he says he wants to see me over the weekend, he can't because I'm working, and I'll be so resentful of work—and him. It's stupid. The other day he offered to clear my five grand debts, and, all I want from him is a twenty pence phone call. I was looking forward to being off and seeing him, and I'm so disappointed.

~~~

It's eight o'clock on Friday night. I haven't heard a word from Mike since we argued on Tuesday Morning. I'm convinced he's finished with me.

I was determined not to be pathetic and whinge at him, but I sent him a brief email asking him to let me know where we stand. Being in a relationship is supposed to make you happy, especially a new one. I'm miserable. I haven't left the damned computer for three days, and he hasn't been on once. I have to work from eight until six tomorrow. I hope he gets in touch to let me know one way or the other before then because I can't concentrate on anything.

I know I'm like a stupid kid. I get emotionally involved too fast and am too intense for men to cope with. I'm emotionally immature.

Last week, he said to me, 'I'm the same, Clara. That's what makes us brilliant, and why we're lucky we found each other.'

And then he dropped out of existence.

I thought Mike could cope with me. All I need is reassurance that nothing's changed overnight, and then I'm fine. He was the one flinging I love you around like bloody confetti.

One of my best friends, Baz, rang to see if I was up for a night out. He wants to know all about the fantastic new man in my life. Meg's been talking. I turned him down because I didn't think Mike would like it. Baz was brilliant and said he understands, but he might not ask again.

I'd have gone if Meg had come too, but as usual, she was too tired. I could do with something to distract me from the damned computer. Sometimes Mike rings at night, and I don't know whether to turn the computer off in case he rings me on the phone or keep it on in case he comes online. I don't know what the hell's going on, and I'm confused, hurt, angry and mixed up.

I hope we're okay after this. If he hasn't finished with me, he's going to be annoyed with my lack of trust. He's told me that he's real and said I don't trust him. I know he isn't running around with other women. If everything's fine, it means he hasn't been in touch because he's swamped with work. I'm waiting, not knowing if we're on or off, or what's going on.

Maybe he's got no intention of getting in touch with me, and the first I'll know we aren't together is when I never hear from him again.

Sounds like the sound of goodbye to me.

I wish he'd turn up on the doorstep.

~~~

11th October 2011.

It's one o'clock Saturday afternoon. I haven't heard a word from Mike since Tuesday. That's going from speaking every spare second that we could, from him skiving work to see me, from me driving into the middle of bloody nowhere for a sneaked two hours with him — to — nothing.

It speaks for itself, and I'm devastated.

I should have pushed him away when he kissed me. I didn't give out any signals that it was okay to. I didn't fancy him. He made me fall for him. He said the only rule was to be faithful. I honoured my side of the bargain.

This one lasted three weeks and never went beyond a kiss. But Emily met him, and that hurts.

I keep my private life away from my daughter until I'm sure about somebody, but he had to turn up on the doorstep. It's a good job I wasn't married. Luckily, I have nothing to hide. I'll be over him in a week, and some tosser will come along who isn't worth having.

Within days of meeting each other, we talked about moving in together, and now it's all over. I was scared of not being sure and hurting him. If one of us had to be hurt, I'm glad it's me, because I'm the fickle one. This will pass in a few days, and I'll be angry and then I'll be over him. He's had time to sit on his moor and think about us. I expect I'm too risky.

I'm a risk taker, Mike isn't. I get it.

I'm pissed off, though. I had him pegged for a man with more integrity than dropping off the planet. If I'd been the one wanting to end it, I'd have had the balls to tell him.

These are the last words he wrote to me: I hope you have a restless night thinking about me. You've brought me back to write this at 1 am. I'm thinking of you, and how proud I am to have such a wonderful, sexy lady as you. I'm the luckiest man to have you to hold and walk through life with. Take care, my love xxx

I corrected his typing. He wrote that email after we'd had words over a week ago. I was expecting to see him the next day. I don't know what went wrong. Part of me is wondering if he's had an accident. I can only assume from his silence that he doesn't want me—but I don't know.

I've sent him a last email. I won't contact him again: Mike, Emily's away for the night. Please, if there's anything left between us, can you arrange for me to talk to you? I don't care if it's only for five minutes. If it's over, that's fine, but please tell me. I don't know if something's happened to you. I'm not stupid and can take a hint. But I am stubborn, and until I know it's over, I'm spending all my time waiting to hear from you. I promise. If you answer this by saying you don't want to see me, I won't bother you again. I'm very easy to get rid of. Clara x.

We were only together a short time and were never intimate, but we talked about all sorts of things. I was looking forward to our weekend in Wales. After that, he said he was going to take me to the Highlands of Scotland because he wanted to make love to me in the snow. He might have only ever had one sexual partner, but he's a kinky bugger. He said he wanted to tie me to a tree in his wood with my stockings. I'm strong, and he wants to make me vulnerable and have me laid bare to do with as he pleased. I've never let anybody tie me up before. That takes trust, and I've never met anybody that I'd want to be that defenceless with. I guess I'll never know if I would have liked it now.

Time: 3:15 pm. Finally, I heard from him: Babe. I love you. Be on here tomorrow at 10 am. I am fine. Sore leg. Don't worry xxx

That's it? Nothing else? It's enough, though. I don't know what's gone on with him, but I guess we're still on.

So, tomorrow we need to talk.

I'm insecure, I don't trust all this love talk, and I don't believe it. It's not ringing true. When I don't hear from him for days, I assume he's not going to get in touch. I get that it might be inconvenient for him to boot the computer up, but I need more contact. Even if it's just a few words like this. It's enough to know he's alive, and everything's okay.

His job is dangerous. He makes his own ammunition for himself and all the guns on the shoot. So, he's dealing with live explosives every day. On the shoots themselves, he's taking out fifteen idiots armed with guns. Anything could happen. He says he's going to be on the Internet tomorrow morning, but I hope he comes in person. It's a week since I've seen him, and I miss him.

It's not easy.

~~~

Phil rubbed his eyes and looked up from the diary. 'Christ. Do women really think like that? She's got no self-respect, mooning around for days. "Oh, no. He hasn't rung me in the last five minutes. He must be shagging a game bird," It's pathetic.

'Give her a break. She makes me want to reach for a puke bucket as well. But look at the way he's treating her. And read what she's saying between all the angst. Alarm bells aren't just ringing, they're being used as weapons to batter her. She knows something's wrong. We can look at other suspects all we like, but this creepy bastard's our man. I feel it,' Brown said.

'If she knows she's being used, she's too stupid to do anything about it. I've got no sympathy for her.'

Brown stood up and snatched the diary out of his hands. She glared at him and clutched the book to her chest as if it was her heart she was protecting. She left the room in a temper, knocking a chair over on her way to the door.

'No Phil. She just wants to be loved.'

Brown slammed the door behind her.

Chapter Eight

Silas Nash had something to live for. He rushed home every evening and either threw something together on toast or put a ready meal in the oven. After his dinner, he'd wash up and feed Lola, but he couldn't wait to get to the laptop and didn't even turn on the news before he powered up to check his messages.

He'd been talking to Legally_yours_64 since he came home from Greece. It began with a few tentative messages, and, as dating app encounters tend to be, giving and receiving information was like pulling teeth. Nash tried to be as honest as he could about general topics while lying to protect his identity at all costs.

In his second message to Nash, his new friend told him his name was Kelvin Jones and that he was forty-nine. The first message was simply, 'Hi. How are you?'

When Kelvin gave him his personal information, Nash panicked. He had to do the same—after all, they wouldn't get anywhere if they didn't speak. Brown had coached him on what to say until the level of trust was there, and he could be honest about everything. Nash told the truth about his age but told Kelvin his name was George Shan.

This was only the second person he'd spoken to on the dating app. He'd stopped messaging, Dave Thorn after being warned off him by the psychic, Conrad Snow. Nash felt guilty when he thought about it. He'd seemed like a decent bloke, and Nash had cut him off, with his only explanation being that he didn't think they'd be compatible long-term. Brown had assured him it happened all the time, but Nash felt as though he was the only person ever to ditch somebody by message on a dating app.

He'd been reluctant to try again, but Brown bullied him into it. And here he was in a pickle. It couldn't be any better with Kelvin. But Nash was a liar. He'd given a false name and told him he was the caretaker at a local school. From day one, every instinct in his body had screamed at him, to tell the truth, but, as one of the top police officers in the country, he couldn't let himself be vulnerable in case somebody outed him as a gay man on the dating scene. He internalised being gay and thought the results could be catastrophic for his career, and that witnesses and suspects would see it as a weakness in him.

Brown had tried to hammer home that the opposite was true, being gay was being him, and his character had made him an excellent cop. He thought it was very sweet of her, but a childhood of schoolyard bullying had ingrained shame into his psyche.

Unlike speaking to Thorn, Nash and Kelvin had everything in common. Kelvin spoke openly about his life. He was born in Nigeria and was raised as the third son of a strict Christian Family. The Muslim religion dominated North Nigeria, and most of the Christian families lived in the south. His surname at birth was Abiola, but when his family settled in Kendal, they'd taken the western name Jones, and the boy, Kenziabal was given the name Kelvin.

Because of his strict upbringing, Kelvin went to university in Manchester and was encouraged to marry young. He finished his education and trained as a solicitor, taking a junior position in the town for work experience. They kept him on, and he moved up through the ranks until one of the old owners retired, and he was offered a forty-nine per cent buy-out partnership deal with the other owner. Wesley Deacon had chosen to stay on as the senior owner of the firm and they made a good team.

Nash and Kelvin passed messages, talking about their interests and things they enjoyed, and it was Kelvin who suggested leaving the dating app and talking on the phone.

Nash was excited, horrified, and scared. He said yes before he had the chance to think too much and talk himself out of it. Kelvin had a deep voice with a rich, educated tone and only a hint of his Nigerian roots. After an hour, Nash was head over heels in love, and he'd never met this man.

They chatted for three hours the first night. Nash was guarded and steered the conversation back to Kelvin when he asked personal questions. But he couldn't avoid the basics. He told him he lived in Barrow but didn't mention that it was actually on Walney Island. He told him about Lola the cat, and about his previous relationships. He found it excruciatingly painful because he had to filter every response to keep his identity private. He told outright lies when he talked about his job and hated himself when he got into his role. He talked too much about painting classrooms and buying plants for the outside areas of the school.

That night he had a nightmare that Kelvin had a tracker on his phone and had walked into the station with a bouquet of flowers for Nash. Kelvin melted, and Dave Thorn stood in his place. The solicitor's suit turned into a gamekeeper's greatcoat, and the flowers were a shotgun pointed at Nash's face. He woke in a sweat.

Kelvin talked openly with nothing to hide and made Nash feel worse. Jennifer, Kel's wife, had given him three lovely children, who he was still very close to. Kelvin was faithful throughout his marriage, and although he knew he was gay, he loved his wife very much. He spoke about having to hide who he was for a long time because of his career, and Nash wanted to blurt everything out. He tried to tell him several times, but at the last second, something always held him back.

Instead, he told more lies on top of lies on top of lies.

He kept his feelings for Kelvin to himself. He wasn't worldly-wise and couldn't tell this stranger that he felt his world would stop turning if he didn't have his nightly conversation with him.

Another feeling had been churning him up inside. It wasn't a pleasant thought, and it didn't make him feel good. Brown passed the Clara Watts diary to Bowes every night to type up, and the following day the badly typed transcripts were brought to him. His first thought was that they were useless.

The pages were littered with typos and grammatical errors. They could never be used for anything other than their personal research. Nash highlighted the relevant sentences, and they amounted to less than half a dozen pages. He retyped the important parts that may be used in court himself, rather than passing them back down the line to somebody else.

But that wasn't what made the pit of his stomach churn. It was the talk in the station about how stupid and gullible Clara Watts was. Here was a woman who fell in love with a man after a couple of meetings and believed every word he said to her. It was like a personal challenge to the conman to come up with the most outrageous excuses. From the reports of other women, he'd conned, they suspected he had his two hours with Clara, and then moved on to the next one, so that he put a full day into grooming his various victims. Clara took in every word because, when you want to believe somebody, you do. She would have blindly followed him to the ends of the earth.

Nash was Clara Watts.

That was how he felt about Kelvin. He hung on to his every word and replayed their conversations in his head until they could speak again. At least Clara had met her man in real life. Nash's feelings for Kelvin were sight unseen. He'd seen photos and adored what he saw. But if he met Kelvin, and he had two heads, it wouldn't make a difference. Nash would still want him unconditionally.

He heard what the lads said about Clara Watts, and he watched Brown going into battle with them to protect her. She said it was admirable having blind faith in her man, and that Clara was in love and trusted her partner as any decent person would.

But Brown identified with Clara, too. She was in a broken, destructive relationship that she couldn't claw her way out of. She knew it was wrong, but they were in love, and couldn't break away from each other.

Nash wanted more. Talking to Kelvin on the phone most evenings wasn't enough, and like Clara if ever Kelvin was too busy to speak to him, the doubts and insecurities crept in. Was he talking to somebody else? With his perfect African genes, Kelvin looked fantastic. Was Nash making a fool of himself in a dating game he didn't understand the rules of? Kelvin was a lot younger than him, he read every one of Clara's doubts—and he knew them.

He could call it off now—but his heart would stop and he'd die.

'Hi Clara, I'm as much of a gullible fool as you are,' he said into the stillness of the room. Lola lifted her head, and through myopic eyes, she slow-blinked and agreed with him.

The night before, Kelvin broached the subject of meeting in person. Nash had nearly choked. It made it too real. He had to get out of meeting him, but he didn't want to. He craved meeting Kelvin more than anything in the world, and he'd take whatever consequences that brought. But when it came to a response his courage left him, he'd made an excuse and changed the subject. He had no idea what Kelvin must have thought. As he put his phone down, he cursed himself.

Kelvin was the first contact in his recent calls list. He had to ring him back and explain. He hit his name and breathed. Oh shit.

Kel answered.

'Yes,' Nash blurted out, without explaining anything.

'Yes, what?'

'Yes, please. I'd love to meet you.'

Kelvin laughed. 'Okay. When?'

'How does now grab you? We could meet halfway. The Rusland Pool, maybe.'

'Crikey, I didn't see that coming. It beats Coronation Street and a soak in the bath any day. Okay.'

'But there's something I have to tell you first.'

'Go on.'

'I'm not a caretaker. And my name isn't George Shan.'

'I know.'

'You can't know.'

Kelvin's next words almost made Silas shut down his phone and never open it again.

'Hi Silas, pleased to meet you.'

Nash didn't know what to do. All those lies he'd told. Just that night he'd recounted a tale about clearing pigeons from the school loft space. He'd talked about fictional children and had even given them names. Kel hadn't said a word.

Nash felt such a fool and his cheeks burned. How did he know? And if Kelvin could find his real name out so easily, why couldn't they track Clara's mystery boyfriend? He pulled his mind away from the case but still struggled to find the right words.

'I am so sorry. I've hated lying to you.'

'It's okay. I get it. I've been there myself and understand why you did. I've spent most of my life living in Denial Village, and I was waiting until you were ready. I knew you'd get there when the time was right. I call you Inspector in my head, and it's very sexy.'

'I feel awful for deceiving you.'

'You weren't adding up, Silas. You drink Martell Brandy, for God's sake—and you told me your special occasions bottle is vintage. Show me a lowly caretaker that can afford that. So, on the first night, after we'd spoken, I did some research. You can't be too careful these days. And you might be a great detective, but you're a useless liar. Anyway, thank you for trusting me, I'll see you at the bar. Mine's a pint of Guinness if you're there first.'

Nash croaked out the word 'Okay.'

'See you in an hour, Inspector.'

Nash was dumbfounded. He had to close his mouth, bite his tongue, and do everything in his power to stop the words, 'I love you,' from spilling out of his emotionally immature mouth.

He felt a lot of sympathy for Clara Watts.

An hour? He had an hour to get changed and drive the Twenty-five minutes to get to their meeting place. He didn't have time to panic about meeting Kelvin because he was too busy getting in a flap about what to wear. He had a two-minute shower and fell over the cat on his way out of the ensuite. It was their time for TV and cuddles, and Lola twined around his legs to remind him.

'Lola, if you have the power to turn into a human and tell me what to wear. Now is the time to do it.'

He contemplated calling Brown, she'd sort him out, but she'd want all the details and keep him talking, and he was never going to make it on time as it was.

He squirted Lynx Africa under his armpits and splashed Obsession for Men on his face after scrubbing over it with his electric razor. What if he had a shaving rash and it went all red and blotchy? He used his Bulldog moisturizer and coated his balls in a cooling testicle cream. He had no time to regret not being kinder to his skin.

Dress up, dress down, look like a dick. Feel like a clown? He wore suits all day at work, and Psychologically he wanted to take his first-date experience as far away from his career as he could get it. He'd be a policeman if he wore his suit.

On a trip to York the year before, the Lambretta shop had a sale, and he bought a polo shirt for a northern soul night at The Forum. Sandy let him down that night, and he never went. The shirt had hung in his wardrobe ever since. It was black with burgundy trim, and he teamed it with a pair of smart light blue jeans that looked more like trousers. He wore his hint-of-red brogues. And, as an afterthought on the way out of the door, he grabbed his grey jersey scarf and draped it around his neck, letting it hang. He thanked his parents for his good genes, and his barber for the neat goatee. At a push, he could pass for late forties.

He got to the Rusland Pool Bar and Restaurant with four minutes to spare. With rushing, there was no time for fear or doubt, only excitement. But, with his hand on the door, fear gripped him. He had to force himself to push it open and walk in. Kelvin was distinctive, and it only took a quick bar scan to see that he wasn't there.

What if he'd stood Nash up? He'd said, Guinness. Should he order? He'd feel such a fool with two drinks in front of him if he didn't come.

'Yes, love? What can I get you?' The woman was looking at him, and he just stood there like a fool. Speak, you dickhead.

'Two pints of Guinness, please.'

'Extra Cold?'

'It is. I should have worn a coat.'

'No Extra Cold Guinness,' she laughed and tapped the pump. 'Relax. And stop worrying, she'll be here.'

Nash had no answer and gawped. He normally drank bitter and had no idea why he'd ordered Guinness. Probably because it was easier than asking for different drinks under the server's scrutiny. Kelvin might think he was a weirdo that was mirroring him, and he wished he'd gone for bitter. What if Guinness made him fart?

He was fumbling with his phone on the card reader when he felt the tap on his shoulder and jolted. He spun around and knew in that second that he never wanted to look at any face other than this one for the rest of his life.

'Hi,' Kelvin said. His smile was sudden sunshine on the darkest day.

'Hi.' Nash was a statue. Then he nodded his head. Noddy goes to bloody Toyland. He nodded and opened his mouth to speak without thinking of a damned thing to say. There was nothing. Some bastard had come along and pickpocketed his brain while his back was turned.

Kelvin pulled him into a hug. Three things floored Nash. The feel of Kelvin's arms around him. He was wearing a grey woollen overcoat, but Nash felt the strength in his arms. The lips that brushed the side of his cheek and made him want to reach up and touch where the kiss had been just to prove it was there. And the warm breath whispering in his ear so that only he could hear.

'Relax,' he said. 'She's already here.'

The lady held the card machine out and coughed to remind him that it hadn't connected. Kelvin let him go, and he turned back to her and pressed his phone to the plastic.

'I never saw that one coming. You're a dark horse, aren't you?' she said.

'No. He's the dark horse. I'm a Palamino.' Nash wanted to cut his tongue out. What a stupid thing to say, but he heard Kelvin laughing behind him. He felt his hand clap him on the shoulder. 'Should we find somewhere to sit,' he said.

They went to a table in the corner, away from the diners. Nash watched as Kelvin took his coat off and folded it before draping it over his chair. He wore grey trousers and a blue jumper. Smart, like a solicitor out of uniform. No suits tonight boys.

'Aren't you cold?'

'Bloody freezing.' Nash said. 'I wanted to impress.'

'Mission accomplished.'

Jesus Christ, he was blushing. Apart from when Kelvin had caught him out on his lies, Nash hadn't blushed since the bullies had given him a wedgie in the chemistry lab when he was fourteen. Kelvin picked up his pint but burst out laughing before it reached his mouth. His breath blew the froth off the top of his glass to land on the table in front of them. It sat there like an island. It was their Switzerland.

'What?'

'Palamino.'

The ice was broken, and from that second there were no awkward silences. They shared a basket of chips fried in goose fat, and Nash wanted to lick the salt from Kelvin's lips. Kel caught him staring and knew the effect he was having. He winked, and Nash melted.

Neither of them wanted to leave, but they had to work the next morning, and it was too late, and too soon, to do coffee at either home. Neither mentioned it, but Nash felt it was an unspoken there between them. Desired but resisted. Of all the parking spaces available, their cars were next to each other in the carpark. It seemed prophetic.

'See, even our cars are making friends,' Kelvin said.

'Did you really say that?'

'You want to hear the rubbish I spout in court.'

'Love to.'

The night was clear. Away from the smog of town, the stars were bright, and there was a rag around the moon indicating frost before morning. It was cold, but not unbearable. 'Come here.' Kelvin put his arms around Nash and wrapped his open coat around both of them to keep him warm.

But it was Nash who put his hand up to the back of Kel's head and pulled him down for a kiss. Kelvin was three inches taller than Nash.

Was this how it felt for Clara when the gamekeeper kissed her on their first date?

The kiss was soft and held a million promises. It was the best kiss of Nash's life.

Chapter Nine

The next day he had a meeting with Conrad Snow. It was the first time he'd been the one to instigate an interview with the psychic, but they were getting nowhere with finding Clara Watt's mystery man and needed anything the psychic could give them. It was time to stop fighting the paranormal and suck it up. If he got nothing, he'd lost nothing. Nash had arranged to meet at the station, but as Snow's car was in the garage, he'd asked that they get together at his home in Lowick Bridge.

It was a nice place, a converted farmhouse that embraced ancient and modern in an intimate tango across the Lakeland hills. He had a plot of land and raised some farm animals, and the smallholding had a sense of calm about it. It was the kind of place you were happy to be.

Snow had a brand-new Genesis electrified G80 in the drive. Talking to the dead must be lucrative. He wouldn't get much change out of a hundred grand for that baby. Nash took a moment to be jealous. Why hadn't he come in that car? Snow had heard him pull up, and the door opened before Nash rang the bell.

'Come in, Inspector. The coffee has just brewed.'

Nash wiped his feet and stepped onto a doormat in a hall with a soft white carpet. It seemed highly impractical for farm living.

Snow pointed to a rack inside the door with footwear on the bottom rung and disposable slippers in packets on the top. 'Would you mind? We normally use the backdoor into the kitchen, it's the only room where I allow outdoor shoes, but I wanted to welcome you cordially.'

Nash would rather have used the kitchen entrance and not had to take his shoes off. He was mortified when he undid the laces of his shiny black brogues and slid his foot out to see his toe poking through the sock. It wasn't like that when he dressed, and he would never dream of putting damaged clothing on. His smart appearance was everything to him. Sod's law dictated that the one time he had to take his shoes off, his sock gave up the ghost. It was embarrassing. He didn't want Snow to think he was a slob. At least his toenail was neatly clipped.

Snow grinned, and Nash was irritated that he was enjoying Nash's discomfort. He led him into a lounge with the same white carpet throughout. The room was stunning, with the entire West wall comprised of glass to look out over the stream at the bottom of his land and the rolling hills of Grizedale Forest in the near distance. A log fire burned in the huge grate, and Nash felt that it had been lit to impress him.

'Nice place.'

'Thanks. We like it.'

We? He had a partner then. Nash had wondered. Snow gave nothing of himself away. Nash sat in one of two ivory silk armchairs and looked around. But there was nothing to confirm whether Snow lived alone or with a partner. There was no evidence of any children. He was a man that kept his cards close to his chest.

He poured coffee from an ornate silver Samovar on a hostess trolley and passed a delicate cup and saucer to Nash without asking if he'd like milk or sugar. Nash was a tea drinker. If he had to have coffee, he liked it white. This was black and bitter.

'You had a good evening last night,' Snow said. It wasn't a question. And it irritated Nash that he made a point of alluding to knowing things.

'I did thank you.'

'He'll be good for you, and if you're both prepared to work on your different lifestyles, you can make it work.'

'I beg your pardon?'

Snow ignored him. 'Watch out for the youngest child, though. She's a Daddy's girl, spoiled, and she has claws.'

'Do you mind if we stick to the matter at hand? I didn't come here to discuss my personal life with all and sundry.'

Snow looked around the room as if expecting All and Sundry to leap up from behind the sofa. 'Of course. What can I do for you, Inspector Nash? Forgive my intrusion into your personal life, but I'm a fifth-generation sensitive. It's my duty to tell you what I'm given.'

Nash took Carla Watts's second diary out of his bag and passed it to Snow. 'I'd like you to have a feel of this and do your divining thing. How much do you want me to tell you about the case?'

Snow had already put his hand up to stop him from talking. 'Don't say a word, it'll stir the mud at the bottom of the swamp. I want a clear reading. And, it's called psychometry, as well you know.'

He closed his eyes and used the palm of his hand on the diary, making circular motions over the cover. 'It belongs to a lady. Carla.' He drew numbers on the cover with his finger and repeated a three and then a four. 'Come on. Stop messing about. Give me her age. Just her age, nobody else's.' He looked up, shook his head, and tried again. 'I'm sorry. I'm trying to get a fix on her age, but I'm getting two distinct numbers, thirty-three and forty-one. I'm seeing both numbers and can't clear either of them away.'

'I understand.'

'You do? Thank God for that. I thought you were going to shout at me.'

'I do not shout at people.'

'Oh, you so do. You're like a grumpy doctor with a terrible bedside manner. The woman was left-handed.'

'Not much help, I'm afraid. We didn't get much from the body—too decayed, but you're right. It confirms what the handwriting profiler told us about her. You were nearly right with the name as well. It's Clara, not Carla, and we're dealing with her at two different ages, eight years apart when she was thirty-three and forty-one.'

'That's good. I'm glad you could take it. If something isn't right, just tell me it's wrong and give me a chance to correct it.'

'The thing is, Snow. I haven't got all day, and I'm not playing parlour games, so if I can interject to speed things up a bit, I'm going to. Anyway, it's her book, but she's not the one we're interested in.'

'No, it's him. I realise that. Oh, I don't like him. Not at all. He's a charmer. I'll give him that. I'm seeing a snake. A big, fat, self-satisfied, lying snake and it's slithering across the pages of the book. All right, darling. Yes. Yes. I've got it, my love. It's not just a book. It's her diary. Oh, Sweetheart, bless you. She's bleeding onto these pages, literally and figuratively, pouring out the hurting words like a purge. There's another one, another diary like this from the first time. This one's the second. She loves him very much, but he leads her on a merry dance. There's an eagle. It's not a metaphor. I see an eagle flying over a field and coming to rest on her arm.'

'Is he there? What does he look like?'

'I can see part of him. He's a big brute, well over six feet. And broad with it. I can only see his face in profile, but it's fleshy and very weathered. There are some deep trenches in his skin, and pockmarks, probably from childhood acne. It looks either scarred or badly chapped. He's dark, with curly hair, either very dark brown or black, just touching his collar. He's wearing a green Barbour jacket. The kind people wear to go shooting. Ah, thank you. Yes. They're showing me a rifle. It's cocked and over his arm. He's got Wellington's on and is quick to smile. He smokes. Roll-ups. And he has a small tobacco tin in his hand. It says, To Dad, love Sal xxx.'

'That's something we didn't have before. Thanks. Can you tell me anything else?'

'I can, but I'm not sure I want to. I see a black oil slick covering the book. It's like darkness covering her life. I'm seeing an older man. White wig and robes. He's a judge.'

'He's got convictions? Has he been to prison?'

'Damn, I'm getting this all wrong. They're telling me the old man isn't really a judge. It's another one of his lies. Somebody just knocked the wig off the old man's head. Does that make any sense at all?'

'No. None.'

'You need to get her out of there, Nash. It's not healthy.'

'Too late, mate, she's already gone. Can't you reach her for us?'

'No. She's not coming through. Nothing.'

'Can you tell us where this bloke lives, or his name?'

'I'll try.' He stroked the book again and traced imaginary letters with his fingers. 'Mike, Steve, Dave, Robin. No. I'm sorry, I'm getting too many names coming at me for this bloke and can't find the right one. I just keep seeing random names with legs climbing a steep hill. As frustrating as it is, sometimes they give me imagery rather than words. It's gone. I'm seeing barbed wire. Sorry, I'm wrong again. It's a plant, a thick vine like a twisted rose stem, with thorns sticking out of it. Maybe watch out for Roses? As to where he lives. I'm seeing owls. Lots of owls. M.I.L.'

'Millom? Is it Millom?'

'Maybe I don't know. I'm sorry. That's all I've got.'

'Nothing else?'

'No. I hope some of it can help you.'

'It's not much, but I suppose if we've got Millom as a starting point. It's better than nothing, and you think he might be called Steve, Mike, Robin, or Dave. We already have the name, Mike. Can you confirm that?'

'No. I've given you everything I had, and I could make guesses all day, but I don't do that. If I start putting my own interpretation on things, that's when we'll get muddled up. Look out for the roses. Oh, and the juicy steaks you've bought for dinner tonight are fine, but you'll have to re-think dessert. One whiff of those strawberries, and he'll throw up all over you and have a three-day vomiting migraine. Allergic.'

'As I live and breathe, it's Madhur Jaffrey.'

Snow handed the diary back, and Nash dropped it in shock. The cover was hot. Not just warm as though it had been held, but hot, far hotter than human body temperature.

Snow grinned, 'Sorry. Should have said. Occupational hazard.'

Chapter Ten

12th October 2011

Mike and I are fine. I'm a stupid overreacting drama queen. I hate the uncertainty of new relationships. Roll on the stage where he comes through the door, and I say, 'You know where the kettle is, and if you want anything to eat, get it yourself. And you can get those dammed wellies off my carpet, mate.' At the moment, he turns up unexpectedly, and my heart does a backflip. How long does that last?

He was dumbfounded that I'd kicked off and didn't realise what all the fuss was about last week. 'Calm down, lass, you're going to give yourself an ulcer fretting like that.' He'd tried to come on Wednesday, as arranged. A tanker had overturned in Lancaster, and he was stuck in traffic for three hours and ran out of time. He got halfway here before turning around to fight his way back. Then he did his leg in, and that laid him up and made his work slower.

'Sometimes, I'll be out of touch for a few days. That's the nature of this business,' he said. He looked tired. As expected, he was disappointed in me. 'Where's the trust between us, girl?' I felt small and knew it was me in the wrong. 'I might not have been in contact, but I've been thinking and talking about you all the time.'

On Friday, he had to buy a new Land Rover for the estate. While he was at the garage, he saw a Frontera Sport 4x4 that would be ideal for me to help him in the woods. 'I was going to pick it up there and then for you, but I figured you'd blow another gasket at me. The big question of the day is. Do you want to come with me and see if you like it? If you do, I'll buy it for you.'

I don't suppose it was a brand-new car, but nevertheless, I bet we're talking thousands rather than hundreds. Doesn't he listen to me? Things got tetchy again.

'I want you to be safe.'

'I am safe.'

'You need a decent car.'

'I've got a decent car.'

'What, that old thing?'

I was speechless. This is the best car I've ever had. It's fast, clean, in good nick, and reliable. I like my car. I see no reason to change it as it's running well and doesn't need anything fixing. Everything in it, on it and connected to it works. That's a novelty in itself. If he'd seen my last car, he'd have cause to worry. By the time it chugged its last, it wouldn't go over thirty and screamed for mercy, leaving big oil puddles in its wake. One car I had didn't have working doors, and I had to climb through the window. I've gone up in the world. My status has elevated with the Mondeo. My only problem is that it's too big for my job.

It's greedy and costs a fortune to run, but I don't want to change it until something happens to stop it from passing an MOT. His son, Dave, is seventeen and learning to drive. He needs a car, and yet Mike wants to buy one for a woman he's known for a month. He frightens me sometimes. It was an emphatic no from me, and he promised not to mention it again.

I haven't seen him yet. We were supposed to meet halfway for a stolen hour today, but he was called to a work meeting about the fuel shortage. I think after getting so wound up about not hearing from him, he expected me to blow, but I'm fine with it. I'm disappointed he couldn't make it, I haven't seen him for over a week now, but all is well, so I'm not hyperventilating.

~~~

'Why couldn't she have been useful and told us where halfway is? At least we'd know if Snow was on the right track about Mike living at Millom,' Brown said.

'I wish she'd open her eyes and see what's in front of her. A lorry overturned in Lancaster? Come on, lady. Wake up. I want to shake her, and then give her a cuddle and tell her it'll be okay,' Renshaw said.

'It could be true. We have the date. I'll check if there was a big overturn that day. One that held traffic up for three hours.'

'I'm going to swap jobs with Conrad Snow. Do it, but you're wasting your time. I'm telling you now, there wasn't. Buying her a car, my arse. He knew damned well she'd say no.'

'Still a gamble though.'

'Not at all. If she'd said yes, the car would have already been sold.'

'DVLA will have a record of every Land Rover sold countrywide in October 2011. That's going to lead us straight to him. Something concrete at last. And we know his son's seventeen and called Dave. We'll have him by the end of the day.'

'I wouldn't bank on it. If he's been in any kind of trouble up to this point, he'll have covered his tracks with false details, and that'll carry through to his legitimate dealings. Can I see you tonight, Molly?'

'Sure. As long as you take me to your local and snog me at the bar in front of your wife's mates.'

He put his hand on her thigh, and she brushed it off. He looked as miserable as sin—because that's what it was, she thought. A big, fat sin.

'I can't do that,' he said.

'I know.'

'This is killing me, Molly.'

'Did you make love to her last night?'

He hung his head and shook it slowly like a polar bear in captivity. 'If you'd asked me that question regarding any other night in the past three weeks, I could have said no. I won't ever lie to you. Yes, I made love to my wife last night.'

'Special night then.' The bitterness and venom dripped from her tongue as she turned back to the diary—She felt as stupid as Clara Watts.

Conversation closed.

~~~

He's been promoted at work. I don't know all the details yet, but he's excited about it. Apparently, it means more work, more hours, and less time for us, but it's what he wants. If it makes him happy, then it's fine with me. He says it's him working towards our future together. In his new role, he'll be responsible for every estate staff member except the Lord. He's already on call twenty-four-seven, so I don't get how it can mean more hours.

'I'll turn it down if you don't want me to take on the extra responsibility.' He looked like a little boy asking to go to the cinema with the big kids. 'I'll even quit work if you want me to. If it means being able to live in Barrow with you, I'll take any menial job that'll have me.'

He's undecided because this opportunity and I have come along simultaneously and thrown him.

He's bought fifteen acres of land to set up his own business next year. I suppose he's taking that into account. I advised him to accept the job and see how it goes. I want him to do whatever makes him happy. Taking him out of the countryside to live in the Happy Hovel with Emily and me would be like asking Diana Ross to live in a ghetto.

He'd be so miserable if I took him away from his work. He shocked me, though. I assumed the estate was something like Holker Hall. A big imposing house, a gamekeeper's cottage, and a few acres of working land. Not at all. The Duke of Westminster owns and works the estate. He's the richest man in Britain. Mike answers directly to him and is responsible for fifteen square miles of land. He has nine beat teams, each comprising half a dozen men. He has a hundred beaters, thirty men with dogs to retrieve, and nearly a hundred gardeners, handymen, security, and other staff under his command. I imagined him getting up in the morning and walking the perimeter boundaries. No wonder he laughs at me.

When we were arguing about him buying me the Frontera, he asked what I'd do when he wanted a fresh flask taken to the wood. My car would never get over the land. I told him I'd walk or tell him to get it himself. He laughed, and I assumed he was laughing at my remark. Now I can see that he was laughing at the thought of me 'just nipping out for two minutes' to find him. It puts the work he does, and the hours we're apart, into perspective.

He's almost certain we can get together for sixty minutes tomorrow, but I have to drive out to a hill in the wilds of Cumbria to meet him. I'm getting one hour. Yippee.

~~~

Brown was typing notes as fast as she could get the words from her brain into her document. 'Did you spot the massive lie?' Renshaw asked.

'The Grand Old Duke of York Stuff? Yes. He told her he worked for the Duke of Westmorland, and we've spent hours clearing intel on it. No wonder everything came up blank. Now he says it's the Duke of Westminster.'

'Back to square one, and more donkey work.'

'Playing devil's advocate for a second,' Brown said. 'What if that was her mistake and not his? It could be a simple typo. She was relating a tale he told her from memory. Westmorland and Westminster are similar. This one might not be down to him, and her simple error could have cost us in time and manhours.'

'Yeah, but only if she's an airhead.'

'Philip Renshaw, I don't know what I ever saw in you. However, I suppose you could come for one cup of coffee tonight. But that's it.'

'I'll see you at eight.'

'Read on, McDuff.'

~~~

13th October 2011.

I could kill him.

Last night I was in heaven, knowing I didn't have to go back to the zoo. I've had to be there at night lately, but I've managed to claw back some of the hours during the day. I talked to Mike on Skype all morning. He couldn't sneak away after all. No surprise there.

I spent the afternoon sulking and taking my frustration out on housework. Praise be to the darling God of chores that the house was spotless even with the after-school advent of Hurricane Emily.

I made tea, washed up and was going to watch some TV with Emily while my hair dye proofed. We had our pet rats out, and they were exploring my desk. They have temporary names that may suffice if nothing else comes about. The black one is called Mink, and the ginger one is called Mouse. I was tired but hauled my backside upstairs to dye my hair in case Mike managed to sneak away at all this week. I got hair dye all over the bathroom, and a bit on my hair and settled down to watch my programme with a plastic bag on my head.

There was a bang on the window, and we jumped out of our skins. The rats were terrified, and Mink fell off the desk and scurried across the floor. They aren't tame yet.

A bar of chocolate flew through the open window towards me. Emily ran outside to see what was going on.

And, to my horror, in walked Mike and Simon in their Sunday best. Mike took it in his stride. He looked at me as if he'd never seen anything better. Simon's face was the one that amused me. He doesn't benefit from rose-tinted glasses and sees what the rest of the world sees. His mouth literally dropped open, and his only comment was, 'Ye gads, are the miners on strike again?'

We're harking on a theme here. Every time they come, I'm either in a state of undress, disrepair, or both. I was sitting on the sofa. For the second time of meeting Simon, I was in my knickers and a T-shirt again. The man might take pity on me and buy me a pair of trousers for Christmas. Added to my sexy as-hell unshaved legs, I wore a particular old nightshirt. I keep this one for dyeing my hair. I've used it so often that it's covered in a spectrum of bright and vivid colours, with a goodly spattering of black all over it. I didn't have a bra on, so at least my knees were warm.

Mike has caught me on the hop three times when he's turned up unexpectedly and found me less than presentable. Three times, I've greeted him with, 'Oh shit.' He says he's going to answer to it.

I wasn't embarrassed. My house was clean, and I was clean though you wouldn't think so to look at me. I just found it amusing.

Simon has been talking to Meg on the Internet since they met, and he made a hasty exit to her house.

Two minutes after they arrived, I had to leave Mike to go for a bath. 'It's not that I have an irresistible urge to get wet and naked as soon as I see you. But this time, needs must.'

However, this time was different because he asked if he could come with me.

I meant to say no, but my vocal cords disobeyed all commands. He came into the bathroom and watched as I undressed. I rinsed the dye off my hair in the shower first. I wasn't embarrassed about getting naked in front of him for the first time. It seemed the most natural thing ever. I sat in my wonderfully clean water and hit a problem. As soon as my hair connected with the water, there was an almighty blackness that put a healthy oil slick to shame. I'd got the worst off under the shower, but with rushing, there was plenty left to contaminate my bath. He sat on the loo seat and watched as I ducked my head, and the water turned to pitch.

'Crikey lass, I was going to ask if I can join you, but I'll give it a miss.'

I washed in the dark water, shaved my legs, and then stood and showered off under the downstairs trickle until the water ran clean. The upstairs shower takes all the pressure.

I wasn't embarrassed because he normalised it. It wasn't sexual. It wasn't even sensual. It was just intimate and nice. I've earned a new nickname. After watching me splashing about in the bath, he calls me, The Black Seal, which is cute.

The last time he turned up unannounced, he was waiting outside my house when I came in from work. That morning, I'd left in my usual last-minute dash to attend a birthing camel. However, I'd found the remains of a half-bottle of vodka in my bag from the previous Friday night when I went to my cousin's house for a drink. Going to work with half a bottle of vodka in my bag wasn't a good idea, so I left it on the dining room table. It was still there when Mike arrived.

'What's with the alcohol?' He was judging me. I explained about the girl's night.

'Yeah right,' he replied.

'No, really. I never drink in the house.'

Tonight, after Emily went to her room, he said, 'Come on. Let's nip to the shop.'

'What for?'

'You'll see.'

When we got there, he pointed to the alcohol behind the counter and asked for a bottle of Smirnoff. I felt awkward.

'What's that for?'

'After seeing the state of your bath water, I dread to think what you might want to do with vodka. Nothing would surprise me, but drinking it sounds like a good plan to me.' This was in front of Kev, the shopkeeper who lives above the shop on the corner. I know him well, and I'll be the subject of gossip tomorrow.

'I don't want anything, thanks. I've got work tomorrow, and I'm happy with coffee.'

But the vodka was bought. We drank it straight because I didn't like to suggest buying Coke as well. And this is where it gets silly. I know for a fact that Mike doesn't drink. He drank a quart of vodka to please me. I never drink in the house and drank the other quart to please him because I didn't want to seem ungrateful.

He didn't want the bloody vodka.

I certainly didn't.

And we both drank the foul stuff, neat to make the other one happy. I already had a splitting headache through lack of sleep, and alcohol was the last thing I wanted. It was another communication breakdown.

We had a lovely night, though. We lay on the sofa and cuddled. He said he wanted to make love to me. 'I want to, Clara, but I can't love you and then walk away. I respect you too much for that.'

We'll make love when he can stay the night, which will be when it snows pink in July.

He asked me ever so politely if he could shoot Mink and Mouse.

I declined his request.

And he finally took the phone that I bought him without any argument or grumbling about who was paying for it.

~~~

'Ha, I knew it. Told you he'd take it. Come on, Brown. Hand it over,' Renshaw said. Molly went into her purse and handed over a ten-pound note.

'Bastard,' she said. 'I hate him even more now.'

~~~

I'm seeing Mike tonight. We hope to meet halfway in seven hours, but I'm expecting a cancellation because he might have a sore head. After drinking the vodka, he picked me up and dropped me in the dog's bowl. Then, he kissed me goodbye and lost his balance, making us both fall over. He deserves a hangover. I can smell his aftershave all over me. And now I'm going to bed to sleep for the first time since Friday night.

Chapter Eleven

15th October 2011.

After Mike came unexpectedly and found me and the house a mess three times, I've had problems with my OCD. I've been struggling to adjust to the gruelling work at the zoo. The extra responsibility means a lot of evening and night work that I didn't sign up for, and getting childcare for Emily is difficult and expensive. Things like housework have slipped. Some days I struggle to fling the Hoover around. I've always kept a tidy house because I don't like clutter and can't settle with it. Mike seeing the house at its worst, shamed me, and I blitzed with a big spring clean. Since then, nothing has been out of place, but it's taking its toll.

I bathed yesterday and showered three times. I smell imaginary smells and it's as though I've brought a lemur home with me, they get in my nostrils and stay there. It's costing me a fortune in Pantene as I'm doing a bottle of conditioner every two days. The housework drives me mad, so I dread to think what I'm doing to Emily. As soon as she's finished a drink, I take her cup to wash up. I refuse to have a litterbin in the house, so all rubbish or kitchen waste must be taken to the outside bin individually. The first spec on the carpet and the Hoover comes out, and if the dog goes to her bowl, I have to sweep the floor and then mop it half a dozen times. That's not as extreme as it sounds. I use flash sprayed neat on the floor and then put washing powder into the mop bucket to make it smell nice. Most of the re-mopping is to rinse the floor and make sure that it's not sticky when it's done. I'm changing the beds daily even though mine hasn't been slept in. Megan says my house is always tidy and to relax. Easy for her to say.

The worst thing is the imaginary, and not so imaginary, smells. Kali is getting old. She's always been a terrier with body odour. It's worse recently, and I've had problems with fleas again this year. I've tried every product on the market and had a hell of a job getting rid of them. Any dog can get fleas, and any child can get head lice, but if your animal or child is infested, it still carries the stigma of being dirty. The imaginary smells are a pain. I'll be sitting on the sofa watching the TV and I smell something.

'What's that smell? Can you smell it?' And then I'm up with the Febreze, sniffing around the house like a demented bloodhound. The air freshener comes out, I follow my nose with a wet cloth and the Flash at the ready, but I can never locate the imaginary smell. Emily laughs. 'Not again. There's nothing there. You're nuts.'

Nuts, I may be, but it's hard work being a screw-up. I'm flipping exhausted. Today I started washing all my quilts again. We've got eight, six doubles and two singles—between the two of us and including the spare bedroom.

Half of them haven't been used since the last time I washed them. They don't fit in the washer, so I have to tread them in the bath and then hang them over the line to drip and then have them around the fire to dry. A fire in this weather, for God's sake. It's not that cold yet. And then the quilts are there, making the place untidy. It offends me, so I move them to hang in one of the bedrooms, but all the bedrooms have been decorated recently, and I don't like them hanging there either, so I move them onto the line again, and the whole fiasco starts again. Me going loopy has a knock-on effect on Emily.

Mike told me he was stuck with his car until it died. He changes the Land Rovers for new ones, both his own personal vehicles, and those belonging to the estate, because they are tools of his job, but he can't get rid of his car.

He bought it years ago for thirty thousand pounds, and it has depreciated in value to such a degree that it's not viable to sell it. It's in perfect condition. He has it, serviced regularly.

What's that? I don't understand what a service is. My cars have never had one. I buy. I drive. I scrap. Repeat.

Mike's is a posh car. It has Sat Nav from when it came out, and, at the time it added hundreds to the value. It has heated seats that go up and down like a dentist's chair at the touch of a button. It warns him of impending speed cameras. I admit, that's nifty. It does this, that, and everything except make a brew. It's all old hat now, but they were add-ons when the car was new. That day, he said he'd keep it until it wouldn't run, and that he'd learned his lesson about buying brand-new cars.

Today I had an email saying he's busy and can't come to see me. He sneaked in a PS after all the mush at the bottom of his email, saying, I've sold the car and have a new one coming next week. He's supposed to be saving money for the business he's launching next year.

I think he's bought a new car to please me. I'm not impressed. He doesn't get that I don't give two hoots about cars. They have four wheels and a steering wheel, and they get you about. What more do you need to know? A nice car works. And an old knacker doesn't. It's as easy as that. It didn't make any financial sense to sell his car. Considering that he's a self-proclaimed tight-arsed git, he seems to be on a mission to spend money. However, if he's spending his money on something he wants, it's none of my business. He can buy ten new cars if it makes him happy.

~~~

23rd October 2011.

I was supposed to meet Mike at Grange-Over-Geri-atric-Sands for an hour today. That's all he could spare. I got home from work after driving like a maniac, flung myself in the bath, and then drove to Grange at the speed of light to be there by eleven. I waited until twelve-thirty, but he didn't turn up. He couldn't make it because of work again. If I'd taken the time to check my email before I left the house, I'd have saved myself a tenner in diesel. He'd sent me an apologetic email telling me that he had two men off and had to work.

I haven't seen him for a week. It was my weekend off, but I didn't see or hear from him until yesterday. I was still annoyed about driving to Grange and being stood up last week.

He'd sent an email out of the blue. 'I can meet you in Grange tomorrow.'

'Sorry. No can do. I'm working tonight.' I could have met him. I was being a spoilt brat and wanted to teach him that after another week of nothing. Not even a phone call, I can't be picked up and put down when it suits him.

'Come on, babe. I need to see you.'

'Okay. I can grab a couple of hours to sleep before Emily gets home from school.'

I dropped my attitude and gave in to him. But after all that, and getting up after just two hours of sleep, he cancelled — again. Is it just a power trip to him?

As well as work, he's got some domestic problems. Daisy, his daughter, turned up on his doorstep the other night, complete with a two-year-old, and an eight-week-old baby. Her boyfriend had hit her, and she walked out.

Good girl. The first time is the last time.

Yesterday, as I was talking to Mike, she was getting the 'I'm so sorry' and the 'It won't happen again,' texts. Of course, it will. You have to stand up to abusers.

I hope she sticks to her word and doesn't go back to him. We spoke for a while on Skype, and she seems like a nice girl. I've invited her to come and stay here for a few days to clear her head. I hope she does, it'd be lovely to have two babies around the place, and it'll give us a chance to get to know each other.

Mike's furious. He never liked the boyfriend anyway and is very protective of his children.

I'm trying to be grown-up and understanding, but this relationship isn't enough for me. When we're together, it's perfect. But two hours on a Monday or Tuesday morning isn't enough. Mike's a workaholic. I was talking to Simon on Skype last night and wishing it was Mike. 'You'll never change him. Accept it, or move on now, before you harm him.'

I've been summoned to a posh hotel on Friday afternoon to meet Mike's father. To say I'm not looking forward to it would be an understatement. His parents have heard about me. His dad's only a bloody JP. He's a high court judge. They've looked into my history, and they've judged me because I don't come from money. His mother's sending his father on a fact-finding mission to see what I'm about. Apparently, Mummy makes the bullets, and Daddy fires them hard. Mike says they're concerned and want to meet me.

That's hard for me to understand. What kind of family vets the girlfriends of their forty-two-year-old son? Is this normal? If I was them, I wouldn't want my son taking me on either, so maybe it's understandable. I've been instructed to wear a skirt, 'But nowt alternative or wacky, none of that hippy stuff you've got—and to try and be reserved.'

'Me? Reserved? That's funny, Mike. But here's an idea. Why don't I just be me, and see if they like me?'

Normally being told what to wear and how to behave would cause an eruption worthy of Vesuvius, but this meeting is important to Mike, and I want to get it right.

However, if he thinks I'm going to play the part of a simpering innocent, he's mistaken. These good upstanding members of society have prejudged me, and I take exception to that. For Mike's sake, I want them to like me. It would be wonderful to be welcomed into their close family, and be a part of something loving, but I'm not ashamed of who I am. I've told Mike that if his dad questions me, I'll answer him honestly, and if he can't handle my answers, that's his lookout.

'Don't worry, love. After five minutes, they'll adore you.'

'Who are you trying to convince?'

'Both of us.'

Simon thinks it's hilarious. The dragon and dragoness don't like him, and he advised me to watch out for the fire and the horns.

Mike's dad is a judge, a member of the Masons, something big on This, That, and every committee, and a pillar of the church and the community. Mike says he's a snob, but he's honest, straight—and blunt.

Mike told him about wanting to buy me an expensive car. What did he go and say that for? No wonder they'll think I'm trash. What would I think in his dad's position? This one's fallen on her feet, she's a common gold digger out for what she can get.

I've already worn into that title well. And frankly, I'm not going to put up with it again. My ex-husband's parents called me that, and it cost me a hundred and twenty-five grand's worth of my share of our house, and all the other trappings of middle-class suburbia. I made a point of walking away from everything with nothing but the clothes on my back.

They refused to come to our wedding. They wanted hubby to have an aids test in case I'd infected him with something unpleasant, and they called Emily a bastard. I was a good wife for seven years. I didn't deserve that. And later, when they tolerated me, I welcomed them into my home, fed them, and ran around after them, trying to be the perfect daughter-in-law. I wanted them to like me.

Before we married, I sold my house to buy one with him. When I left him, our house was valued at two hundred and fifty thousand pounds. I brought sixteen thousand a year into the house, and okay, he tripled that, but I did my bit. I left everything we had without any regrets. I think he did well out of me.

I can do all three of those things, honest, straight, and blunt. I can also do charming, proud, and disarming. But mostly, I can just do me, and if that's what I've got to sell to this man who is coming to judge me, then sobeit. He can take me or leave me. It's not him I want to be with. But, if he wants to label me, then he'd better be prepared to back it up. This porcupine has prickles.

Chapter Twelve

Brown stretched her back, and Renshaw's hand went to her shoulder blades to rub them. She jerked out of his reach. 'Not at work. What are you doing?'

'Sorry. You've been bunched over the diary for two hours, and I wanted to help. Anyway, what are we doing? Do you want to go back in and present what we've got to Nash, or go for lunch and pick it up later? This simpering cow's boring me now.'

'Let's crack on for a bit longer. Just one or two more entries.'

'Hey, don't you get ideas about this crazy woman's relationship. We're nothing like them?'

'Aren't we?'

Sensing a storm brewing if Brown got onto the subject of him leaving his home again, Renshaw flipped the page to the next entry. The next three dates concerned arguments with Emily, Clara's work and looking for a new place to live. They skim-read them and highlighted them for exclusion.

They argued about leaving some of the zoo stuff in, but Brown reasoned that it showed Mike's state of mind and cruel character, so they left them to be typed up. If Nash didn't want them as example pieces to help with profiling, he could drop them.

~~~

30th October 2011

Mike cancelled twice this week, so we've kept postponing a meet-up. It's no bad thing today. I'm exhausted. I did a day shift at the zoo yesterday and then worked all night. I'm working again tonight, and then have to go back in tomorrow. It's good not having to dash off to Grange today. I'm intrigued, though. Mike said to bring a coat and decent walking shoes because he had something to show me. As far as I know, he hasn't been to Grange since we met there on our first date, so I can't think what it is.

Yesterday at the zoo, I gutted every one of my vivariums. Normally I'd do one a day, but yesterday I had my work head on and decided to give them a good do. I emptied and scrubbed out the python pond, which isn't a pleasant job, but it's another box ticked on the worksheet.

All the snakes are sloughing properly now that I've got the humidity up to eighty per cent, but the owner overruled me about euthanising the Burmese pythons. They've put on weight with proper force-feeding, and maybe I can kid myself that they look better, but they'll never come back to full health, or eat for themselves. I wish the poor buggers would hurry up and die. But, there's not much chance of that when they're being kept alive artificially. They could carry on in this half-life for years.

The reptiles bring good revenue. People expect to see a decent reptile house at a zoo, and with the greatest will in the world, ours is not a decent house. I would like to have the sick snakes put to sleep. They might look like big, impressive animals to the general public, but to anybody with herpetological knowledge, they aren't a good advertisement. I wouldn't dream of destroying a healthy animal, but these snakes have no quality of life. The other keepers like them because they're docile and can be used for talks and petting time. They're docile because they're half dead.

I could re-stock the reptile house without it costing him a penny. I have contacts and could re-stock with unwanted pets, and other zoo overspills. It would mean clearing the vivaria and leaving them empty for six months to decontaminate. And that would mean a loss of revenue—the board won't agree. We can't put healthy snakes in with the sick ones. I'd like to clear all the snakes out and start from scratch. They should never have got into this state in the first place.

I've had better success with my lizards. Before I arrived, they were on dead food only. They were eating little, and then only salad and some dead meat products. I've got them on crickets, meal and wax worms and locusts, as well as their still food. They've gone from being lethargic, bored, branch potatoes to mad charge around things chasing their live food. With utilising the outdoor enclosures, the colours are up on the iguanas. I'm pleased with them. From being half dead when I took over Zone-Six, they have come up to tip-top condition.

Mike worried me. He said to hide until after closing one night, and he'd euthanise all my snakes for me, and it would be reported as an act of cruel vandalism. I do want to put them out of their misery, but only because they're suffering. Mike said he'd never killed a snake before, only a few slowworms. It was the way he said it. It felt like some kind of trophy kill, rather than what was best for the animals.

Tomorrow I'm boxing up the new hognose snakes for hibernation. I was concerned about the weight of one and considered not hibernating him this year. We took them as a rescue package six weeks ago, and Amigo, one of the males, was underweight.

They store fat through the summer months to carry them through winter. I stopped feeding them last week to give them a fast week to clear their gut.

Anyway, common to their species, they have all proven to be good feeders, and Amigo has put on enough weight to go down with the rest.

Tabitha, one of the Brazilian Blue tarantulas gave me a scare yesterday. I took her out while I cleaned her terrarium. Normally she's placid and sits on my shoulder, but yesterday she made a bid for freedom and shot off, losing herself in a crack behind the units. And there she stubbornly sat, just out of reach. I got her out with the coaxing help of a stick. I had to be careful not to hurt her, and she shot out and scuttled up the back wall, where it was fairly easy to trap her and get her back into her case before, she ran again. But she was mad. Tarantulas don't like being poked with sticks. I didn't have gloves, preferring to handle all my animals with skin-on contact.

But there was no way I was touching her when she was rearing up and flashing her fangs, so the best I could do, was to strip out of my T-shirt and fling that over her. The shirt, spider, and fingers all went in the case, with the latter being extracted very carefully. It meant I had to stay in the tropical room, in my bra, until she moved away from my shirt and gave it up. I'd locked the tropical room from the public, but people were passing the viewing windows outside.

'Daddy, why is that lady standing there in her underwear?'

'I don't know, sweetie. Let's move along to the next window.'

Mike said he would've stamped all over the spider. I don't like it when he talks like that.

We lost one of our Ibis this week. Scarlet is the sweetest, most loveable red panda you've ever seen. She is also a keen hunter. A couple of months ago, she had a seagull, and in her time, she's lain waste to several of the free-roaming lemurs.

It happened while I was off, but apparently, it was a spectacular kill and stopped the viewing public from their awing at the cute panda. The Ibis flew onto a tree on Scarlet's island.

Scarlet came out of the branches stalking it. The Ibis saw her and took flight, and Scarlet made a lunge, grabbed it by its feet and dragged it to the ground where it stood no chance. The Ibis is five feet tall, and Scarlet barely makes two. She's very shy, but she's coming around to me now and will sit on my shoulder for as long as it takes me to hand-feed her some fruit. She's like a soft teddy bear but looks can be deceiving, and she has mean teeth, as the Ibis found to its cost. Again, Mike said that he wished he'd been there to see it. I don't like this cruel streak in him. It's a bloodlust, and it scares me.

~~~

1 November 2011.

This morning I had an urgent phone call from my landlord asking me to be available between ten and one tomorrow because he's having the house valued. I've just paid a fortune for new carpets and decorating. What am I going to do? Houses don't often come up for rent in Dalton. And I haven't got three million points to make us eligible for a council house. I dare say I'll find something.

Moving in with Mike isn't an option. If I choose to live with him, it'll be because it's the right thing to do, not because we're homeless and he's an instant fix to a problem. Damn and blast my bloody life. It's always two steps forward and five situations back.

I think Mike and Simon might be coming to see Meg and I tonight, but as usual, Mike hasn't been in touch to either confirm or deny. If they come, I'll cook cheese and onion flan, baked potatoes and salad. With pineapple upside-down cake.

~~~

2 November 2011.

Mike asked me to marry him last night. He said it's getting harder every time he walks away from me, and he's sick of going home horny and frustrated. 'I want to sleep with you, Clara. Can we spend the night together very soon?'

'Can you do Friday?'

'I'll try my best, but listen,' he sat up, grabbed my hands, and looked at me in one of those mental photograph moments to be re-played later. 'If we sleep together, I'll have to marry you. My rule is, don't bed them unless you're prepared to wed them. Will you marry me, Clara?' And there was not a thee or thine in sight.

He scared me silly, but he says he knows he wants to be with me forever, I believe him. And that's terrifying.

If I married Mike tomorrow, and if it only took one person to make it work, he'd do that, and I'd be with him for the rest of our lives. I don't doubt him for a second. Mike is a settler. 'You can't take a wife out and shoot it, so you have to make your marriage work.' He was horrified when his wife left him. It had never occurred to him that his marriage could break up. Yet he was miserable with her for years.

I've had his side of the story, the other men—and women—the clubbing and drunkenness and the neglect and abandonment of her children. Even though I've never met her, I think I know her side too. She had a husband who neglected her. He was out working all the hours God sends, being what he considered a good husband, and bringing home money for her to spend, but never being there for her.

Mike loves his work, and any woman who takes him on must understand that, and not try to change him.

I don't know if I can. I already feel neglected two months in. We go days without contact and get together for a few hours when he can make it. Mike will give me the world, but he won't give me his time. I think I love him, but how long will I love him when he's never there, and I always feel as though I'm dangling at the bottom of a long list of priorities?

I have my family and friends here. I have my work. Forgetting that terrifying marriage word, just living with him is enough of an ordeal to contemplate. If I live with him, I'll also work with him, something his wife never did. But if I'm left alone for too long, I'll make new friends. And there lies the route to all trouble. What happens when, say, seven years later, some man turns my head? My partner had no time for me, but a new man gave me attention. I'm fickle and can fall out of love as fast as I fell into it. I need affection.

My ex-husband was a workaholic. He was never home, so I built my business in reptiles. I created a life that ran alongside my life with him. I made friends, and my ex and I were blissfully happy for six and a half years, and I never looked at another man.

My husband wasn't a good lover, or at least he didn't please me very often. Mostly it was for his gratification, and I made love like doing the ironing or changing the beds. It was another household chore that had to be done. It didn't matter. I compensated for an unsatisfactory love life with other things.

I didn't have anywhere near the passion for him that I already feel for Mike, and we've never even been intimate. My husband and I made a great team until things went bad. I enjoyed his company, and spending time with him, and when he wasn't there, I had other interests to keep me busy. I loved being faithfully married.

I was happy being a wife and having a home and family to look after. I took pride in doing it well, and we were content. Who's to say that I can't do it again?

I've always been in long-term relationships. Marriage scares me, but being married doesn't. I don't want to marry Mike, but not because I wouldn't want to be his wife. I've been married and failed. I don't want to fail again. Marriage is serious and sacred. I'm sticking by what I said and won't move in with him until I've cleared my debts and can contribute to the household. That gives us time to decide if it's what we really want.

They came last night, and we had a brilliant time. I cooked for the masses. Meg and Simon seem to be getting close. I'd love for them to get together, but I'm not sure that Meg's right for Simon. She's involved with another man who she's been seeing for the past year. It's all fireworks and chemistry, but he's living with somebody else. It's not a good situation, and somebody like Simon would be great for her.

The valuer has just been to assess the house. I expect I'll be getting my marching orders any day. I think I'll have a month's notice to quit. I'm not worried. Now that it seems to be happening, I'm looking forward to finding somewhere new to live. It'll probably be the next town down in Barrow-in-Furness.

Chapter Thirteen

Bronwyn Lewis glared at Nash over the eleven laptops he'd signed out of stores.

'No.'

'I'm asking you nicely. Don't make me go behind your back.'

'You do, Nash, and you're out of here. You aren't as indispensable as you think you are. Don't test me.'

'And who's going to run the department? Bowes?'

'Get out and take your computer shop with you.'

'Okay. I'm sorry. That was an unkind remark. Bowes will make an excellent detective one day. I'm frustrated and lashing out.'

'And you're barking at the wrong people.'

'I know. But the fact remains that I need you to sign off on this.'

'Another covert operation is bad enough. Unlimited overtime, until we get a result, is out of the question, and you're mad if you think I'm going to agree to this nonsense. We're a police department, not a lonely-hearts club. And that's my answer to the first part of your request. The second part isn't even worthy of a response. Putting one of your team in danger, Silas, what's got into you?'

'We're getting nowhere. This killer has gone to ground. No. Not even that. He's vanished. He's the invisible man. I take that personally.'

'And because the great Silas Nash can't get a result, he goes all gung-ho and stops thinking rationally. Even if we went along with this—if we get him. At best a honey trap would be inadmissible in court, and at worst, it could jeopardise the trial. No, it's not happening.'

It took another half an hour before he got Lewis to agree to his demands.

'For the record, Silas.'

'Yes?'

'The woman in me is right there with you. Go and catch this bastard, and when you do, nail his balls to the incident room wall.'

Before he picked up the box of laptops, Nash went behind Lewis's chair and kissed her on the top of her head. With her fire-red hair pinned in a severe bun and her pin-striped suit, she looked like a ball-breaker but smelt like an angel. Lewis always wore scarlet lipstick and Nash figured it was her stamp in a man's world.

'Thanks, Boss.'

Nash waited for them to settle down, and then looked at his team. 'Come on then. Which of you bright sparks has caught this bloke?'

His question was met with silence. Nobody answered him, and Nash stared at them as they refused to look him in the eye. 'Come on, guys. You must have something on him. This is ridiculous. It's been three days. Renshaw, what are you doing all day?'

'The first diary was a hundred-and-ninety-thousand words. That's a lot of shit to trawl through to find the relevant bits—and that's just the first time they met.'

'Get him fast, or I'm pulling you and Brown off it.'

'I'll be glad to come off it. She's a whinging cow and so pathetic she gives women a bad name. She could put me off sex for life,' Renshaw said.

'Watch your mouth, Renshaw. That's our victim. Respect her like you respect your mother.'

At the same time as Nash tore a strip off him, Brown jumped down his throat. 'You're such a knob, Renshaw. She's not pathetic. She's vulnerable. This player's giving her the run-around, and she's hurting.'

'You two can tear chunks off each other elsewhere. Keep it out of my incident room. I want to hammer this animal. We have a lead, so let's kick a killer in the coccyx. He lives in Millom. I want every rock, stone and pebble turning over in that town until you find him. He may have a daughter called Daisy, and a seventeen-year-old son called Dave. Snow mentioned a tobacco tin with the name Sally.

'I'm checking all the census records for a man named Michael with those children, but so far it's coming up blank,' Lawson said.

'Like your paycheck this month if you don't get me something, lad. Pull every firearms licence in Cumbria. Go back ten years. I met with Renshaw earlier this morning, and this man's dangerous. If it's the same guy, the firearms shopkeeper was wary of, we're pretty sure he makes his own bullets. Do you know how scary that is if he's still at large?'

'It's worse than that,' Renshaw said. 'The shopkeeper said he bought gunpowder and detonators in bulk and drove around with them loose in the back of his truck. He bought enough explosives to blow up the shipyard, or at least put some hefty dints in it.'

'Bowes, get over to the shop. The man's name is Simon Shaw. I've got a laptop here for you. Spend the afternoon going over mugshots with him. I've arranged for, Collins, the mugshot artist, to go with you and get a drawing of him in case you don't get a hit. Ask Collins to make up a couple of impressions if he can. It's a strong lead, but bear in mind, this creepy guy might not be our perp.'

'This shop,' Bowes paused for effect, 'Cocked and Tackle.' He waited, enjoying his moment as the team laughed. 'It's in Lancaster. But, that's a fair old trek from Millom, and there are some nasty old roads to get there. We think he moved to Millom and I'm guessing that's why he changed shops. While I've got the Rogues Gallery on my Laptop, do you want me to scout any firearms shops between Broughton and Millom while I'm out?'

Good thinking, and interview Labrador breeders. Patel, I want you in Dalton. Get a clear trace of this Meg woman. Don't come back until you've found her.'

The team made the relevant end-of-meeting noises, and Renshaw peeled his left buttock from the table it was resting on.

'Oi,' Nash said. 'Did I say you could go? Sign for these.'

He hefted a large container onto his desk and let out an audible grunt. Jesus, it was true. He was getting old. He read the name stickers on each laptop as he handed them out. 'Okay, homework, new tactic. Listen up, team.' They all stopped opening their laptop lids and gave him their full attention. 'The good news is you can all have as much overtime as you like. The bad news is you can have as much overtime as you like. I want you all on this. We've split you into three teams. Don't take the piss out of the system, you can't cheat it. You'll be required to log into your timesheet, and your calls will be monitored. You'll be rounded down to the nearest fifteen minutes.'

There was a collective groan.

'Why not rounded up?' Bowes moaned.

'Because you rabble would be logging off every ten minutes. Right, pay attention. You've been given your personal account login details. However for those of you with the pleasant job of hitting on women, once you get onto the dating apps, you only have one collective identity. Keep it nice, team. Remember this is work.

'For those of you assigned to trawling accounts to look for our perp, the contacts on all the relevant dating apps have been split between you. You will be speaking to men aged between thirty-five and fifty. They've been ordered by importance, so you must work down your list in order.'

'Aw, that's not fair, why do I have to chat up men, when Brown's going to be hitting on women?' Bowes asked.

'We all know which of your heads governs your brain, Bowes. We wouldn't want you to get distracted. The police commission is not paying for you to get your jollies.'

Murmurs rippled through the room as they took in the information, and Nash brought them back to attention by banging his hand on the desk.

'Listen up. For those of you posing as potential targets, to draw in our perp. Men get in touch with your feminine side. Put on a splash of lipstick if you have to. I'm told it works wonders.'

'What the hell? No way,' Bowes said.

'I'm joking, you idiot. All joking aside because Bowes can't handle it. Let me run through your character, and the dos and don'ts. You are Molly Turner, 39, and you're divorced without children. Your parents are both dead, and you have no siblings. We want you to be as isolated and vulnerable as possible. But make no mistake, this man is not a fool. You've been given a script, and while I understand you can't be a robot, I want to stick to it as much as possible. Do you understand?'

There were general assents around the room.

'Why have you used Molly's name?' Renshaw asked.

'Need to know basis, Renshaw. Team. On me.' They stopped what they were doing to look at Nash. 'Let me make this as clear as can be. Your job is not to engage in conversation. You get in, you find out the information on your brief to see if he fits our perp's intel, and you get out. Got it?'

'Sir.'

'The more you say, the more likely it is that you'll blow your cover. Stick to the script. We want the name, age, location, occupation, kids, and family pets. Get in-get out. Fill in your spreadsheet for each attempt you contact. The columns are *Date*, *Time* and whether contact is made. Next fields, *No matches*, and *Possible matches*. Fill in every cell with the relevant information. Dead simple—even for you lot. Got it?'

'Sir.'

'Dismissed. Catch me a killer.'

The case was getting to him. It was as though this man had vanished—or never existed in the first place. They had a lot of information on him. Everything from The Earl of Westminster to a father who was a judge, but every angle drew a blank.

He remembered Snow's warning about the man in the white wig, and it being symbolically knocked off. It was another direct hit for Snow. He'd warned that the perp's father isn't a judge, and it was another of the perp's lies.

He'd managed not to think about Kel for the duration of his meeting. But he couldn't wait for their second date later. Nash was a worrier, and he fretted that seeing Kel two nights on the bounce was too much. He didn't want to come across as too keen, but who was he kidding? He'd met a man from a dating app in the flesh, which was a huge thing for Nash. After three hours in his company, he'd walk over hot coals for him and was counting down the seconds until he saw him again. He couldn't concentrate on work and had packed his things up before four o'clock. In his present state of worry and distraction, he was no good to either man or beast. He needed to pick up some groceries for the meal he was cooking, and going to the supermarket took him past the refugee centre on Bath Street.

His heart leapt into his mouth when he passed the gate and saw two familiar figures grappling in a street fight. Sebastian Whitehouse had Aiden Lawson on the ground and was on top of him. Nash broke into a run, but when he got closer, he heard Aiden laughing.

'Give it to me,' Sebastian laughed, trying to get something from inside Aiden's coat.

'You'll have to take it from me, you big pussy.'

The young men wrestled until Seb pulled a basketball from Aiden's jacket. They got up, grinning at each other, and went back into the yard where a hoop had been put up. Nash smiled when he saw Seb tap on one of the windows to the kids inside the classrooms. He pointed to the ball. 'Break time, guys. Come on, two teams of seven. Who's up for a thrashing?' He bounced the ball three times and threw it to Aiden Lawson, who slam-dunked it in the hoop.

Pleased with a good bit of work, Nash grinned. He'd put the troubled young men together, and it could have been an unmitigated disaster, but he'd had a good feeling about it. Aiden's troubled family had a lot of problems, but the kid had never been in trouble, and Nash wanted to keep it that way. It'd be great to see him make good. Seb, the wild stallion, would go either way. Being the proverbial bored rich kid opened a lot of dark doors. With money in his pocket, and a caution for taking his dad's car and being caught in possession of marijuana behind him, now was a critical time for him. He was still at that vital crossroads and had choices to make.

Before he died, Max Jones had volunteered at the refugee centre for young people. Nash had blackmailed Sebastian, to follow in his late uncle's footsteps and help people his own age and younger build a new life in this strange country. It looked as though the kid was coming good.

He made a mental note to tell Kel about it over dinner that night. He hadn't come down from the success of their date the night before yet.

At home, he prepared everything he needed, and he'd flash fry the steak when they were ready to eat. With an hour to kill before he needed to shower and change, he went to his office and stared at his whiteboard.

The Westminster and Westmorland thing was bugging him. He wrote the two words and drew lines from Clara's name and Mike's to meet the headings. Then he wrote underneath *Who said it?* It made a huge difference. The mystery man might have said Westmorland all along. It's what Clara said in the beginning, and only changed it half a dozen entries later when Mike said he worked for the Earl of Westminster. He stared at the board for a few minutes, then took the line full circle back to Mike.

It was him.

It had to be. There were no estates in the Westmorland area of Kendal that covered fifteen square miles. She repeated that specific distance which could only have come from him. Neither the Greythwaite nor Low Jock Scar estates were anywhere near that big. Again it showed him as a liar. Nash didn't understand why she'd been so blind to him.

Guilt rinsed him and hung him out to dry as he replayed all the lies, he'd told Kelvin. Nash was mortified, but Kel thought it was funny and said he could never see him as a caretaker.

'Maintenance engineer, if you don't mind.'

'Got your Corgi certificate, have you?'

'No. But I almost bought a Great Dane once.'

'It's okay,' Kelvin had said. 'But you've had your free pass. That's it, Detective. No more lies. Right?'

'I promise. I will never lie to you again. I'm not dishonest by nature.'

'I should hope not. If you can't trust a policeman, who can you put your faith in?'

Me. You can put your faith in me, he'd wanted to say, but it was too heavy, and too soon.

Kelvin knocked on the door bang on time. He brought roses, red ones, and a bottle of red wine. The gifts brought a shyness to Nash that he'd never felt before. They went into the kitchen while Nash put the flowers in water, and Kel sat on a stool at the island where they chatted while Nash took the clingfilm off the salad and tossed it in his special homemade dressing as the steak sizzled on the griddle.

'Apple Charlotte okay for pudding?'

'That sounds fantastic.'

'Can I ask you something? This might sound odd, but I don't suppose you're allergic to strawberries, are you?'

'How the hell do you know that?' Kelvin laughed at the randomness of the question.

Without going into case details, Nash told Kel about Conrad Snow, and it kept them talking through the meal. Like Nash, Kelvin wasn't a believer, but he was far more open-minded about the possibility of supernatural abilities than Nash had been. Over dessert, Nash reached for his wine glass, and Kel caught his finger, and their hands intertwined.

The difference in skin tone entranced Nash. Kelvin's hand was as black as an onyx charm, while he was pale even by Caucasian standards. Nash couldn't tear his eyes away from the beauty of the contrast.

Chapter Fourteen

Brown and Renshaw sat in her lounge with a laptop each. 'We're going to work, and then you're going home. No bed, no sexy time. I mean it this time, Phil.'

'What's brought this on?'

'Nothing. Everything. I saw Sal in Asda last night.'

'Yeah, I know. She said she'd bumped into you, but you seemed stressed and blamed it on work.'

'Your wife wanted me to go to the bloody café with her for a coffee and a catchup. She said we haven't had a gossip for ages. What do you suppose I could gossip about Phil? "Oh, by the way, Sal, he left his tie on my bedroom floor last night. Will you give it to him for me, please?" Or maybe we could chat about the fact that her husband's playing away. "Hey Sal, sorry to be the one to tell you this, but there's a rumour in the canteen that Phil's having it off with someone. Who do you reckon it is?" Jesus Phil.'

'Are you done?'

'With you? Yes.'

'Behave.'

'What am I supposed to do, Phil? Sal and I were friends. We used to go for coffee all the time—and moan about you, mainly.

Now I cross the street to avoid her. I once saw her coming to meet you after work, and I crouched down beside my car in the carpark so she wouldn't see me. On CCTV, Phillip. I had to pretend I'd dropped my keys. I would love to have gone for a drink with her—but I can't. And that's your fault.'

He put his hand out to stroke her face.

'Don't touch me. Get to work.'

'Can't we read the diary together to get it finished?'

'No. You swipe the dating apps, maybe you'll find my replacement. I'll read.'

~~~

3 November 2011

I was supposed to meet Mike's father on Friday. There was even talk of Mike taking a day off and being able to stay over Friday night. It didn't happen, nothing happened, and our arrangements had to be cancelled. I was devastated.

Two weeks ago, he finished the goose shooting early. It's supposed to go on until October when geese are replaced by ducks, and that season lasts until the geese come back from Iceland in late January. It's always time to kill something. When is it time for us?

He called off the shoots because there are still some geese about, but not enough to re-populate for next season. He's clever enough to think ahead to future breeding programmes and make that call. His level of responsibility is massive, and I'm in awe of him.

On Friday, the estate manager over him overruled his decision and laid on five goose shoots for the weekend. Originally, before Mike closed the season, it was only two.

My doubt-o-meter crept in. Surely five shoots can't just be laid on at a moment's notice? Aren't these things booked, planned, and sealed in goose blood months before the actual date? Anyway, that's the way it happened, and our plans were scuppered.

I thought Mike was the estate manager, that's what he told me. He said he was the top dog below the owner, but the lines are grey and blurred. This pen-pusher oversees the paperwork. He's not above Mike in rank, and Mike isn't answerable to him — but the manager can pull rank when he sees fit. I'm sure Mike said he had full control of everything. I must be mistaken. When I spoke to him, I said he should go over the prat's head to the Duke of Westminster and tell him he can't work with the man.

But, by then it was too late — and Mike had already hit him.

I was talking to his best mate, Simon, on MSN last Thursday night when we got the news. It literally kicked off while I was talking to him. It's almost two weeks since I've spoken to Mike this time, and the only information I can get comes to me via Si.

'Oh hell. Hang on, Clara. I've got Mike on the phone. He's in trouble.'

Si was gone for over an hour before he came back and told me Mike had blacked the estate manager's eyes and had him up against the filing cabinets by his throat. Si said he had to dash because he needed to go to the estate to calm Mike down, but all our arrangements for Friday night were off because he and Mike were running the five goose shoots together. I asked him to tell Mike to ring me when he got the chance. I speak to Si more than I speak to my boyfriend. It's not fair for him to be kept so busy that he can't have a life.

I was worried sick about him. That job is his life. After beating the estate manager to a pulp, he'd lose his career. I didn't know what was going on and sat up by the computer all night in case Mike or Si came online.

They didn't

In fact, I had no word from him at all from speaking to Si on Thursday until Saturday afternoon. Had Mike been arrested?

Also on Friday Daisy was due to go back to the man who hit her. This, combined with hassle at work and having to cancel our plans had put him in a black mood.

He hadn't had a second spare to ring me. I know he works day and night. When there's a shoot the next day, he has to be up all night skreeing the game and checking that everything's in order. He had to make more rounds of ammunition than usual, and he didn't have time to talk to me. He said he'd sent word with Si through Megan, and he felt that was enough.

I didn't.

I feel pushed out and neglected.

I don't like receiving third-hand information about him via Megan, through Si, from him.

'Would a two-minute phone call be too much trouble?'

'Aye lass, but you haven't a clue what it's like.'

The man infuriates me. He's the most inconsiderate oaf I've ever met, and yet, when we're together, he's perfect, and nothing is too much trouble to please me. He makes my core tremble and has no idea the effect he has over me – or maybe he does. I wish he'd keep in touch.

Anyway, he had to do the shoots because they'd been laid on. The guns weren't happy because the geese were scarce and they'd paid a fortune for the experience.

There were repercussions regarding his assaulting the estate manager, but he seems to have got off lightly. It's odd, but he wasn't even suspended. The incident has been dealt with in-house. The manager may be an officious prat, but I think Mike owes still having his job to him.

My man has a volatile temper. Does his feisty attitude stop at estate managers? We've spoken about violence and he says he's never hit a lady in his life. I don't care about his past or anything in it. The more I see him the more I want him, and when he doesn't make contact, it tortures me.

We talked on MSN on Saturday and again on Sunday afternoon. He said he'd meet me on the computer at ten this morning. It's now twelve fifteen and he hasn't come online. I last saw him from eight-thirty until midnight three Wednesday's ago. He doesn't know when he'll get away again.

And I haven't been invited to go there.

He put Dave, his son on, yesterday. He's seventeen and a nice lad.

'Hiya. I'm glad you're online, my dad's smiling. Are you, okay?'

'Always.'

'That's good.'

'Well apart from when your old man's being a prat.'

'Lol, I'm looking forward to meeting you?'

'I'd like that. First round's on me, we can plonk Flask Man in a corner to moan about not liking pubs.'

'You know him already. If you're my new evil stepmother, I want to see what all the fuss is about.'

'You're not missing much, love.'

'That's not what Uncle Si says. He says my dad's a lucky bugger to have found you. Anyway, Dad's here grinning and wanting to get you back, so I'd better go.'

Bless him. He's a credit to his dad. I felt all warm after speaking to Dave. It was great to hear that I make his dad happy. But more than that, it validates, Mike, and proves that what he tells me is real.

We're going to a Christening next Sunday, but it's doubtful that Mike can make it. He said he'd try, and added, 'You know I want to get you in a church.' He's persistent. I'll give him that much.

They only had an hour before they were due on the skree, but my wild, man-beating boyfriend was baking scones for the beaters.

~~~

4 November 2011

Mike ended our relationship yesterday. He finished with me without a second's hesitation. Last week he asked me to marry him, the month before he wanted to buy me a car, and this week he finished with me.

He came online yesterday. He was happy, said he'd missed me, and tried to make me smile, but I was tired and in a bad mood. I hadn't heard a word from him since Friday and hadn't seen him for over three weeks. I was spoiling for a fight. He doesn't have any time for me and it's getting me down. I hit him with it—again.

I whinged, told him I wasn't happy, and that I need him to make more time for us.

'Babe, you know it's the start of the shooting season. I'm up to my eyes in it.'

'It's an excuse, Mike. Everybody's entitled to time off, it's the law. If you don't take your days off, it's not because you have to—it's because you choose to.'

He was quiet for a few minutes, a sure sign he was battling with a reply.

'I hear you. I know you want more than I can give. I'll give your phone to Si to give to Meagan, and we'll call it a day. This isn't worth the hassle. I'm glad I never slept with you because I couldn't bear that. I'm too tired to fight with you, Clara. It's over.'

I read the words again and couldn't believe what I was seeing. I felt sick and grabbed my throat. There was nobody in the house but me, and I could let my emotions out without alarming Emily. I released a long moan like the cry of a grieving whale. The pain was biting and physical. I couldn't bear the thought of never seeing him again, and I felt the tears pouring down my face until I was choking on snot. The misery engulfed me and tore at my skin.

My reply was short as though there was no feeling there at all. My pride and anger bit him.

'No problem. And you can bin the phone. I don't want it back.'

I logged off before he had the chance to reply. And I cried for hours until dehydration came at me with a pounding headache that was nothing compared to the pain of his loss. I've deleted him from both of my MSN accounts and deleted and blocked him from my email. He's gone from my phone, and my life, as if he'd never been. I have nothing of his. At least it made for a clean break. Usually after a breakup, there's a divvy up of belongings. A post-mortem, and aftermath. But there was none of that. Mike was like a dream, the months that never happened. But the pain I felt was palpable in reality.

If he can throw away what we had without a second thought, it shows he was never real, anyway.

He threw 'I love you' around as though it meant something. The words had no value. Mike never said anything he didn't mean. So maybe I didn't live up to the ideal in his head. And when he said it's over, he meant it.

We were into our third month. I so wanted to make him happy. I've never met anybody like him before, but the end result is always the same. I didn't think he'd end it, and I didn't want to break up. I needed a compromise that we were happy with. One day a week, and a weekend once a month wasn't unreasonable.

Knowing I had his support made me strong. I have a hell of a time coming up with work and finding somewhere to live. I feel weak. They are challenges I have to face and deal with. I didn't need him to do anything for me. I look after Emily and me. It's the way it's always been. But knowing he was there was enough.

And then there's Christmas. Another Christmas alone. This will be our eighth with just the two of us. Each year I pray that next Christmas will be a family celebration, but it's just me and Emily. She eats pizza because it's her favourite treat, and I gave up forcing her to eat a Christmas dinner she hated, years ago.

I cried until I dried.

When I found out that Rick had been unfaithful to me with three other women—one of them a famous Coronation Street actress who is his next-door neighbour—I bawled so hard that I made myself puke. This hurts just as much, but it's different now. I'm tired and over it. I can't be bothered with anything and spent the morning going through the motions of housework. I'm hurt, and it's all tied up in a great big nothingness.

I cut myself yesterday after he told me it was over. He never cared about me, and the relationship was just another round of bullshit, with another man. I have special scissors I keep for the job, but Emily's had them for her crafting, and they're as blunt as hell. I only made two cuts. They'll scar with using blunt scissors, but I flung them against the wall in a temper before I did any real harm. The irony is, they were still sharp enough to put a hole in the wall.

And then I got really crazy. I ran downstairs to get one of my super sharp chef's knives. One slice and I'd have amputated something. But, it's not about how much damage I can do, or about attention. It's the opposite, it's furtive and secret and deeply shameful because that's not the person I want the world to see. It's something to do with bleeding. I don't even know what it's about myself. When I'm in a self-destructive rage, the only person I want to hurt is myself. It's getting the bad blood out, and it's about pain. The sting is acute, and when you're hurting physically, it takes your mind off hurting inside. I stopped myself from using the knife, but the need to cut was blazing like a roaring fire inside me. I thought about hacking myself with a razor, but it's a stupid lady razor with a guard on it. When I'm getting ready to go out on a Friday night, I can make chopped liver out of myself without even trying. *Intuition: the super lady razor that doesn't cut!*

Like hell, it doesn't. It wouldn't have been satisfying enough for what I wanted to do to myself, anyway.

I sat on my bed and laughed. I am so worthless that I couldn't even find anything suitable to mutilate myself with.

And then, after laughing at myself, the urge was gone, and the shame and loathing slipped in. I don't want to hurt myself. I only made two cuts opening old scars, and nobody will know. They're high on my right arm where the tattoo is. I hate my tattoos and keep them covered, so it's easy.

Mike and I are over so nobody's going to see me without my shirt on. A light bandage is enough to keep the wounds clean. I could use a couple of stitches in the second one. The first was a scratch with the blunt scissors, so I used more force on the second. I've cleaned and dressed it and stuck the wound together with Micropore. If any questions are asked, I'll say I did it on brambles when I took the dog out. This is the same old story, a different man, but the same scenario. Whatever's lacking in my mental makeup is always going to be lacking, so I'm going to meet men, fail, and go again.

~~~

'My God, he really did choose the vulnerable ones. This woman's got some serious mental health issues.' Molly wasn't one for crying, but she was upset and tried to hide it from Phil.

'Hey, what's the matter? It's getting to you, isn't it?'

'She's self-harming. Cutting herself with a pair of scissors, for God's sake.' Molly rubbed the top of her arm where Clara had described cutting hers. 'Can you imagine how worthless a woman would have to feel to do that?'

'No. She's just nuts. No sane person would do that to themselves—and all over a man that she barely knows. It's an attention stunt. She's a screwed-up lunatic and should be locked up. Maybe she should think more about her daughter than a stranger who's as weird as she is.'

'Just because we don't understand it, doesn't make it something we can hide from.'

'What's that meant to mean?'

Molly thought back two weeks to her own moment of shame. The table, the candles, the hunter's chicken in the oven for when he arrived. She was going to make a joke about the hunter and say she'd caught the chicken herself, to tie in with the case. And then there was his call to say one of the kids was ill, and he couldn't get away. He whispered into the phone, and she could hear Sal calling him. And then Sal was there, 'Who's on the phone, love?'

'Nobody, darling. I'm just coming.' And the phone went dead without another word.

Dismissed.

She hadn't had a cigarette in two years—but there was that packet at the back of the drawer for emergencies. They were stale and strong, disgusting, but she smoked two of them in six minutes—and felt sick.

She was punishing herself. Self-harming.

Just like Clara.

And that wasn't the worst of it.

She puffed, and the end of the second cigarette burnt orange.

'Nobody,' he'd said.

She drew on it again. You're nobody—nothing.

Looking at the end of her cigarette, she flicked the ash into the yogurt pot she'd found in the absence of an ashtray.

Nobody.

She cupped her other hand under the cigarette—and for a split-second, only that. Just that one faction of time, she imagined stabbing the end of the cigarette into the flesh of her palm. Who in their right mind would do something so ugly? 'Nobody,' she'd said aloud. She spoke into the vast space of her empty kitchen with the cheerful yellow and black checked tablecloth. It had to be there because Phil had cut deep trenches into her table when the idiot had used it as a saw bench. She only asked him to help with some DIY that once. He cut other deep trenches in her life, but they were less visible.

She was better off on her own.

Chapter Fifteen

10 November 2011.

Despite keeping my distance, my so-called friend, Megan has forwarded several emails. Sentences, really, from Mike. I haven't replied.

I love you xxxxxxx. Let's talk it through. This was yesterday when I got home from work.

Love u. You, my babe x. While I was off work on Monday morning.

If u want me, I'll be on MSN. I hurt and miss u. Yesterday morning when I got home from work.

Morning sexy, just filling my flask. It's wet and cold xxx. This morning when I got home from work.

It's the most he's ever contacted me since the first week. He wants to talk, but can't make the time until Monday, and then only on MSN. The last two emails talk as though nothing's changed between us.

I've been so unhappy. Despite deleting him so I wouldn't sit at the computer all day, I did it anyway. I should have gone to bed yesterday, but I didn't. I'm off tomorrow and Sunday, but he hasn't got time for me. I'm back on shift Monday and Tuesday when he has four hours off, and then that'll be it for another ten days.

Do I give it another go? I could take a crash course in extreme patience and see how it pans out. He says it won't always be like this when we have our own pheasant business. I'm not a pheasant plucker. Should I call it a day now, and cut my losses? He can go back to his geese, and I'll be a lonely man hunter for the rest of my life. A dating butterfly.

He never rings me. The last time he did was a week after we met. I've had two texts from him on the new phone, and I'm lucky if we talk on MSN once a week. My life revolves around sitting by the computer day and night, waiting for contact.

If he cares about me, he'd find time. I'm busy, too, but I make time. I'm not happy on my own, but I'm a lot more content.

~~~

15 November 2011

Si and Mike messaged me through the night on MSN. Against my better judgement, Si persuaded me to add Mike to my contact list again, and at least hear him out. I went to work and accidentally left MSN on all night.

Mike's contribution was, 'Babe, why aren't you asleep?'

Because I'm at work, which you would have known if you'd cared enough to listen.

'Close your eyes and go to sleep thinking of me.'

Why the hell would I want to do that? You dumped me, remember, or have you forgotten that, too?

He made me angry and I didn't reply.

Si didn't wind me up, 'Hey you. I thought you were on the last of your three tonight. You haven't pulled a sickie, have you? You all right, girl?'

That was nice, but I couldn't be bothered replying to him, either.

I haven't seen Mike for over a month, but he wants to talk. The worst of the hurting is over. I don't want him back. I'm tired and moody. I've had three shifts from hell and haven't slept since Tuesday night. What's the point? If he wants me back, we'll go through this again in a week or two when I feel neglected. And if he doesn't want me back, I'm going to feel rejected all over again.

Megan wants me to get Baz to come out with us tonight to make up the numbers as she's seeing Si. I don't even want to do that. Giving up a Saturday night out is unheard of. I'm already supposed to be going out with Baz tonight. I asked him to come out last Friday, but he was skint. He said he'd come this week. I feel bad about cancelling on him, but my heart isn't in it. He's my friend and I'm letting him down.

~~~

26 November 2011

So, I met a man who might be capable of loving me. But his work stops him from having any time for me. I haven't seen or spoken to him for over a month. He seemed so genuine in the beginning.

Megan came around last night. She couldn't wait to tell me her news and wore smug like perfume. 'I was talking to Mike on MSN last night.'

'What did he say?'

'You're not going to believe this, but he's asked me to go for a day out with him.'

'What?'

'He's taking me for a day's beating.'

'And you said, yes?'

'Of course. Why Wouldn't I? I thought he was insensitive asking me when he'd never asked you, but you've split up, and I'd love to get on that fancy estate. You can't expect me to say no. You don't own him.'

I was so hurt.

'He never asked me.'

'I know,' she grinned.

'Why wasn't I good enough to ask? What have you got that I haven't?'

I went into rant mode and called him all the bastards under the sun. As for her, I could barely look at her smug face. I told her I'm washing my hands of both of them. She's supposed to be my friend, but she's going out with my ex-boyfriend a few days after he's finished with me.

'Stop being such a drama queen. I don't think there's anything romantic in it. And if he wants sex, he's got no chance. I don't see what your problem is.'

She said it as though there was nothing wrong with her going out with Mike. She justified it with the fact that Mike and I are over. 'And let's face it, my friend, you barely knew him. He's fair game now, I'm afraid.'

I told her I couldn't care less what they do. She'd done me a huge favour because I'd been pining. Stupid me again. Enough is enough. I wasn't very kind to her and screamed at her to get out.

'Bitch. Bastard. Bitch, bastards.'

'Clara, you get so nasty when you're tired.'

She'd told me she was seeing my ex, and she doesn't expect temperament. She left on very stiff terms.

I stayed in with no intention of going out and watched TV with Emily, and that was that. I rang Mike's phone, not expecting him to answer. He never does. So I left a voicemail.

'Megan came tonight and said you've asked her out for a day's beating. You bastard. Don't ever contact me again.'

She's welcome to him. He'll have her tied to the first tree they come to, and I hope he bloody leaves her there. Good luck to them.

~~~

16 November 2011.

It seemed so out of character for Mike to ask Megan out. He couldn't stand her. She's been seeing a married man for well over a year and she's stringing Si along. Mike's a straight person. He'd never want to be with somebody who was seeing other people. It's not him. It didn't ring true.

I was waiting to see if he'd come online on Monday, to find out what he had to say. After my email, I didn't expect him to be there. But he was. My heart jumped into my mouth when I saw his messenger go green. I wanted him so much, and for all my big talk I was nowhere near over him. But I did get the truth out of him.

He'd seen Megan on MSN and hadn't spoken to her, but she'd hit on him. What he'd actually said was, 'If you see Clara, ask her if she'd like to come for a day's beating on the estate.' He sent me the conversation as proof. What was Megan playing at? In his next message, he'd said that she could come too, so I'd have somebody I knew with me, and Si might be there as well.

How did that morph into, 'Would you like to go out with me?'

He told me Si had finished with Megan because he'd caught her out on some lies. Mike said he'd never considered us as finished. It was just a heat-of-the-moment argument on his part. I've been through torture, and he doesn't think it's a big deal.

We're giving it another go. But we're going back to basics. I'm going to try not to nag him, and he's going to get as much time for us as he can. We're not going to get heavy and talk about living together. He's furious about Megan coming between us. He said Megan called me a slut and told Si that while Mike and I were apart, I'd been out with other men.

I haven't been anywhere with anybody. I was supposed to go out with Baz on Saturday, but I cancelled. I'd told Mike about him and wanted him to meet Baz. If I had gone, we'd have had a drink, had a laugh, and had a dance. I've had my head so full of Mike that I'd never look at anybody else.

Other people have put their oar in our relationship. From now on, my loyalties lie with Mike, and nobody else. Because of he-said-she-said, I've sent every conversation that I've had with Megan and Si on MSN to Mike. I have nothing to hide. I'd never lie to him.

He's going to do his best to come tomorrow morning. It's been a month since we saw each other and a lot has happened. I'm not going to get my hopes up too high in case he can't make it. He's invited me to a day shoot on the Solway in Scotland. I'm not going as a beater. I'll be there as his guest. He said when we see each other he wants to forget everything we've said before. He wants us to make love and commit to each other.

He's done a U-turn on that one, but so have I. I was ready for sex the last time we were together, but he wasn't. He said he wouldn't make love to me until we could spend the night together. I was happy with that. It's nice to be treated with respect, but if he'd changed his mind, I wouldn't have needed any persuading.

However, this time, I changed my mind. I don't want us to have sex. We've got too much re-building to do. Megan has called me a slut, and I want his respect. If sex with him lasts forever, then it's worth waiting for. And after recent events, I'm not as sure that we're going to go the distance. He said it was just a stupid fight, but it's more than that. He rejected me and that smarts. He was so tired that day and wanted to spend a happy time with me on MSN before going to bed. He'd been up all night preparing for the shoots. 'I didn't mean to end it. I'm a prat, but girl, you can't half fight.'

'I never got started, that was just a warmup.'

'Jeez Clara, you said you've got a temper, but I wasn't expecting that.'

I rang Megan and told her what she was accused of and she was horrified. She said that she never called me a slut. She never said anything that could be inferred as that, and when Mike had asked her out, it definitely didn't include me. I don't know why she did it. She's supposed to be my friend. She told Si that I was going out with men, and he passed it on to Mike and warned him not to trust me. 'Clara, we're supposed to be friends. How can you even think I'd call you something horrible?'

'I didn't think you'd be capable of going out with my boyfriend, but you would have.'

I know Megan tells lies. As far as I know, Mike has never lied to me. And an MSN conversation can't lie. Megan is no friend of mine. I sent her the messages and told her we were done. She denied it all and said that Mike had manipulated the conversation from his end. My boyfriend struggles to read and write, he can't hack a bloody computer.

I'm going to continue being a hundred per cent honest with Mike, and I believe that he will too, everybody else can go to hell.

~~~

1st December 2011

Here I am, and here he isn't. He cancelled again. I'm disappointed, but I'm too tired to be annoyed. He says he's got definite time off to come tomorrow, and it will be better because I'll have had some sleep. It'll only be a couple of hours in the morning, but we can talk and get things back on track.

~~~

'The stupid woman got rid of him—but she's going back for more. It's as if she had a death wish.' Molly despised Clara's weakness—but not as much as her own.

~~~

3 December 2011

Despite going to bed after three and not sleeping, I was up at six to clean the house for Mike coming. This was a definite because he'd arranged the morning off.

I was ready by nine and wrote to my diary for an hour to kill time. He wasn't here by half ten and he had to be at work for two. If he didn't get here soon, it wouldn't be worth it. I'd avoided going online because, for the first morning in weeks, I knew he was coming to see me. I didn't want to go online to see his red man turn green and have his picture appear on the screen showing that he was still at home, and not on his way here, but by a quarter to eleven, I had no choice.

I tried to log on but didn't have an internet connection. I needed to be online. The panic was blinding, what if he was trying to contact me and thought I was ignoring him? My frustration was manifest and I hurled a mug across the room and felt a split second of satisfaction as it shattered against the wall.

At noon, I knew he wasn't coming. I rang Virgin and found out the fault was theirs—for my lack of internet at least—and they weren't expecting a connection in my area for at least twenty-four hours. It goes without saying that Mike's phone was dead.

I bought it and put ten pounds worth of credit on it. It had five as part of the package. In the last month, I've had two texts, and for the last three weeks, his phone has been dead. He charged it once when he took it home and hasn't bothered since.

He didn't ring to let me know he wasn't coming. He never does. He just didn't turn up.

This is ridiculous, but I don't know where he lives. It's a big country estate, and I know the general area, but I don't have his address. He's never given me his home phone number because all calls are connected through the office and are screened. He likes to keep himself private. In our early days, he always called me and withheld the number. The internet was down. The mobile I bought him was dead. He's my boyfriend, but I have no means of contacting him.

As afternoon turned into evening. I gave up waiting. Maybe he didn't let me know because he was going to spring one of his surprise visits in the evening. I spent two hours getting ready in case he turned up. He didn't, and at nine o'clock, I gave up waiting. I feel used and worthless again. This morning I got up to find that my internet has been restored.

There was an email waiting for me from Mike. It was sent at three yesterday afternoon, six hours after we were due to meet.

Sorry. I have just got home. I broke down on the motorway. I'm going to the garage tomorrow and will sort it out xxx.

The last time he was coming and couldn't use work as an excuse, he got stuck in the wake of an accident. This time his car's broken down. We don't have a lot of luck, and I'm trying so hard to believe him.

I got his email, and for the first time ever, I couldn't be bothered sitting by the computer all day on the off chance that he'd come online to talk to me. I went to bed early and slept solidly from eleven until seven. I got up feeling tired and worse than before I went to bed. This morning I was exhausted, so I checked my emails and went back to bed. If he paid one of his unexpected visits, he'd just have to knock me up.

~~~

9 January 2012

It's been a while. Check the dates I haven't written for ages. I've been very sad and not in a good place.

Let's start by getting rid of Mike, and then we can move on.

So paraphrasing as we skip merrily on.

I met Mike and wasn't impressed.

He came on strong, so damned strong, and he won me over.

He was all hot and heavy — though never physically, and that was weird. 'I love you. Let me pay off your debts. I want to buy you a car. Marry me? We'll start a business and be together forever.'

And then the broken dates started. A month in, he let me down, work, work, work. 'I love you. I want you. Too busy to have time for you.' And then, in a strop, he finished with me.

I was heartbroken, but after a week, I was more or less over him.

He said he'd been hasty, that he loved me. It was my fault that I didn't understand his lifestyle.

So we got back together, on-screen anyway. I never saw him in person again after the second month. Our relationship was an hour on MSN on a Monday morning if I was lucky. In the end, I hadn't seen him, or even spoken to him, in over five weeks.

I wanted to see my boyfriend. He'd gone AWOL. For those final three weeks, there wasn't a word. I hadn't had so much as a sentence from him, and he hadn't been on MSN. I wrote to him to cross the Ts and dot the Is.

Crikey, I don't want him popping up in ten years saying, 'Hell, that was a long shift. I've finally got a night off to come and see you, my love.'

It's finished, done, over — and I mean it this time.

He never cared. It was just the same pretty words, spouted in the same pretty order, with the same broken dates and the rapid cooling-off period. I wonder how he'd have wriggled out of it if I'd taken him up on his offer of six grand to pay off my debts. That was a pretty big gamble.

The stupid thing is, I don't understand why? It wasn't to get me into bed because apart from all his talk of tying me up to a tree there was nothing — and that was his mild fantasy, the big one involved a twelve-bore shotgun in my intimate place, and it was terrifying. But he didn't want to have sex with me. We never did more than kiss. What did he get out of leading me on?

His fantasy was way out there, and the stupid thing is that I'd have done it to please him and give him the ultimate sexual experience. I'm a pleaser, I'll do anything to make a man happy. This has shown me that I do mean anything.

Mike was all about dominance and control, but not in the usual S&M way. His kink was linked to the countryside. He wanted to take me to his private wood and tie me naked to a tree. He said I'd be bound, gagged, blindfolded and helpless. All tame stuff, until you add a loaded gun, 'Safety catch on, perfectly safe. It's all about trust, Clara.'

No, it's about power and control. He wanted to masturbate me with the barrel of a loaded shotgun. In the weeks we were together, he never talked about making love to me properly. He talked about tying me up, bending me over the sink and using a vibrator on me, slapping my bottom, biting my pussy, tying me naked to a tree and leaving me there for an hour while he went to fill the feed bins. It was about humiliation, not trust.

I thought I was in love with him. I wanted to make him happy and fulfil his fantasies. I told him I'm uninhibited and would try anything once.

'But would you? How far would you go, Clara?'

That's when he told me about his gun fantasy. It freaked me out. He wanted to insert a loaded shotgun into my vagina, and I agreed to it. It was all fantasy. When we were together, and he held me, he was gentle. His kisses could be hard and passionate, but he was soft-hearted and seemed caring. I'm so eager to please that I'd let a man insert a loaded gun into my body for sexual gratification. I don't know if I'd have gone through with it until the time came, but I think I would. I had total trust in him. A gun can discharge at any time. He told me it was a million-to-one chance that it would go off with the safety catch-on, and in that case, it would discharge backwards and kill both of us, not just me. Well, that's okay then. Being masturbated with a big gun does nothing for me, but the thought of fulfilling the ultimate fantasy for him does, and if it led to gentle lovemaking afterwards, the prospect excited me. How sick am I?

I suppose I'm thankful that it never got that far. For all his kinky talk, we never did more than kiss. His hands never strayed, and his kisses were hot, but never got out of control. I thought I had him where I wanted him. He seemed besotted, but I think he had the potential to be dangerous. It's over. We never made love. We never went out anywhere. He never saw me dressed up, hair done, make-up on. I was always in outdoor walking wear, or in a state of dishevelment because he'd sprung a surprise visit. It's over.

I haven't heard from him for weeks and couldn't believe it when my phone rang at teatime tonight.

He sounded terrible.

'My darling. I've missed you so much. You have to help me. There's nobody else I can ask.'

'What's up?'

'I can't go into too much detail, but my son's robbed the estate. I've taken the blame to protect him, and the owner's going to ring the police if I don't replace the money by tonight.'

'How much.'

'Ten grand. If you can get a loan, I can stall them until it comes through. I wouldn't ask, but I've got nobody else to turn to. Will you do it for me, my love? Meet me at Foulshaw Moss Nature Reserve at eight tonight. Get an emergency loan and bring the money. I'll meet you in the car park. I love you.'

'I haven't got any money. Goodbye, Mike.'

I hung up.

~~~

'Yes. Good Girl. He's asked her for money, and she hung up on him. I hope she didn't cave—we have the link to Foulshaw here. It's the same place her body was found eight years later.'

~~~

18th April 2012

There is an end to the Mike story. I haven't spoken to him for four months. I didn't forget to write the epilogue. I'm just sick of writing about that waste of space. I hadn't heard from him since the night he asked me for money...until a few weeks ago when I had a phone call from him.

'Hi.'

'Hello. What can I do for you?'

'I need to talk to you.'

'Go on. I'm listening.'

'God, this is difficult. First, I want to tell you a massive truth.' There was a long pause for effect. 'I fell in love with you the day I met you.'

'Go on.'

'Shit. Damn, you're cold.' Another pause. 'This is hard. But everything else that I've ever told you has been a lie, and I'm so sorry.'

'I don't understand. What do you mean, everything?'

'Everything. I made it all up to con you. I was playing the long game but didn't plan on falling for you.'

'Explain. You've got three seconds before I call the police.'

'It's all I deserve, but please hear me out. I'm not and never have been a gamekeeper. I'm an unemployed, married man living on disability in a council house with a wife and children. I haven't had a job for nearly twenty years. And I'm not forty-two. I'm fifty-three.'

It was too much information to collate in one go. I didn't reply.

'It's over, Clara. I told her about you and that I want to be with you, and she's taken my children and left me. Everything, even down to the name I told you is all lies, except that I love you.'

'But you're Mike Thornton. You work for the Duke. He trusts you.'

'No. That's not me.'

'That's not even your name?'

'No.'

'But you brought two gundogs to my house. You wouldn't let me stroke them, and said they weren't pets.'

'Borrowed from a friend. They weren't mine.'

I should have asked his name, but it seemed irrelevant.

'But I spoke to your children, and even your dad.'

'I had to have somebody to confide in. My dad was really old Jimmy from down the street. I was going to buy him a bottle of whiskey to meet you and play the part.' I laughed at that. It seemed funny that he'd said my worth was in question from his posh parents.

'Your kids said you were happy with me. Dave asked when he was going to meet me. He didn't sound like a thief.'

'And I don't sound like a conman, but that's what I am. You see, you never spoke to my children or my dad. You spoke to people I know in the pub. I bought them a pint to pretend. It seemed funny at the time.'

'You thought doing that to me was funny. You're sick.'

The kids did know about you. Well, the oldest two, did. They don't get on with my wife. My daughter, Jenny, you knew her as Daisy, laughed when I told her you'd invited her to stay with you. She was never beaten up by her boyfriend.'

'I can't take all this in.'

'I gave them false names so you couldn't track me. I know the Duke of Westminster's estate from days out there, and if you turned up, you'd never get past the gatehouse. I had to cover my tracks.'

'Where do you live?'

'You wouldn't believe me if I told you, but it's not very far away from you.'

'What about all the times I drove to Grange-over-Sands to meet you halfway?'

'You drove past my house to get there. I said it was halfway so you'd think I was trying, but it was only five minutes from where I live.'

I couldn't believe what I was hearing. This was the man who told me, 'If you bed them, you've got to be prepared to marry them.' He said if he ever caught me kissing another man, that'd be it. We'd be finished, and all the time, he was going home to his wife. He brought guns to my house. They weren't his. Even his gundogs were borrowed. The man said he shot pet dogs on his land. He said he'd beaten a man up. Mike was a fantasist.

'It's all different now, Clara. She's gone. You can have a key to my house, free reign, do what you like.'

'Everything you ever told me was a lie?'

'Almost. But not everything.'

'How could I ever trust a word you say?'

'I do drive a four-by-four.' He didn't care about admitting he was a lying, cheating bastard, but his ego couldn't cope with me not believing that he has whatever kudos driving a Land Rover brings, it was pathetic. Who cares what he drives? He bragged that he got it on his disability scheme.

'What about Simon? I met him.'

'He's real, different name of course, but he's a mate.'

'He told me stuff about the estate. He said you'd beaten up the manager.'

'Yeah, you were clingier than a lot of them, and we had to get inventive with our excuses. But you haven't asked me what I want.'

'Haven't asked you what you want?' I sounded like a demented parrot. 'I couldn't give a shit what you want. It's not relevant to anything.'

'I was hoping we could pool our finances, a few grand each would build us a life together. I've got my share here. We could be living together by tomorrow, my darling.'

'You're crazy. I'm not giving you any money.'

And that's when his voice changed. So hard, it sounded like a granite slab covering a vault. 'Okay, Clara. I can tell you aren't up for being with me. I won't trouble you again.'

Click.

And that was that. I haven't heard a word from him since.

I'm expecting him to get in touch. Baz thinks that somebody as unhinged as him could come to my house with a bloody big goose gun — he has access to them because I've seen them. He could hold us hostage. Either way, I don't think I've heard the last of him — but I hope I have.

All the signs were there, and he might as well have told me outright that he was married. I was a fool not to see it. He implied that I'm one in a long line of conquests, and yet he professed to not like women much. He seemed so set in his ways. He seemed stable and faithful, everything I wanted. But he was a thief and a liar. I can't believe there was no estate. His story was elaborate with every tiny detail coloured in.

I had a lucky escape.

~~~

'Wow, he admitted to her that it was all a big con.'

Brown stretched and closed the diary after marking the end of the relevant piece. 'That's it. The first book's finished. I'll put the kettle on. How're you getting on?'

'I've just engaged with a man in Garstang, right age. I've spoken to nineteen men tonight, and after hearing what some of them want to do to me, I feel dirty.'

'Welcome to the world of everybody that ever dipped their toes into the murky sperm-filled sewage water of internet dating.'

'Cynic. A quick coffee for me, please, and then I've got to make tracks.'

'Of course, you have.'

Phil ignored the jibe. 'So what have you got from The Wailing One's diary tonight.'

'Didn't you hear me? He confessed.'

'What?'

'He admitted he was a conman out to take her for money.' Other than that, pretty much more of the same. Except. This guy was messed up in the head. He wanted to tie her to a tree in the woods and leave her there for an hour while he fed his pigs or whatever.'

'It was pheasants. But, yes, we know all that. What else?'

'That's just the entre. The sick bastard wanted to insert a loaded twelve-bore shotgun into her vagina and masturbate her with it. I did gasp at the time, but you were deep into your homoerotic conversations with other men.'

'Steady. We'll have less of that. You know I only have eyes for you. Seriously though it shows his depravity.'

Molly was hurt by the word seriously, of course, the thought of only being interested in her couldn't be serious.

'We'll take it to Nash in the morning. His confession is massive. And the kinky stuff is something he might have suggested to other women. I don't want to even think about him actually doing it to anybody. Another thing is, Clara told Megan to get lost. We need to know if it was a permanent falling out,' Brown said. 'And don't forget, it was around this time that the friend went missing and hasn't been seen since.'

Chapter Sixteen

Nash had a headache. He'd been out drinking with Kelvin, and it had turned into a late night. He'd almost asked him to stay over. The spare bedroom was made up, and when Hayley had come to clean the house for him, he'd asked her to change the linen and freshen the spare room—just in case. He figured the sleeping arrangements would take care of themselves naturally, but it didn't hurt to be prepared for all scenarios. In the end, the only thing that stopped him from asking the question was the doom of having to be up for work hanging over them. It was Wednesday morning, and they were seeing each other again on Friday.

Nash smiled because he was happier than he'd been in years, and then grimaced when he heard the noise coming from the incident room. They were all talking about their exploits on the dating sites they'd been allocated.

'Some of the things they come out with in their first sentence make me want to scrub my phone with bleach.' Bowes said.

'Listen up, team.' They stopped what they were doing and turned in their seats to face the front. 'It sounds as though you've got a lot to tell me.'

Patel jumped out of his seat and handed Nash a conversation printout. 'I think we've got him, sir.'

Nash scanned the paper with answers to the relevant questions. 'Great work, Patel. Good teamwork from all of you. But, why the hell didn't you ring me with this as soon as you got it?'

'Sir, it was turned one in the morning. This has waited all these years. I don't think another eight hours is going to hurt.'

'What if he's smelled a rat? He'll be up the nearest drainpipe before you can say dirty vermin. Patel don't delete your account yet. We don't want him getting suspicious. But if he contacts you again, do not respond.'

'I'm just checking the chat again now. I have three messages from him asking if I'm there. The last one was forty-four minutes ago.'

'Good work. Leave it to us now.' Nash turned to the whiteboard. So, we have a hit from Patel. Steve, aged 42, Username Hunter. And he says he works as a gamekeeper at Brampton house country estate near Levens. He has two grown-up kids and three grandchildren. I reckon we've got our man. Make sure all your laptops are logged out, and return them to my desk before you leave, please. It looks as though our Molly Decoy is a popular girl. We'll monitor all the chat lines for a few days.'

While the team congratulated themselves, Nash spoke to Brown. 'I'm going to grab Lewis now to see how we're going to proceed, and as discussed in our last meeting, it's highly likely we'll be bringing you in, Brown. I'll try and arrange a briefing by ten, it shouldn't be any later than that. You'll need to be ready to pick up the conversation where Patel left off. Tell the suspect you went to bed with a migraine, but don't make contact until after the briefing. We need to strike while the iron's hot.'

They'd already started to leave the incident room when Lawson burst in. 'Sir, you need to see this. I've got him.' He was excited, and his cheeks were flushed as though he'd been running. Lawson had taken that morning off for a career meeting at the school concerning his nephew, Aidan.

'All right, slow down, lad. What have you got?'

'I had our meeting with the careers officer and was waiting outside while he had ten minutes with Aiden. I figured while it was quiet, I'd have five minutes on the dating app. He was my third chat.' He passed Nash a sheet of handwritten notes, and Nash read aloud. Alerted to the new intel the couple of officers that had left the room came back to listen. 'Steve, 42. No kids. Okay, that's an anomaly, we know he has kids, but he could be lying here. Username Gotabiggun, another difference. Says he works as a gamekeeper at Brampton House.'

'Dirty git,' Lawson said. 'He says he wants to sing to me in bed.'

'He's using a load of different accounts,' Bowes said.

'It looks that way. Certainly two at least. While you've been away this morning, Lawson, we've had another hit from Patel. Well done.' Nash gave him a grin and wrote the whiteboard up with the latest intel.

'Sir, I'd like to revisit what happened to the friend, Megan, who seemed to just vanish,' Renshaw said.

'Where are we with that?'

'It's a mystery. I don't want to shout my mouth off too soon, but I think this Megan may be an earlier victim.'

'I thought she went to live with family. And then she buggered off to London and vanished, innocently into the smog and without any suspicion of foul play?'

'That's what we thought, but I've been digging. She did go to live with her eldest son but didn't get on with the daughter-in-law. However, that's the least of it. They found out she was sneaking off for a couple of hours to meet a man. It could be our guy. Anyway, the family were suspicious and put a nanny cam in, and it turns out she was putting the kiddies down for a nap, and then leaving them on their own. The son went ballistic and threw her out. She said she was going to London, but there's no record of her staying there long. No phone records, bank details, nothing after the first few months.'

'The lady vanishes,' Nash muttered, he was tapping his teeth with a marker, a sure sign that he was mulling things over.

'Sorry?'

'Just thinking out loud. Renshaw, you stay on that enquiry. I want everything you can dig up on where she went.'

Renshaw was in the middle of his reply when Lawson shouted, 'Oh my god.' He was visibly shaken. 'I've got another message. Sir, you need to see this.'

Nash sat on one of the desks, and the team gathered around. 'I was checking my laptop was logged off the app before handing it back, when it pinged with a message.' Lawson turned the laptop around for Nash to see.

He read the message to the team. 'Hey, sweetheart. Where are you? You haven't been answering my messages. You seemed keen last night. Haven't gone off me already, have you?' The user sent that message and wrote another, they watched his typing alert, and when the message appeared, Nash shook his head in disgust. 'Guys, I'm sorry, it's disgusting. "I just want to check. You are a pure English rose, aren't you? I want to be the first man to taste your sweet English nectar." He's a monster.' Nash stopped reading and looked around everybody before continuing. 'This guy needs to be stopped, he's an animal. I'm sorry you had to see this, Lawson, and you Patel.' Nash nodded a silent apology to Patel. 'He goes on to say, "There's been an influx of dirty bloody," and he uses the derogatory P word. This is strong evidence to put him away for hate crimes on top of everything else. And if he isn't our guy, I'm going to have this bastard anyway. He says, "I'd round the lot of them up and shoot them dead in the street. I want to check that you're white all the way through and aren't one of those softie snowflakes that wants to let them take over our country. And another thing, my wife was turned gay by a queer, so I don't like them either. We need to clean up our country." That's it for the racism and homophobia, thank God, after that, he goes back to flirting. Interestingly he signs off with "I can't wait to hold you in my arms and sing you a sweet lullaby, my geese love it." And, did you all pick up on the other tie-in?'

Molly jumped in, 'There's a passage in the first diary where he told Clara Watts, that his wife had a lesbian encounter.'

'Exactly. This is circumstantial at this point, but it's all evidence that weaves the cloth together.'

'That's what he said to me, all that singing malarky about his goose. He even used the same words,' Lawson said.

The team were stunned into silence by the blatant hate crimes, and Renshaw had his arm around Patel's shoulder. Nash coughed, 'What kind of sick world do we live in? I think this is the same man as Steve with the Hunter username. I also think it's our person of interest, but let's not get too excited. It's too early to tell. I wanted this guy before—now I want him so bad it hurts.'

Nash spent time with Bronwyn putting safety measures in place to protect Brown and talking through every possible eventuality.

'I still don't like it, Silas.'

'Nor me, but we have every reason to believe he killed the best friend as well. A woman called Megan Hartley dropped off the planet after The Gamekeeper showed an interest in her.'

'The Gamekeeper? Don't we usually leave the sensationalist names to the titillation-hungry media?'

'We have to call him something. And, we're not having any luck tracing Hartley. Her family haven't spoken to her since an argument when the son threw her out of their home. It's very telling that she left two young kids home alone to meet a man she met online. Every instinct is telling me it's got to be him. I think he killed her, Bronwyn. The worst of it is, it was eight years before he killed Clara Watts. I can't believe he was dormant during those eight years. We don't have enough to go with Hartley yet, and she may be living her best life somewhere. But I'd bet my hat on it that she isn't.'

'It doesn't make me feel any better about sending Molly into his lair,' Lewis said.

'I can't come up with anything better. She's waiting outside, shall I call her in?'

'Yes. Let's get it over with.'

Nash went to the door and called Brown into Lewis's office. When she was settled, a sombre mood fell over the room. They'd already discussed what was going to happen, and the meeting was to talk Brown through wires and surveillance information and to see that she was still set on going ahead.

'Molly,' Lewis said. 'What we're asking of you is highly dangerous. If it leads to a conviction, nothing can ever be used in court. Legally, we're sailing close to the wind regarding coercion. I've put it across to the High Court Commissioner that it isn't just a honey trap, but our only means of gathering information. She didn't buy it for a second, but gave us, if not a green light, then a high amber one.'

She paused to let what she'd said sink in. 'My question, Molly, is are you sure you want to go ahead with this assignment? It's dangerous, and while we'll take every precaution, we can't guarantee your safety.'

'Yes, ma'am. I've read a diary about this guy. I know him. And I know what makes him tick. I understand his triggers, and I'm confident that I can draw him out.'

Nash touched her gently on the arm and smiled at her. 'We're going to be there when you meet him. We'll lock this down so it's cast-iron tight. Your safety is more important than nailing him,' Nash said. 'You'll be wearing a wire, and the van will be parked outside. You'll only meet him in a public place, and we'll be less than fifty feet from you at all times. We'll have eyes on you in the pub or restaurant, and you'll have safe words and gestures. At any time, anytime at all, if you want us to get you out of there, you use your safe word or make your gesture, and we'll have you out within thirty seconds. Is that clear?'

'Yes, boss. You make me feel safe, and I'm confident.'

'Good. Right, let's discuss your approach. You can't suggest a meeting, that's too forward, and he'll back off. He's a controller, let him do the running. If he's in, it won't take long, and I'm guessing he'll ask before the end of your first chat. There's a good chance he's still married, and he'll gear towards coming to your place. That can never happen. Got it?'

'Yes.'

'Your backstory is that you've come out of an abusive marriage and you're staying with an aunt for a while until you get a deposit pulled together for a rented flat. She's in the mid-stages of dementia, and she's your only family. The inference is that if you did go missing, she wouldn't be raising any alarms for a while. He goes for vulnerable easy targets. So you play everything down. You've seen the Molly Turner decoy profile. The photo we posted is an AI image with a strong similarity to you, however, she's a lot bigger than you. When you meet, your weight loss will be down to the stress and anxiety brought on by your divorce, and the physical demands of looking after your wealthy aunt. We'll provide a suitable wardrobe for you—you'll hate it.'

Molly scowled, and Nash laughed.

'You want me to be seen in public dressed in sackcloth and ashes?'

'Something like that. He doesn't like women to show off their assets, as it were. See it as humbling.'

'Don't you think, if I'm wearing a dowdy, beige monstrosity, it'll rouse suspicion if I run into somebody I know?'

'I wouldn't have thought so. People don't examine others that closely. But avoid places where you know people. Your dress would be the least of our problems if anybody came over to you. Are you good?'

'Yes, sir.'

'Great. We'll try and make first contact tonight.'

'I'm ready. I'd still like to read the other diary though, the one eight years later. The first one has given me a lot of insight into his character.'

'No problem.'

They wrapped up the meeting and Brown pulled Silas to one side in the corridor. 'I didn't want to say anything in front of the super, but something's been bugging me. I've been waiting for you to mention it, but you haven't.'

'Go on.'

'What about that bloke you were messaging in Greece?'

'What about him?'

'Come on, boss. Join the dots. He's the right age, and he was a gamekeeper too.'

'No. He worked as a groundsman, didn't he?'

'I'm almost certain he said gamekeeper because I remember you calling him a poacher. It's ringing all kinds of alarm bells to me.'

'Don't be ridiculous. He was a gay man looking for men. Your guy is a homophobic woman stalker. It's not even close enough to be a coincidence. And never once crossed my mind,' Nash lied.

'It should have done, Nash. You're too close to see it. It's been running through my head for days. Your guy was called Dave Thorn. This one is Steve Thornley. It's giving me the ick.'

'You're barking up the wrong tree. It's nothing to do with him. But, if it's a cause for concern, I'll take a step back on it due to personal involvement, and I'll get Renshaw to check it out.' Nash's face said it all.

'I know you're a private man, and hate the idea, sir. But we need to at least check it. Let's not involve anybody else at this stage, and I'll delve into it. I'll need access to your account, though. I don't need to look into any other chats if you get my drift, but I'll need to pull the ones with him.'

'At ease, Brown. It's okay. I've got nothing to hide. The few conversations we had were all very respectful.'

'Thank God for that. There are things I don't need to know about my boss. I promise I'll be discrete. If he's our man, it doesn't bear thinking about. Thank God for Snow warning you off him.'

'Quite.'

Chapter Seventeen

Molly settled on the sofa and psyched herself up to chat with a possible murderer. She'd interrogated several, but this was her first intimate encounter with one, and she had to be careful not to blow it.

She logged on and swiped on his profile, hoping he'd take the bait. If it didn't work, the tech team would create a new profile tomorrow, and she'd try again until he did bite. He needed to make first contact with her. Brown couldn't be forward in any way. They'd done as much profiling as they could from the information they had and were confident that Molly Turner was exactly what he went for. She was dumpy and dowdy. She didn't come across as very intelligent or worldly and was a perfect mark for a conman. She was the exact opposite of DI Molly Brown. She hadn't travelled and wasn't adventurous. There were no photos of her skydiving with her face G-force affected and distorted. She had the obligatory photo of a cat, and her username was, *Lovesreadingromance*. Brown hated her.

Countryboy: Hi.

Bingo!

Lovesreadingromance: Hi.
Countryboy: You have a lovely face.
Lovesreadingromance: Thank you, but I don't.
Countryboy: I think you do. What do you do?
Lovesreadingromance: You first. What do you do?
Countryboy: I'm a gamekeeper on a big country estate, sweetheart. I'd love to show it to you sometime, sweetheart.

The patronising repetition of sweetheart was annoying her already.

Lovesreadingromance: I'd like that. I like animals. Have you got any pets?
Countryboy: No. They aren't pets, but I do have two black Labradors. They're working gun dogs, sweetheart. Mother and daughter. They answer to Bess and Jude. What about you?

Molly hated him already.

Lovesreadingromance: We've got a cat called Pearl.
Countryboy: We?
Lovesreadingromance: I live with my Auntie Lottie at the moment. That's why I can't work. I'm normally a bookkeeper, but my auntie has dementia. She's my only relative, and there's nobody else to look after her.

Countryboy: It sounds like you need cheering up, sweetheart.

They carried on chatting for another half hour, and Molly dimmed her intellect and let him groom her using every trick in the book. She drip-fed him the information that she wasn't short of money and that the old lady was loaded and on her last legs.

He wanted to meet at her house for a coffee, but Molly explained that it would frighten Lottie. Brown's blood ran cold with his next idea.

Countryboy: I'll tell you what, do you know Foulshaw Moss? It's beautiful out there, and we could go for a walk and get to know each other, sweetheart.

She felt sick at the mention of the beauty spot where Clara Watts had been murdered. She had to think fast and said she couldn't because she'd sprained her ankle a couple of weeks before and still couldn't walk on it properly. She asked if they could meet in Wetherspoons in Barrow, and her hands shook as she read his next reply.

He said it wasn't good for him. He wouldn't be able to get away from work for long, and the best he could do was an hour in the morning. It was like reading Clara Watt's diary again.

He said it would be better if they could meet in The Commodore pub at Grange-over-sands. Better for him, and it was another of his hunting grounds that he'd taken Clara to. This guy was despicable, and she felt her skin crawling with a thousand metaphorical maggots.

They planned to meet at ten the next morning, soon after the kids went to school, and his wife would be at work, she presumed. Brown tested him further by asking if she could ring him.

She played to his ego and said she wanted to see if he sounded as nice as he looked. Gone were the days when married people could get away with listing profiles without pictures. Living in a visual age, presence was everything, but it was easy enough to download a fake image.

She had.

She'd been given a burner phone for any communication between them but didn't need it. He fed her the line about not having a mobile phone. And used the same joke as he'd given Clara about his sheep not needing a phone. Brown felt physically, horribly ill. This guy may well be a murderer, but he was also a bloody creep. All the similarities added up to hard-written corroborating evidence. There was no doubt that this was the one Clara Watts had been seeing. When he'd taken the bait, and their date was arranged for Grange, she couldn't get rid of him fast enough.

She left him with two kisses in her last message. He replied with three, and she watched his account disappear from the screen with a beep before she downloaded the conversation and sent it to Nash.

Brown rang Silas to tell him how she'd got on, and so they could have the sting in place by the next morning. Nash said he'd been expecting her call and must have been sitting with his thumb on the phone because it barely rang before he answered. He listened to a recount of their chat and then downloaded it to read.

'Excellent work, Brown. Well done.'

After speaking to Nash, she couldn't settle. A chill permeated her body, and she couldn't get warm. A soak in the bath would thaw her and warm right into her blood, but she would be vulnerable, naked, and up to her neck in water. It was ridiculous, this evil man didn't know who she was, or where she lived, but she couldn't stand the thought of braving her vulnerability. She changed into pyjamas, and a fluffy dressing gown made hot chocolate, and switched the fire on full. Then, she turned on the new series of *Unforgotten*. The programme was about cold cases, and the first screenshot showed a naked woman on an embankment. It was too close to home. She didn't want to watch anymore and turned it off fast.

Molly was aware of a crazy connection with the dead woman. She felt close to her, and more than any other victim, including the murdered children she'd seen, this one resonated with her. Steve, who had called himself Mike sometimes, was the bridge that linked them inextricably together.

She imagined a string from beyond the grave, running through her killer and reaching all the way to Molly. She shuddered but was compelled to open the second diary. This one was written in 2019, eight years after Mike had conned Clara for the first time. She noticed it was only part-filled, and after flicking through the used pages, she wanted to finish it before meeting their monster the next day.

~~~

30th July 2019.
And the strangest thing has happened to me. A bad person from my past has popped back into my life.

~~~

Molly stared at the words with an impending sense of disaster. What are you doing, crazy girl? Run.

~~~

Eight years ago, I met a man. I fell in love with him and thought he was a good person. We were together for three months. During that time, I was his double-life woman, one of many, and a dirty secret.

When things cooled on his side, he rang me and confessed that he wasn't a gamekeeper living in a tiny cottage on the grounds of a huge estate. He was a married man, living on the dole with his wife and baby in a council house. Apart from a few menial jobs when he was young, he said he'd never been employed. He'd drawn disability for an invisible bad back for most of his adult life. Everything he ever told me was a lie. We never slept together or had sex, and that was the only positive thing in the sorry mess.

I don't know what drove me to curiosity when I'd barely thought about him in eight years, but after watching a TV show about the cesspool of online dating, I was compelled to go back onto the dating site where I met Mike—call it morbid fascination. I wanted to see if he was still in there and conning other women the way he did to me. I found his profile. His username was the same, *Baycrawler*, and I felt like committing murder. I got out fast. If only there was a way of warning his other contacts. I feel it's my duty to let them know what he's like.

I was in and out, but it was still enough to register my presence. Damn!

He messaged me under a different username, a new account, and with a single word.

Boo!

I was livid. Eight years, a destroyed life, and he comes at me with Boo. I ignored him and couldn't believe what was happening. I've been over him for years, but the old feelings resurfaced, the memory of being in love, the hurt every time he let me down, and the ultimate betrayal when I found out he was a cheating liar. He messaged me again and called me his Black Seal, the old nickname he gave me after seeing me in the bath with hair dye on. It cut me like a knife. Then he sent me an email address and told me to write to him—as if I would. I told him I would speak to him, but only on the telephone. I don't know why I said it. Curiosity to see what he had to say, I suppose.

I didn't want anything to do with him but ignored my instincts screaming at me to get off that site and shut down my phone. This man was a dangerous predator, and he'd stripped me of every particle of self-worth last time. I hated him. He didn't have my number, and I knew he couldn't get it—unless I contacted him on it.

He tried to wriggle out of speaking to me and wanted me to email him. I refused and said the only way this conversation was continuing was if it was over a telephone connection. He said he couldn't give me a number for me to ring him and would explain why. Of course, he couldn't, but he said he'd ring me instead. I don't know what kind of voodoo bewitched me, but against every fibre of my genetic makeup, and all my ancestors screaming at me not to do it, I gave him my number. It was only a telephone number. I could block him at any point. I thought I was in control—but he'd already twisted and manipulated me into doing what he wanted.

The phone rang instantly.

I ignored it and counted the rings. When it got to thirteen – unlucky for some – he rang off.

I opened my desk drawer and threw the phone in. The drawer slammed shut so hard that I hurt my hand.

It rang inside the drawer.

I wrenched it open, desperate to answer it before he gave up and disappeared again. I couldn't let that happen.

I had to know what he wanted to say to me. It was curiosity pumped to the max. It was a need for revenge. And, It was sheer stupidity.

I pressed ANSWER but didn't speak.

'Hello, my Black Seal. My darling, I messed my life up letting you go. God, I've thought about you every day. Did you really think I'd let you just walk away from me when I saw your beautiful name? You're the best thing I ever had in my life. I went back to your house to find you, but you'd moved.'

The voice transported me back eight years. His speech was normal, with none of the old, affected dialects, but it was him. So deep. I'd forgotten how deep it was, and how sexy, but there was nothing sexy about this man. He was a monster.

'You deserve an Oscar. I had the impression back then that you really disliked me. Otherwise, why did you treat me so badly? But I didn't know you had a wife locked away. It was an explanation of sorts I suppose but nowhere near enough reasoning. I blamed myself.'

'I know.'

'Why did you do it to me? I was loyal. I still am and will tell the man I've been seeing that we've spoken.

'You never married?' He asked.

'No.'

'There's still a chance for me, then.'

'No. None.'

'Don't be like that. What have you been up to all this time?'

'Avoiding pricks like you.'

'Oh, my darling. That temper. God, I miss you so much. You're being hard on me. But I deserve it, and so much more. I fell in love with what was in your head and how well you treated me. You taught me that treating people right matters above everything. I can see you've put on a bit of weight since I saw you. I want you to know, it doesn't matter to me. I hope you're eating better than you did before. I bet your Emily has grown up since I saw her. Please let's have a walk. We can go to The Commodore at grange-over-sands, do you remember it? Just tell me when xxx my little black seal, you'll always be that to me. I was bad at telling you how much I cared about you, and still do. You aren't saying anything. Talk to me. Stop being hard.'

'Hard? I haven't even begun. You're good, very smooth. Patter in place, all the right words, in the right order. Coming in that hot and heavy so soon might be a mistake, though. You've overplayed your hand, and how quickly you slid my weight gain in. Nice. Subtle, Flaskman, subtle. I expect you're an Adonis now, are you? Seeing as you can look down on me. If that's the case, you must have done a hell of a lot of self-improvement over the last eight years.'

'Go on. Get it all off your chest, and then we can talk.'

'Damn, you're patronising. I feel nothing speaking to you. You're a fly for me to pick up with tweezers and stick under my microscope. I'm interested to know what makes you tick, how you feel, and why you do the things you do. Are you a psychopath, sociopath, totally delusional, a heartless game player — or just the most incredibly child-like man? I never had answers to my questions — not really. Everything from your name to your occupation, to your marital status was a lie. You offered my daughter a little job with you that didn't exist because you didn't have one yourself. You borrowed dogs from a friend to make me think you were a gamekeeper. You are one of the most interesting, but sad and sadistic people I've ever met. You even took me on a night shoot because you told me you had a licence, and yet you never loaded your fancy gun. The one you borrowed, along with the dogs. I bet you can't even shoot. It would have been ironic if we'd got caught poaching geese when you had no intention of trying to shoot one anyway. If you did try, I was going to have a sneezing fit so that nothing got killed.'

'See, you remember, too. That was one of the best nights of my life, sweetheart.'

'And one of my worst, sitting on a cold beach waiting for damned geese to fly past in the middle of winter. My idea of hell. I see you're still married?'

'I'm in the middle of a very messy divorce.'

'Yeah, yeah, heard it all before. How honest of you to put it on your profile, you are getting bold. I wonder how many more women there have been since me. Have you been prowling the same dating site for the last eight years, picking off women to cover in your lies? How many poor sods have you fed your double life to? I was gullible. I admit, you fascinate me, but not in the way you did, it's morbid disgust on my part. It was never about sex with you, was it? You made me fall for you and then made me feel inadequate by putting off being with me. What was it all about? You didn't want me physically.'

'I wanted you more than you can ever know.'

'You messed me up and twirled me around, and then left me confused and dizzy. Grange isn't happening. I met a man I liked there once, but he was a made-up man, with a made-up name, and everything about him was fake. I don't even know your name. And I don't care anymore. We were built on a foundation of games, Dave, Mike, Flaskman, Dickhead, it doesn't matter to me now.'

'My name is Steve.'

'Is it? Why should I believe you?'

'Because I'll never lie to you again.'

'You came to see me in Dalton. Why? I was there for a long time after you left me.'

~~~

'Tell me about your boyfriend?'

'He's none of your business.'

I wasn't truthful to him earlier. I'm not seeing anybody, it's already over. I wrote to tell him after he let me down on Sunday. It wasn't worth a trip to Workington to tell him in person. I didn't sleep with him either, and only knew him for a few weeks—par for the course.

'I still remember the excuses you made to avoid sleeping with me. When I found out you were married, I figured you had the crazy idea that if you didn't have intercourse, you weren't being unfaithful to your wife. I get it now, and this dumb fool worked it out all by myself. I didn't know she existed. I wish I had because I'd never be with a married man.'

'I know. I tried so many times to tell you, but I knew I'd lose you and I couldn't.'

I never lied to you. Not once, and I'm not starting now. Nothing changes for that fact. I have no interest in meeting up, ringing, chatting, or having any contact with you.'

I can be your friend, pen-pal, whatever you want to call it, and I won't push for anything more.'

'How's Simon? And, here's a thing. Did you ever hear from Megan after we broke up?'

'Not a word. Why?'

'She left town. I haven't seen her for years. Not since you.'

'She was trouble, that one. She needed to leave you alone. I bet someone's taught her a lesson about the way she treats people. She wasn't kind to you, Clara. I'm glad she's gone.'

'Me too, as it happens. She came onto the pathetic excuse for a man that I called my boyfriend.'

'Ouch. Have you got nails in the bottom of those kinky boots of yours?'

'You have some audacity. I'll play for now, but if the game stops being fun, this time the tables turn, and you won't know who I am.'

'I just want to talk to you.'

'Anyway, I've got to go. Laters Flaskman. You've got my number. If you're man enough to ring me, which I think you will because it's all games to you. But there'll be no flirting.'

I took great satisfaction in hanging up before he could speak. But he had affected me. As much as I say I don't want to hear from him again, I can't wait. I don't want him back. I hate him, and that's the truth—but I do need to know why? I never deserved what he did to me.

~~~

Molly felt the overwhelming urge to speak to Phil. But like Clara, she had no way of contacting the man she was having an affair with when he was at home with his wife.

Chapter Eighteen

The difference between Clara and Molly was that Clara never knew what she was neck deep in. Molly was in a position to tear Renshaw's family of four people apart and knew exactly what she was doing. But she couldn't help herself. She was as weak and as pathetic as Clara. The diary was devastating. How could Clara be so stupid as to have anything to do with a married man who had already hurt her once—never mind Clara? How could she?

Her elbow clicked as she raised her arms over her head in a long stretch. She was stiff and realised she'd been sitting in the same position for over an hour. The diary had pulled her so far in that she didn't know she was thirsty until she took a break from reading. She went to the loo and made a coffee before getting back to it.

~~~

1 August 2019
He rang me again the next day. I wasn't going to answer, I'd slept on it, and the flutter of excitement after hearing his voice again passed as I remembered the horrible things, he did to me. He befriended my daughter, too, and promised her the earth. He hurt both of us. I needed an-

swers, and at that point, I was still playing him. I answered the phone and needled him for an explanation of why he treated us so badly.

'I've never understood why you came clean to me. Why, after you dropped off the planet for six weeks, did you ring and confess? You'd been gone for nearly two months. I was getting over you and piecing our lives back together without you. It would have been better—cleaner—if you'd stayed gone. It's crazy stuff from crazy times. You told me you'd leave your wife for me. The wife I knew nothing about. And here we are eight years later, and you're still with her. Unless the one you're divorcing now is a different wife. Did you expect to come and live with me that night? Was I supposed to melt into your arms after not hearing from you for six weeks? I've never taken another woman's man in my life, and I didn't want her cast off. Trust me, sweetie. You weren't all that.'

'And breathe. Wow. And hello to you, too. We have this custom in England when we answer the phone. We usually start with, hello.'

'You're a bastard.'

'And you're an angel. Black seal to Bishop 3. Your move.'

'Go to hell.'

'I'm sorry. I'm trying to tease you into being kind to me. You're right. I owe you a massive apology, but I wish I'd never let you go. I've thought about you every day since and will always love you.'

'What is your real name?'

'My name is Steve. I've got a lot of explaining to do. I did, and still do, love you. I conned a lot of women out of money—a lot. But, you're the one regret I have. I can't do this over the phone. Meet me please and let me explain.'

'Steve. I never knew you at all, and it's like stepping back into another lifetime. An unhappy one.'

'You're wrong. Remember back, Clara. We were so happy together.'

'No. You don't get to do that to me. I wasn't happy, I was bloody confused and miserable. I was happy for two hours every six weeks when you dropped back into my life out of nowhere. This time, you've picked an unfortunate time to appear. I've been treated badly by another man, so I'm not feeling it for mankind. And let's be honest. I hate you. I despise you. I want to hurt you the way you hurt me.'

'And the way he hurt you?'

'Yes. However, I want answers to my questions, so I'll be civil to you. Or I'll try. See? Honesty. I'm playing you to get the answers I need, nothing more. I think you're despicable. And being right up front about it. Last time we spoke, you told me that even your name was invented. So, how can I believe a word you say? I don't believe your name is Steve, but whoever you are, you make my skin crawl.'

~~~

The phone rang, and it was Nash checking that Brown was all right before her meeting the next day. She stretched and made another coffee as she nestled the phone between her chin and shoulder. She told Nash that she wanted to say up and finish the second diary before meeting the perp the next day.

'I'll stay up all night if I have to, boss.'

'Take it easy, and make sure you get some sleep, Brown. I'm not sure it's a good idea reading it when you're tired. What if you slip up tomorrow and let something out that you're not supposed to know?'

'Jesus, credit me with some professionalism, Nash. I have to read it. I need to know him before coming face to face.'

~~~

'You say you love me. You didn't even have sex with me. Was that so that you could tell your wife you weren't unfaithful? What you conned me into believing we had transcended the act of sex. It was built up of feelings, on my part at least, and from the second you contacted me, you fell slap-bang into the category of infidelity. So don't try to kid yourself that you weren't unfaithful.'

'I've always expected to see you, Clara. One day you'd walk into the same shop, or we'd pass in the street. It would be a chance meeting. And after all this time, here you are, my darling. And still so angry with me, but that will change. You'll see.'

'You're deluded. I don't bear grudges. There's no point. But you're only words down a phone. You changed the subject, and I want to hear the truth. I've got questions, and if there's any man left inside you, you'll do the decent thing by me. I've been reading my diary from when we were together. It wasn't all your fault because I allowed you to treat me that way. I was a gullible fool. I wanted to believe every word. And when the truth was obvious, and I doubted you, I didn't want to believe it.'

'You can still talk the legs off a donkey, I'll give you that. It's a long story. Meet me.'

'You could write everything in a letter. I'd appreciate that. I won't be meeting you in person. I've got nothing to gain by it.'

'You want the truth. I'll tell you everything. Please, let's go for a walk,' Steve said.

'You broke my heart.'

'There's a long answer to that. Too long for a phone call.'

'You tried to make me take out more debt. You tried to con me out of money. You asked me to marry you. You did that to me when you were already married. How could you be so cruel? Are you a sociopath? Have you been diagnosed? I need to understand why.'

'Okay, you win, but I didn't want to do it like this. I divorced in 2011, when we met, but was still tied up in property and living with my ex-wife. I messed up, and yes, you're right, this is a different wife. I married a second time after a case of entrapment while we were together. I was so messed up, and that's why I kept disappearing. She was pregnant by me, and I had to marry her. But I swear you're the only woman I have ever truly loved.'

Three of us. His wife, me, and a third woman that he went on to marry and have a child with. My God. My hand was shaking so hard that I couldn't hold the phone to my ear any longer. And I didn't want to. I hung up on him.

He rang back three times. I ignored him. And then he stopped.

Half an hour later my phone rang with an unknown number. I stared at it as though a name would appear on the screen. I wasn't expecting any calls, and every instinct told me it was him and not to answer it, but curiosity got the better of me. I answered, 'Hello.'

'Is that Clara?'

'Yes. Who is this?'

'This is Steve's son, Jay, I know all about you. My dad loves you, and I'd like to meet you with him to see if we can sort things out.'

'Hi. I think we may have spoken before, a long time ago. Or, maybe not. I don't know what's real, and what's a sick game anymore. There's some stuff that I'd like to ask him if he is your dad. I don't even know if his name is real this time. But nothing changes the fact that he's still a married man and has been since the day I first met him. I didn't know he had a wife and wouldn't have had anything to do with him if I did. I wasn't given that choice. I won't meet him. But I'd like to have my say. I want to know why he did what he did to me. However, I don't think you should be dragged into this.'

'Please. What harm can one meeting somewhere public do? You can both have your say and if there's nothing there, you go your separate ways knowing that at least he tried.'

'God no. I despise him.'

'Then you've got nothing to fear from meeting him and getting the answers you want. If nothing else it's closure for you,' the person calling himself Jay said.

'If you were there, it might be okay. I won't meet him alone. I don't mess with married men, but I suppose if you were with him, I could. I don't even know if you're real this time or just one of his friends in the pub pretending to be his son again. That's what he did last time. See how suspicious I am? He did this to me.'

While we were talking, I had a text from Steve. And still didn't know if that was his real name.

My son is speaking to you. Meet him. Grill him. Do whatever you like. It's all truth between us now. Nothing to hide. Steve x

I told Jay I needed time to think and would let Steve know. Later that night, Steve rang me again. It was late and I was in bed. It was an unusual time for him to be able to ring one of his bits on the side. I told him I was tired and confused and couldn't be bothered with him. But he said he wanted to tell me more. I let him speak.

'I have only been married twice, Clara. I loved my first wife in the beginning, but it was nothing like the love I have for you. We were too young and once the kids came, it turned bad, but we stayed married and were happy enough in a comfortable way for twenty years. My second marriage was a mistake. I had to marry her to see my son. I wish it was different, and I'd married you instead.'

'This is such a mess. I wish I hadn't bothered looking on that damned app.'

'And I'm so glad you did. Listen, I had a one-night stand not long before I met you.'

'So much for only having slept with your wife.'

'That was a lie, I had dozens of women, and conned most of them out of money. Ask yourself, why you were different. I didn't sleep with you because you weren't one of them — you were special. The other one came back telling me she was pregnant days after we met. It tore me apart. I was stupid and married her because my family told me it was the honest thing to do. You were never a dirty secret. You were the love of my life. I don't have a loving relationship with her and never did. It's only ever been you.'

'Your material hasn't altered much. You need a new script. What do you want from me, Steve, if that's your name? I want to talk about what happened. But what's in it for you? I don't have any love for you, and we aren't getting back together, ever. So what happens after we've met? What then?'

'You can walk away if that's what you want.'

'It will be. You fooled me once. You won't do it again.'

I'll meet up with him and his supposed son to find out what I need for closure, and then I'll drop out of his life again. I don't want anything to do with a married man. I have no feelings for this idiot. He played me for the fool I was. Fool me once, shame on you. Fool me twice, shame on me. I feel so sorry for the poor deluded cow he married.

He's just sent me a text saying he'll change everything for me. He'll leave his wife if we can be together. I thought he was leaving her anyway and waiting for a divorce to finalise. A real man would leave his wife first and put his house in order. And then come with a clean slate and a new start. He's a disgusting human being. I can't believe he's trying to pull me in again. He makes me sick.

I'll never believe a word that man says. He broke my heart once. He won't do it again.

Chapter Nineteen

3 August 2019

I was playing with Steve, and the lying fantasist deserved it. And, I was enjoying myself. It filled the breaks in my eleven-hour shift. He told me how much he loved me. I told him he was a wanker. I admit some things he said left an impression. He has clear memories of our time together. To me, it's just a haze, but for the most part, I'm ambivalent. I loved him once and lost him. He wasn't the man I'd loved. That one never existed, apart from in the mind of a stupid gullible woman. The sick bastard played me. I thought about him sometimes, but it wasn't with love. It was bitterness and anger. I was still in love with the man I thought he was, but that was only a fantasy created by him. He left me with a parting gift, though. He left me with a lot of curiosity. I had questions in the urgent folder, and more in the queries file. When he came back into my life a few days ago, all I wanted was answers. I'm being honest, and that's the truth.

I still hate him.

The other night, my friends, Jess, and Nigel, warned me to be careful. They know about him from the past and about how he almost destroyed me. I told them I'm playing games with him, and that I want to hurt him. They said I'm playing with fire, and I know that, but I can't stop. He destroyed my plans for the future and devastated me. I want revenge. I want to see hurt in his eyes when I tell him how despicable he is. I need him to feel some of the pain I did.

Yesterday, after one of his texts, I wanted him to say he loved me on the phone again, so I could tell him how little the statement meant. The thought had just formulated in my head when I got his next text. It said to phone him because he wanted to hear my voice. I refused. I won't be at his beck and call and said I had to pay for phone calls, whereas texts were free.

I said he could call me. And there he was, straight in with the excuses. Just like the old days. He had no credit. Wifey must have been around. It's a hard life when you don't get what you want.

I should never have given him my number. That was a mistake. Until the minute I texted, giving him access to my phone, he was just words on a screen. Anybody with a mind to, wouldn't find me difficult to track down, but to that point, the situation was similar to playing an RPG and, he should have been good at that since our relationship was a running role-playing game. He made his move. I combated it and upped the ante with a cleverer one. I got cocky and raised the stakes by taking it to a live phone call, and checkmate. He got inside my head and won. I gave in again. Control. Grooming. Again.

The first time I rang him this time around, his first words were, 'Hello, darling.' I didn't think it was him. He was different. The farmer-yokel accent was gone, and he sounded like a younger man. For all my big talk about not caring, my stomach left the top of the roller coaster and didn't stop flipping until it landed at the bottom of the track. The silly dialect was gone. He sounded like a regular man, but it was the person I'd known as Mike. I'd forgotten how sexy his voice was. I could have listened to him talk all day. I didn't want to end the call, and in that second of voice recognition, I knew that I'd made a huge mistake.

This wasn't my game anymore. It was his—as it had always been. He sounded more sincere. I didn't believe him, though. We've been here before. The words were irrelevant. He could have been reading the bible, but the sound of his voice had a huge impact. What he said, and the emotion in his voice didn't affect me. It was an act. But the resonance of his tone rang in my muscle memory like the tolling of a church bell.

I rang him again when he told me to, on command, because I couldn't do anything else. He hypnotised me. His voice was the hardest thing to come to terms with. I hated him but was enthralled by his voice. I had to put a stop to this before it got out of hand. I rang him on demand, and of course, there was no answer, he was playing with me, so I left a message for him to ring me.

When he did, I came clean and told him without dressing it up that I hadn't lied to him. Everything I'd said was true. I was careful about that. I wouldn't give him the chance to call me a liar. But I told him that I'd been playing games with him. I said I had no feelings for him, and that I'd been laughing at him. I even told him about my conversation with Jess and Nigel the night before, and other conversations I'd had with Baz about him. I said I'd mocked him.

He took it on the chin. 'No more than I deserve,' he said. 'However, I'm sensing a, but?'

'And now I've heard your voice, and it's taken me back to all those years ago. You've thrown me, and I'm confused.'

'We have to meet, Clara. I have to know if you have any feelings for me. I know how I feel, but I've got to see you and find out where you stand. My marriage is over. It never really began. With or without you in my life, I'm leaving her. It's you I want. I'm not losing you again. I need to know if this is real.'

He needs to know if it's real. That's rich coming from a man who built a separate existence for himself.

'If that's true. Sort your life out. Do what you have to do and meet me as a single man. Then we'll talk.'

'I'd lose you. There's a lot to sort out that you don't understand yet. I'll tell you everything, I promise. No lies. The honesty and truth laid bare. But if we wait until I'm single, you won't be. Somebody will have snapped you up, and you'll be gone again. More years will be wasted.'

He tried to push me for a meeting, but I stood firm. I told him I'd meet him when he was in a position to talk with a clean slate. But even then, there's too much past for there to ever be an us. He's still a liar and a cheat, and no amount of sorting out can put that right.

After speaking to him, Baz rang me for a catchup, and I blurted out that he was going to be annoyed. He dragged the story out of me and was disappointed in me, and worried for me. 'Clara, you've got to get out of this now before he hurts you again, love. He's a married man. This isn't funny. Delete all contact with him. Tell him not to contact you again. For God's sake, quit now while you can. Don't make me have to pick up the pieces and put you back together again when he hurts you. Been there. Done that. Got the snot and tear-stained T-shirt.'

Baz is important to me. His opinion is a good one, and I hate him thinking I've let myself down. I've always been a woman of principle, and I stick to my morals. I hated the disappointment in his voice.

Steve made me giddy, and Baz sobered me. He banished whatever madness had crawled inside my brain and eaten all logic and common sense. After talking to him, I was in control and strong. I didn't want anything to do with this useless, spineless, lying, no-good toad. He'd broken my heart once, and even speaking to him gave him the opportunity to do it again.

Coming back into my life, he's stealing what makes me a good person. Last time I didn't know he was married. This time, I know exactly what he is. Baz was right. I couldn't have any more to do with him. I told Baz I'd ring Steve back to tell him.

'Don't you dare. Honey, I'm scared for you. I don't know what hold this joker has over you, but I can see you talking hard talk, and it means nothing. You're fooling yourself because you're already halfway to getting drawn back into his sickness.'

'Okay, I'll text him.'

'No. Promise me that you'll cut him loose as of this second. You don't respond to his texts or calls or any other contact he tries to make. He'll soon get bored and move on to the next mug.'

I knew he was speaking the truth.

'Listen to yourself, Clara. You're telling me you know what you're doing, and you're playing with him to exact your pathetic revenge. It's bollocks. You're talking to him because you want to. The only revenge you need comes by getting on with your life. Stop and look at yourself, girl. You're walking headlong into a viper pit. That's what you're doing.'

'Okay. Get off my case. I won't contact him.'

My phone vibrated with texts from Steve, and I deleted them without reading them. I was strong.

It lasted for half an hour, and then I couldn't stand it. I answered him. I've let myself down again, and I've let Baz down. I know I'm stupid, but I've agreed to meet him and made a half-hearted joke about him coming through tonight. I didn't expect for one second, that he would. He was just playing games with me, for old times' sake. I got home, put him out of my mind and got ready to go out.

Chapter Twenty

10 August 2019.

I am madly and disgustingly in love.

I went to the pub a week last Friday. Steve and I had been texting all day, he said he was going to turn up, but I didn't believe him.

Jess had just got me up to sing on her karaoke when I got a text. I motioned for her to answer it. She looked shocked and held out my phone. 'It says he's on his way to Barrow, and where are you?' she told me.

I went to pieces, and Jess spent the next ten minutes giving him directions to The Pheasant, while I had a nervous breakdown. If I'd thought for one second, he was going to arrive at that pub, I'd have made more effort with my appearance. I was wearing a pair of cut-off jeans over black tights with purple Docs. I felt ridiculous, though several people said it looked okay. I wanted to go home and change, but I didn't have time. He'd thrown me a curveball, but then he always did.

My nerves got the better of me, and I felt sick. This man had broken me, and it took a long time to put me back together again. I'd been in love with him and remembering the electricity between us had me shaking and hyperventilating. I felt sick and scared and nervous about feeling like a fool either in front of him or in front of my friends, who knew what he did to me before and thought I was insane. I was a wreck.

He walked in, and I met him at the door and backed him out. I wanted to inspect my first reaction to him without the entire pub looking on. I took him outside, 'Are you going to give me a hug then?' I had to say something. But it was bravado. I felt ridiculous. I was dressed like an idiot. I felt a mess. But mostly, I thought I was going to pass out because the second I laid eyes on him, I fell in love all over again.

His face. His beautiful, old, craggy face was exactly the same. He was already old and didn't look any different. I broke at his smile, and it was love at second sight.

It was that powerful.

He hasn't aged in eight years. He always looked like an old bugger. He may have lost a bit of weight, and he looks slimmer than I remember. It was as though he'd walked out yesterday and come back today.

I've changed. I know I've aged. My skin isn't as good and looks older, but the biggest change is the weight gain. I read his eyes in that split second before I ushered him out of the door. I waited to see the shock or the disappointment. It wasn't there. He gazed at me with big, puppy dog eyes, and I was more in love than last time. My feelings for him had been given time to ferment.

He took me in his arms, and his body was shaking. 'I've missed you so much. I love you.' He crushed me to him and smelt into the side of my hair.

He held me and I would have been happy to die in that hug. It was all I ever wanted and more. I needed him like I needed air. And the past didn't matter. Nothing mattered but this. I moved away because I was embarrassed.

We went inside, and I introduced him to Jess and Nigel. And then we had time to take stock of each other. He sat next to me and spent the night staring at me. When he wasn't telling me with his mouth that he loves me, he was saying it with his eyes. He has lied to me so convincingly before, and I felt stupid under his gaze.

I put one hand on top of the other to stop them from shaking and then rolled them up in the bottom of my top to stop him from seeing.

'You still do that when you're nervous, then?' It was a reference to our past, and it was so bloody intimate. It was a tiny thing, me bunching my hands up inside my top, but it was too intense. There wasn't enough air in the pub.

'I wish I could hold your hand to stop us both shaking.' he said.

'You're a married man.'

I was so nervous. I told him it was twenty times more terrifying than the first time we'd met, and he agreed. He was visibly shaking, and it was endearing. With all the old feelings flooding back, just being near him, and not being able to touch him was torture. His hair had flopped onto his forehead just the way it used to. I wanted to touch it.

I remembered his first-ever touch when he'd tucked my hair behind my ear, and I wanted to recreate it.

He was a married man. I had no right to touch him. The people in the pub were staring at us. Jess was glaring at me. But I just wanted to touch his damned hair.

Three times his index finger came out of his bunched fist and stroked my thigh. We went outside for a smoke. He still smokes roll-ups, and it was so familiar, the way he held the pouch between his fingers to roll the cigarette on the top of his index finger.

'Can I have one, please?'

'You don't smoke.'

'No, but I need something.'

He finished rolling two cigarettes and held out a light for me. My hand touched his, and I left the contact too long. I took my hand away and stroked my finger along his thumb. He knew I was as in love with him as I'd ever been. I didn't need to say it. My actions, and my eyes which never left him, said it all. He had me again, and he knew it.

His expression told the same tale of love, but I didn't know if he was the same liar that I used to know. Standing a foot apart, we talked. We were unconsciously replaying our first date. He'd leant against the wall, and I stood in front of him. It didn't occur to me then, but our positioning was identical to the first intimate moment. He told me he loved me and that he'd never stopped loving me. I'm the only woman he has ever wanted, and it's only ever been me. He said his marriage was long-dead, and they only shared a house for financial reasons, and because she refused to leave his property.

I was hard. I told him I was affected by his presence, but there was no future for us. He hurt me too much last time to risk going through that again. I said that if he ever found himself single, he could look me up, and we'd see where we stood, but I had nothing to offer him while he shared a home with his wife.

While I was talking, I picked tiny hairs from the front of his shirt. I felt his heartbeat through his T-shirt. He shuddered under my touch. I kept picking when there was nothing left to pick, anything just to touch him.

He was coming home with me so we could talk, but the electricity between us was unbearable. It was too intense. If I'd taken him into my house, either the building would have blown up, or I'd have dragged him into my bed within seconds. I suggested going home to pick the dogs up and taking them for a run. We could talk on neutral ground.

He drove because I'd had a couple of vodkas. Away from the pub, I was calmer but no less excited by his presence. We took the dogs to The Bowl and let them off to run. I think they knew him. They seemed to, but that might have just been fancy. It was dark, and the ground was unlevel. I stumbled, and he called me a townie. He grabbed my hand, and I didn't pull away. We walked for a few minutes, deep in thought and getting over the awkwardness of first handholding.

Having his hand in mine was better than any sex I'd had for years. I couldn't get enough of his touch, even though it was only that small contact. My hand made love to his as we walked. At the same time, it was enough, and a million miles short of what I needed.

I was in love. Our second chance.

We talked, and he told me about his wife. Within six weeks of marriage, they couldn't stand each other. He said she was money orientated, and that's all that ever mattered to her. And he told me about his son, Matt, and how he was born a few months after our relationship eight years ago.

There wasn't a day in eight years that he didn't think of me. Even on family days out to theme parks, he wanted it to be me and Matt with him instead of Alice, his wife. Manipulative words, perhaps.

Ten minutes into the walk, he stopped me and turned me to face him. 'I love you, Clara.'

I knew he was going to kiss me. I went in for a cuddle and buried my face in his neck. He smelt good. He was called Steve, apparently, but smelt of my Mike. He put his fingers under my chin and forced my head up towards him, and he lowered to me. His mouth opened, and his face touched me. I moved my head to the side, and his lips grazed my mouth.

He literally growled at me, 'Kiss me,' he said.

'I can't. You're married.'

'In name only. We share the same house. That's all.'

'Come to me as a single man, and I'll never let you go, but I can't do this now.'

He let it go. We walked. He talked. I listened.

'She was a one-night stand a few months before we met. He couldn't even remember if he enjoyed their night of sex. He was so drunk he could barely get it up, but he managed to come inside her without protection. It didn't ring true. He wouldn't make love to me at all. He had an answer for that, too. He found out she was pregnant the day after we met, and being with me wasn't fair while he had all that going on in the background. He didn't know if he was the father, and he was torn.

We met. We fell in love, and two months later, she came back saying he was the daddy. He didn't want to know, and told her he'd met somebody else, that they'd get a DNA test when the baby was born and take it from there. She went to his father's offices. His father is a judge, a prominent person in the town. At least that story was consistent from last time, even though he told me it wasn't true in his confessions. He'd said I'd spoken to an old drunk in the pub, pretending to be his dad, and I didn't know what to believe.

Alice told Steve's father, 'Your son's got me pregnant. What are you going to do about it?' His dad called a family meeting, and Steve told him about me and how in love he was. But his dad was hard. 'You've pupped it. Now you've got to wed it.' He was told to dump me and marry Alice.

He did and lived to regret it.

It accounted for all those long torturous absences. It stung when he said it was no hardship at the time. We hardly knew each other, and he thought he could get over me to make a go of it with her. She's fourteen years younger than me, slim and prettier than me. He was flattered to have a pretty, younger woman on his arm. He put me behind him and tried to make his marriage work all those times he disappeared on me. She never loved him. He never loved her. It was a disaster. And I kept drawing him back to me.

His wife was a vicious, mercenary cow. I don't know if this is true, but he says he came to Dalton to find me, and somebody told him I was married and living in Ulverston. He let me go. But continued to search supermarkets and public places for me.

He tried to kiss me again.

I refused.

His words sounded sincere, but they always did. I didn't believe him and didn't trust him.

'I'm leaving her. I'm not letting you go again. I'll give up my house, my truck, everything if you'll give me a second chance.'

He tried to kiss me, and I stopped him with a question. 'If all this is true. What about in six months when you're bored of me, and another younger bit of stuff takes your eye?'

'It will never happen.'

I made a derisive noise somewhere in my throat.

'I'm going to marry you, Clara.'

'You are hell.'

'I'm not asking you. I'm telling you. We're getting married the day after my divorce comes through.'

I suppose if ever a sentence of over-the-top words was meant to get a woman to drop her knickers, that one wasn't so bad. I started to say, 'In your dreams,' but never finished the words because he was kissing me.

His mouth covered mine. It was amazing. He was kissing me with more passion than I'd ever been kissed. 'I love you, Clara. Tell me you love me, too.'

'I hate you.'

'No, please, say it.'

And like a demented fool, I did. 'I love you.'

It was done. I'm an adulteress for the first time in my life.

We went home. I was cold. We went to bed. We were fully clothed. He held me, and we kissed and touched each other — but not sexually. He stayed all night.

I am in love.

That was on Friday.

~~~

8 April 2020

I haven't written for months. I haven't been able to. The misery is endless, and the pain and loss are unbearable.

Steve and I are over. He dropped out of my life over a month ago. He disappeared, just like last time. No word. No explanation. I didn't know if he was alive or dead. He just dropped contact. The same as before.

After a fortnight, I had a text telling me that he had some domestic problems and that he loved me.

And then, two days ago, I received a voicemail.

'Clara, my darling. I hope you're missing me. We need to talk xxx'.

'No. We don't. Go to hell.'

Haven't heard from him since.

He broke my heart eight years ago, and I've let him do the same thing to me again. What kind of deluded fool am I? He said he loved me. You don't treat somebody you love like that. My life was okay until he forced himself back into it like a bloody hurricane and smashed it to smithereens. But it's my fault for pulling my door wide open. Now everything is colourless and pointless. I got over him before, I'll do it again, but how many times can you take a kick in the teeth and shake yourself off as though nothing has happened?

My life and everything in it seems worthless.

~~~

18 July 2020

I am angry and upset. I've lost about twenty thousand words of this book. I have no idea what those missing words are. I can't replace them. They have gone. I'm assuming it was the beginning of the end of Steve if that was even his name. What an utter fool I've been.

I'm still deeply in love with the fantasy man that never existed. He was a figment of my imagination the first time he came into my life as a pretend gamekeeper and conned me, and again this time when he came back full of lies and deceit. I hate, loath and despise the man behind the mask. He has broken my heart again. I've hit the point of acceptance. I realised last week when I sent him the final, spleen-venting email that I was only hurting and torturing myself. I've deleted every means of contact I have for the man. I thought about revenge. But there's no point.

In the end, all I did was cancelled the booking for our weekend away in Scotland this week. I found out he was taking his latest conquest to the hotel I'd booked and paid four hundred pounds for. I can't begin to explain how much that hurt. What would have happened on Friday when he was due to pick me up for our holiday? How did he expect that to go down? It was our weekend, but he was taking somebody else.

Now, instead of feeling jealous of that woman, I pity her. She's sleeping with a married man who has as little feeling for her as he does for his wife. I sent a barrage of texts to his mobile phone over two days. Sometimes as many as twenty or thirty a day at all times of the day and night. He'll have had his mobile number changed. A minor inconvenience to him, I suppose. But that's the sum total of my revenge.

I told him I was going to the police to present evidence proving him unstable to have his gun licence — if he even has one — I wanted it revoked. I was going to take him to the small claims court to get an order against him for the three hundred and fifty pounds I paid for the Harris hawk I bought him. And I was going to storm the Mason's lodge meeting — if he ever was a Mason — and expose him as a man of low moral fibre. I was going to turn up on his doorstep and confess everything to his wife. And I was going to make the whole world know what he was.

I did nothing.

I'm a better person than he is, and I don't need revenge. I just need to cut him out of my life like a cancer and move on. I have one last thing to do and then I can.

I was a fool and gave him money. It isn't hard to guess how much — he asked for the same amount last time. I handed over ten grand to start our business. I fell for it. Again. I could die of shame just for being such a fool.

Fool me twice, shame on me.

My texts worked. I'm sure they were sent to a second—safe—phone. When we got serious, he had to give me a number, but he'd never give me the number for his main mobile. He realised I won't just shut up and go away, and I will go to the police. I'm not daft enough to believe that I've pricked his conscience. Anyway, he's agreed to give my money back. I'm meeting somebody tomorrow night. I said I didn't want to see him and refused to meet him. So, he's sending a friend with the ten thousand pounds I gave him to start our pheasant-rearing business. If this person doesn't turn up, I've made it clear that I'll have no choice but to go to the police.

Today I have put the wedding dress I bought up for sale on eBay. We were due to marry in four weeks. I've cancelled the venue and the entertainment. He told me his divorce was almost complete, so I'd booked St Mary's Church. I kept asking him for his paperwork to complete the legalese, but there was always an excuse. Our banns were due to be read and had to be posted four weeks before the date—and well, I suppose it was all too much for him. The game was up that he wasn't divorcing, and he went down his rathole and disappeared underground again.

And that was it, no argument or big bust-up. No screaming or smashing of crockery—he just disappeared—again.

We planned our entire wedding, right down to the entertainment and flavour of the wedding cake. We had a venue booked for a hundred and fifty people.

My heart is broken, but at least I'm getting most of my money back tomorrow. The man will turn up with it. Steve knows I'll go to the police otherwise.

I haven't cut myself for eight years, until tonight. I'm bleeding inside and out. I probably need to go to the hospital, but I'm too ashamed. I'll patch myself up and finish the mess with Steve once and for all tomorrow.

And then there's nothing. My future is a black hole of nothing.

~~~

Molly closed the diary and wiped a tear from her cheek. It was the saddest thing she'd ever read. She was crying for Clara. And she was crying for herself. It was over with Phil. She owed it to Clara for her mess to be over, too. She was connected to the dead woman. And by God, was she going to rip the balls off the man who hurt her twice.

Chapter Twenty-One

Phil Renshaw knocked hard and stormed into Lewis's office while she was in a meeting with Nash about using a honeytrap.

'You bastard. What the hell are you doing, Nash? And frankly, I'm surprised at you for going along with this insanity, ma'am,' he said.

'Okay, Phil. Calm down. I know you're upset, but this is my decision. And, it may be our only shot at catching this man,' Lewis said.

'And you think using Molly as bait is, okay? If anything happens to her, I'll never forgive you for this.'

'We're taking every precaution, Phil,' Nash said. 'If there was any other way, we'd do it.'

'I want in.'

'Renshaw, control yourself. Know your place and apologise to DCS Lewis,' Nash said.

'I'll apologise when you stop trafficking your officers like pieces of meat.'

'Enough.'

'It's okay, inspector. Let him speak,' Lewis put a hand on Phil's arm and smiled at him.

'I'm going to be there when she meets him. I want to be one of the shadows.'

'I've already chosen the team, Renshaw. You'll serve the case better back at base.' Nash kept his voice even. Renshaw was a loose cannon and needed to be contained before he lost it.

'Put me in the field, or you'll have my resignation on your desk by Lunchtime.'

'I'll put you in a field, alright. I'll put you on a bloody stakeout in Macclesfield if you don't get a grip.' He put his hand on Renshaw's shoulder and squeezed it to deflate the tension in the room. 'You're too close, son. One angry twitch and you could blow the case wide open. I blame that red hair of yours for your fiery temper.'

Nash heard Lewis draw in her breath, and he knew he'd said something un-PC again. Phil laughed, and with the tension broken, they spoke calmly. 'I'll look after her, Renshaw. She's precious to all of us.'

'You can't guarantee her safety, though. I need to be there.'

'We'll have six officers in situ around the room. She'll be wired, and we have her safe word and gesture. There are another six guys in the truck, and we've got officers posing as a street cleaner, a pot-hole crew, and probably a bloody chimney sweep. Trust me. She'll have more people around her than the pope.'

'Excuse me, Brown, but try to grin and bear it. My OCD dictates that I have to supervise this myself for your safety. And it offends me a lot more than it does you, trust me on that.' Although a female officer should have tapped Molly, Nash asked Brown's permission and took personal responsibility for checking her wire. He ran his fingers over the microphone attached to the top of her bra cup. Satisfied that it was secure and the wire invisible under her clothing, he nodded.

'What if he tries to cop a feel?' Bowes asked.

'I'll break his sodding arm, and yours too, sir, if you ever go inside my clothing again.' She winked and Nash blushed. 'Showtime,' she said, and Nash knew she was putting on a brave face and trying to cover her fear with jokes.

They'd talked about the last diary, on the phone the night before, and he heard the emotion in her voice. He'd never known Brown to cry, but a couple of times he thought she might be. She told him this one was personal, and that she felt an enormous affinity with the dead woman. Nash wondered if she was too close and if he should pull her. He was torn between what was best for the case, and the knowledge that he was putting Molly in danger, and he'd jump at the slightest provocation to call the sting off.

An officer dressed as a telecom engineer jumped out of the van and checked the street. They'd watched on the monitors, and the perp had already gone in.

Another screen showed him sitting at a table with a pint in front of him and a glass of white wine for Brown. He was drumming his fingers on the table, either in annoyance or with nerves. He was ten minutes late, and Molly Turner hadn't arrived yet. Nash wanted to make him stew.

Brown brushed away Nash's apprehension like releasing a bird to flight. She jumped out of the van and walked around the corner for her first date with a killer.

She burst through the door of the Commodore Bar looking flustered—she was massively on edge, and that part required no acting skills. She stopped and looked around as though she didn't know where he was sitting. He waved, and as she went to him, he stood. He had manners. She liked that in other men.

'I'm so sorry. The taxi was a nightmare. Have you been waiting long?'

Wow, that smile, it hit her right in the loins. She hadn't expected that. Clara, you poor cow. I'm starting to get it. The beast had instant magnetism, and it knocked her for six. She didn't know what to do, or if she should offer her hand to shake. But he knew what he was doing. He'd done this before.

So had she, but never under these conditions. He pulled her into his arms and his hug was warm. Flipping heck he smelt good, too. She recognised the aftershave from a man in her past, but she couldn't remember which one. Brown usually had an excellent memory. It was one of the things that made her a good cop, but it took her a second to place the name. *Nautica Voyage*. Nice.

'Molly, my darling. Stop fretting, I'd have waited for you all night. You're going to give yourself ulcers if you don't calm down, sweetheart. Relax, and get a drink down you. You know what it is, don't you? You're short of a good man to sing you a lullaby at bedtime.' He laughed. 'Sit down, love.' He pulled her chair out for her.

Steve had released her from his hold, which was fortunate because he'd have felt her stiffen. Her blood ran cold. These were the exact word he'd used on Clara. The ulcers, the fretting, but particularly the lullaby line. It was the same old chat.

'White, okay?'

She was repulsed and couldn't speak, so she nodded and tried for a smile.

Steve sat right back in his chair. His fingers steepled under his chin and he gave her that killer smile.

'What?' she asked.

His finger raised to rest over his lips. 'Shush. Don't speak. Let me just look at you for a minute.'

Twat, Nash thought.

When the animal touched Brown, Nash slammed his fist on the desk in the van. That wasn't part of the deal, He shouldn't be laying his filthy hand on her. He felt Bowe's hand on his shoulder, the kid got it. Nash wanted to break the perp's neck for touching Molly. His fist was clenched so tight that his knuckles were white and the bones protruded from the thick coverage of flesh.

One of the lads put a coffee in front of him, but he was too engrossed in the screen to know who it was.

'Thanks.' It came out as a growl. Daddy Bear wasn't happy. 'Look at her smiling at him. Stop flirting, Brown. Dammit,'

'Isn't that what she's supposed to do? I thought that was the point.' Bowes asked.

'It is, but I don't have to like it.'

Brown must have brushed her hand over her chest because the mic crackled and they lost sound. Nash keyed his mic to speak into her earpiece.

'Keep your hands away from your neck. You're killing the sound,' He whispered.

Brown twirled her bracelet to show that she'd heard.

As he listened to the chat-up lines, the colour drained from Nash's face. He was taken back to a conversation he'd had with a stranger on a dating site. The man said he was a gamekeeper and wanted to date him. Nash made the mental adjustments to fit his own conversation. 'Silas, my darling, stop fretting. You're going to give yourself ulcers if you don't calm down. You're short of a good man to sing you a lullaby.'

'Are you all right, Boss?' Patel asked.

The man who contacted him on the dating app called himself Dave Thorn. And, he'd gone on to sing him a lullaby over the phone, '*Hush little baby, don't say a word. Daddy's gonna buy you a mockingbird.*'

'Nash?'

He didn't acknowledge Patel. The suspect preyed on men, too.

'Boss, what's wrong?'

'I want her out of there, pull it. Get her out. Now.'

Patel engaged Molly's mic. 'Abort. Repeat. Abort. Now.'

Nash stood up from his chair and banged his head in the cramped space of the van. He swore, and the guys knew better than to interrupt his thought process. His mind reeled with the horrific revelation. He'd fallen prey to the man they were trying to catch. The memory of their conversations played like cinefilm in his mind. The way Dave Thorn charmed him with sickly words made him feel ill. He heard the man singing to him on playback. At the time he'd thought it was goofy, a little bit nerdy and cringeworthy, but so damned sweet and appealing. Nash had been flattered, foolishly thinking that he'd found someone who understood him.

It was with regret that he'd broken contact with Thorn after the warning from Conrad Snow. Nash's world was the polar opposite of the man on the dating site. His career, home life and interests were miles away from the outdoorsy contact, but that was one of the ways Thorn trapped vulnerable people. He was the perfect chameleon. But he didn't try to fit in with his victims' lives, he was too arrogant for that. He set out to bend them to his life and insinuated his perfect, fake existence into their routines. His interests became their interests—it was genius.

Now he knew better. Dave Thorn was a monster, preying on vulnerable men and women, luring them with his charm, and then snuffing out their lives. Nash was repulsed and felt the familiar creeping burden of self-disgust for being taken in. He hadn't picked up a single thing that seemed off over hours of conversation with Thorn, both on screen and on the phone. His yearning to find love had blinded him to the truth.

However, it gave a new dimension to the case. He'd been an outsider examining the file in retrospect. Now he had a personal insight. Though his role was minor, and brief, he was inside the case looking out. He was impatient to get back to the office and pull his chat history with Thorn on the dating site and from his telephone records. He'd try and work on this angle himself and keep his private life out of it for as long as he could—but it was evidence.

Jesus Christ, he was another victim of this man. He was so grateful that they never got as far as meeting in person. Thank God for Conrad Snow and Maxwell Jones.

Nash couldn't shake the feeling of unease settling in his gut. His ability to read people had always stood him in good stead, but it was off-kilter in this case. He relied on intuition. It was what made him a good cop, but he'd missed the darkness in Dave Thorn. As he watched the monitor, he saw Molly give the signal for, No.

'What the hell is she doing?'

'Looks like she's refusing the abort, sir,' Patel said.

'Stupid damn woman. I'll have her balls over the table for this.'

Bowes laughed.

'Take that smirk off your face, Bowes. This isn't a laughing matter.'

'She's doing well, sir. I can get the guys in there to cause a diversion and have her pulled out kicking and screaming if you like, but it'll blow the cover. It seems to me, we have no choice but to trust her and let it play for a while,' Patel said.

'I'm going to bloody kill her.' Nash needed to get out of there. He had things to do that didn't involve sitting in a stuffy van watching Brown playing footsie with a murderer. He reached for a piece of gum from his pocket, offered it to the team and calmed himself. His personal involvement in the case and the startling new lead had waited this long, it could wait another hour. He was torn between trusting his men and leaving them to complete the stakeout, and not being able to leave Brown with the creep.

This was personal on so many levels—and the bastard was in the same room as Brown. She was like Nash's daughter. His thoughts were confused. The fact that Thorn was targeting men, as well as women, was vile. He couldn't have predicted that. Max had said through Snow that nothing, in this case, was as it seemed, and he was right.

But then there was Molly. His paternal relationship with her was teetering on the borderline of unprofessional and was at the point where it was interfering with his decisions. She wasn't his daughter. She was a competent cop on his team. He had to get a grip.

They huddled around the monitors, aware that Nash was fuming with Brown for directly disobeying an order. She was in no rush to leave and was dancing to her own drum. On the abort command, two of the undercover officers acting as a couple, moved from the bar to sit at the table next to the one Brown and Steve had. When the surveillance team in the van returned to the action, Molly had thrown her head back and was laughing at a joke. They watched for another hour and a half and Nash's temper didn't ease.

'I'm having a great time,' Molly said to her date.

'Me too, Molly. You know this means that there's no question about a second date. We're going to see each other again.'

She was coquettish. 'Really? You want to see me again?'

'Are you kidding me? Of course, I want to see you. Honey, you need to scrap those photos on your profile, they don't do you any justice at all. You're so much more beautiful. I'm going to take some photos of you. In fact, scrap your profile altogether. You're coming off the dating app. I could see myself marrying you.'

'Crickey, Steve. You don't mess about, do you?' Brown said.

'When you know. You know.'

He'd said the same thing to Clara, and it wasn't lost on any of the team. Profanities flew around the van, but Nash didn't say a word.

'So Steve, are you a V or a PH?'

'PH all the way. No white Englishman of a certain age would ever bastardise the name to the V level,' They laughed at his joke, and Nash knew it would be killing Molly, she'd ranted about his latent, and sometimes not so latent, racism and homophobia, as she'd read it in Clara's diaries.

'And what's your surname?'

She dropped the questions in casually and distracted him from the impact of her probing by rubbing her finger suggestively around the rim of her glass. Could she have been any more obvious? Nash was livid.

Steve didn't like her prying and registered it in the way his head turned sharply to study her face, but he didn't miss a beat. Not even half a beat. 'Thornley. Steve Thornley, at your service ma'am.' Nash would have bet his hat on it being another false name, but it was something to check out.

'Good girl, Brown,' he muttered.

The date lasted over two and a half excruciating hours, they had one alcoholic drink and switched to Coke because they were both driving. Three times, Nash had tried to call an abort, but Brown was having none of it. And, she seemed to be enjoying herself far too much for Nash's liking.

But she did her job and did it well. She fed him her cover story and stabbed him subtly with questions. She asked him about former girlfriends. Where he lived, worked and about his family. He trotted out the line about his father being a high court judge. This had already been checked and verified as a lie, but it was further confirmation that Brown was talking to the same person that Clara Watts dated.

Nash was relieved when Brown was wrapping the sting up. They did the in-person equivalent of You hang up. No, you hang up. No, you hang up. And stared into each other's eyes for far too long. Nash threatened to go in and drag her out by the hair, and the team kept their heads down and out of his firing line.

Molly stood up from the table, and Nash noticed that as she turned her back on Thornley, her expression altered, and he saw that her face was pale and drawn.

The toll of the job had got to her. She'd played a blinder, and even had Nash believing she was having a good time. He made a note to see that she had a counsellor available for her debrief the next day.

'What's happening?' Nash asked, his heart pounding.

The couple at the next table created a diversion so that Brown could get out without being followed. They had a vocal argument that involved Jackie Woods, lurching back from the table, and spilling a drink.

'Brown's leaving,' Patel said. 'We're getting her out of there.'

They watched as Molly hurried out of the restaurant, her steps quickening as she put distance between herself and the suspect. Before the brief in the van, she had stashed her car a couple of streets away, around a network of alleys she knew well, should she need a fast escape route. If a few more people were loitering around the alleys than usual that night, the civilians wouldn't notice. When she was safely in her car Nash keyed his mic. 'Are you okay?'

There was a pause before Molly replied. 'I'm fine. But I need a shower.'

Nash chuckled, grateful for the levity. 'You did well,' he said. 'We'll get him this time.'

'Thanks, Boss. Sorry for—you know.'

'And Brown?'

'Yeah?'

'See me in my office. Nine sharp.'

As the team packed up their equipment, Nash thought about the victims. He knew what it was like to feel trapped and alone and to struggle with a part of yourself that you couldn't control. In his case, it had been his loneliness, and social awkwardness around people outside of work—but that was before Kel. He had a job to do, and he couldn't let his personal life get in the way. If he had to bring his dirty laundry into the open, he would. He'd hidden his private life on a case before, to the detriment of the team. It was a lesson learnt. This time, if he had to divulge, he wouldn't hesitate.

He looked at Bowes, who was putting away the last of the gear. 'We'll catch him,' Nash said. 'We'll make sure he never hurts anybody again.'

Bowes was watching him. 'Are you okay, sir? You look as though you've seen a ghost.'

'Is there something we need to know?' Patel asked.

'I need to go, it's urgent,' Nash said, his voice just made it to a whisper. 'See that Brown gets home, and make sure she isn't followed.'

Bowes nodded, understanding the weight of the situation, but not having a clue what had changed. His boss was affected by something he'd seen or heard.

Nash checked the street on the monitors and slipped out of the van to disappear into the shadows. He couldn't shake the feeling of unease settling in his gut. He'd always prided himself on his ability to read people, but he'd missed the darkness in Dave Thorn.

While Patel watched the live feed, Bowes rewound the tape on a separate monitor three times and played the moment when Nash's attitude changed. He muttered to himself, 'What did Nash see?' The guy was flirty and a bit slimy, but nothing happened as far as he could tell to elicit the response it did from the boss.

'Man, keep your head down, and just do what Nash told you. If he needs to bring us in on a line of enquiry, he will. But let him go off shooting rabbits if he wants to. It's his way, and our job is to see Brown home safely, and without arousing suspicion.'

Chapter Twenty-Two

DCS Lewis's office was a pleasant contrast to the noise and bedlam of the station's backrooms—where the magic happened. It was a calm place in the busy station, with a relaxing plethora of indoor ferns and greenery to ease the mind.

The office reflected Bronwyn's personality, she presented a calm front, and while she could be as tough as she needed to be, mostly she was a calm and maternal influence in the station.

She'd called a meeting with Nash, and Brown. Lewis had never been onboard with the honeytrap mission and was dragged along on Nash's ideas with reluctance.

It strayed from formal procedural practice and skirted the line of what was considered ethical. But she'd been granted permission to go ahead, and despite her better judgement, she gave Nash her support. The honeytrap operation was for fact-finding purposes only, and to keep the suspect close. Every meeting between Thornley and Brown would be recorded, and documented in singular detail to bring forward should any litigation come from it. Anything they gained was useless as evidence and would be inadmissible in court, due to the way they obtained it, but the more information they had on him the better.

With this in mind, Lewis was ready to pull the operation at a moment's notice. She was as cool as her office. She wore a grey skirt suit and three-inch stiletto heels. Nash admired her style. He and Brown were like unruly children brought before the head, and Nash was damned if he was going to squirm under her direct main beam—but he did anyway. Only Bronwyn Lewis could have that effect on him, and only when she turned her grey glare on him. He focussed on the bookcase behind her which shone honey-gold. Hayley Mooney cleaned it every night, and it gave off the wonderful smell of Pledge polish, but it would be a very brave speck of dust that settled on DCS Lewis's furniture. She loved green and while her backdrop wall was painted white with green accents, she filled the rear corners with a gorgeous display of indoor plants.

Nash's office was spotless, but spartan. It was his workspace, but Lewis kept hers like an extension of her home, right down to a beautiful Persian rug on top of the emerald, green carpet.

Nash watched her manicured nails tapping as she read over the notes and gathered her thoughts. That day, the talons were polished in dark muted red—the colour of a pool of congealing blood. He gauged her mood by the speed of the drumming. She was calm, that was good. She'd reviewed what they had and agreed that it was useful in that it had confirmed Steve Thornley was the same person as the Steve Thornley and Mike Thornton who conned the victim. Nash had another name to throw into the mix, but battled with himself over how relevant it was to the case, and whether it should be brought into the open. He'd never actually met Dave Thorn.

'My concern is that we know this man is a consummate liar. Ergo, nothing that comes out of his mouth is the truth. We know from the Watts diaries that all we achieved last night was proving his words were lies. We never gained much in the way of hard evidence.'

Molly opened her mouth to speak, and Nash was still trying not to smirk over her use of the word ergo. Lewis could turn him into a juvenile thirteen-year-old. She raised her hand to stem Brown's outpouring.

'Not yet, Brown. You'll get your chance. What I have to balance, is the probability of evidence gained, over the danger we're subjecting a member of my staff to. And bearing in mind, we can never use any of it at trial.'

Molly sat to the side, with her phone resting in her lap as she listened to the conversation. Nash knew she was almost combusting from holding her tongue until Lewis let her speak.

He was on edge, and his voice was terse as he argued for Brown to be taken off the case despite it being his idea in the first place.

'I want her off. She's too close,' he said.

'Not true, sir. I am a professional doing a professional job.'

'She's reckless. She'll get herself killed.'

'I'm not a child. I'm a highly skilled officer, trained in hostage situations.

Brown's eyes smouldered and she glared at Nash as she leaned forward. Oh, Christ, he thought, two pissed-off women baying for my blood.

'I can handle myself. And I want to see him again. I know I can get him to talk, and not just crap. Clara was a doe-eyed fool who refused to see anything but good in him. I know the truth, and I can use my interrogation training and subtlety to draw it out of him, and cut through the BS.'

Nash snorted, and both women turned on him like a pair of hawks. 'What was that, sir?' Brown asked.

'You subtle?'

'Enough. Both of you. If you're going to squabble, I'm shutting the operation down right now.' Lewis's tone was measured. 'However, I agree with Brown. We need this opportunity to gather as much information as we can. We can't afford to let him slip the net.'

Nash scowled. 'Your call. But If I ask for resources, I want free rein on protection. I'm not taking any chances.'

Lewis waved her hand in consent.

Molly watched the exchange. Nash knew the potential danger to Brown, but the focus had to be on catching the killer.

Lewis told Molly to arrange another meeting with the suspect, and Brown turned her phone on to a barrage of Thornley's messages. She responded, keeping it light and flirtatious, and then asked when they could see each other again. He put her off with excuses, claiming that his job as a gamekeeper on a busy estate left him with limited free time.

'Here we go. He's on about a pheasant shoot for some rich people,' she said, as her thumbs flew over the screen. Nash marvelled at her speed. How was it possible to do that and not end up with a random jumble of characters?

'It's so identical to the diaries, that he might as well call me Clara. There were poachers on the property again, too. Just like he told her,' Brown said.

She tried to pin him down to a specific date and time, but he was evasive. Nash was incensed when she agreed to meet him in a layby half a mile up the road from the Gilpin Bridge Hotel.

Nash couldn't believe the plan. 'This is idiotic. You're walking into a trap. It's where he took his other victims. There's open land for miles, interspersed with swathes of forestry. We can't keep her safe out in the open.'

Lewis and Brown assured him that they'd have officers hiding all over the woods.

'He's playing the long game.' Lewis used common sense to calm Nash. 'He's not going to try and extort money from her yet, let alone kill her. We have plenty of time.'

'Yes, until he smells a rat and makes us. And then he'll strangle Brown in the middle of a bloody moor, while we're hidden, like children of the bloody corn, three fields away.'

'Chesterfield, Huddersfield and Macclesfield?' Bronwyn injected humour to lighten the mood, and Nash grinned at her.

'Something, like that.'

'Nash. Trust your team. Brown is only one rank below you. She's trained in armed combat and restraint. Have you seen her take the pissheads down on a Saturday night?'

Molly dropped her head, focusing on Thornley's messages as she read them out loud. He was gushing about how excited he was to see her again. He said he couldn't wait to show her his favourite place in the woods and knew where there was a badger set.

Nash felt a chill run down his spine as he realized how dangerous it was. But they had to go through with the plan, no matter the risk.

'Renshaw's going to kick up,' Nash said. And a look passed between him and Lewis.

'Put the hard word on him, Nash, I don't want him interfering,' Lewis said.

He'd been putting it off. He'd tried to justify not bringing his private life into the investigation. But, at this point, he was the only one who knew that Thornley targeted vulnerable men as well as women. He had no choice.'

'I have new evidence.'

Both women stared at him, and Brown's head shot up as if it was on a spring.

'And you're only telling us this now?' Lewis said.

'Yeah, it's personal. Not easy for me.'

'Go on.' Lewis took her reading glasses off to give Nash the full benefit of her open expression.

'He doesn't just target women?'

'What?' Brown said.

'He uses a gay dating app to pull men in, too.'

'How do you know this? I haven't seen any intel,' Lewis pulled a sheaf of papers to her as if the answer was in them.

'No. There isn't any. I haven't made it public.'

'Well?' Lewis said.

Nash saw the penny drop for Brown, and her hand went up to cover her face. 'Dave Thorn,' she said.

'Yes. You're not going to believe this Bronwyn, but I was nearly one of his victims. I'll give you everything I've got, but I'd be grateful if this can be kept out of the locker rooms.'

'Of course. Your intel will be used on a need-to-know basis. But you should have brought this to me from the beginning, Nash. You know I've got to write your delay up and express my concern about withholding information.'

'I understand. I just ask for as much discretion as you can give me.'

'I'm not happy about this Nash, and we'll discuss it further in a private meeting. Men, too? My God, his reach is wide.'

'Now we have to protect the whole country, not just the female half,' Brown said. 'It was really him? How do you know?'

Nash blushed, 'He sang the lullaby to me down the phone.'

Chapter Twenty-Three

The day of Brown's next meeting was overcast, and the sky was dull grey as they drove to the hotel they were using as a base. Brown was dressed in plain clothes. She wore strong walking boots, jeans, and a hoodie under a sensible coat. It was hardly second-date attire, but Thornley wasn't your average dater. If he wanted a country girl, that's what he was going to get.

Nash joked that she'd left her cowboy hat and spurs at home. Her hair was pulled back in a ponytail and they checked her wire again before she strode through the lobby ready for business.

Molly drove to the layby and her heart was in her throat when she saw Thornley. He was leaning against his 4x4 rolling a cigarette. He was a lot older than Brown, and what was once taut muscle was turning to flab, but not enough to detract from his manliness. That's how she saw him, and if she had to describe him in one word, it would be masculine. He was tall with tousled dark hair and bright blue eyes that twinkled even from a distance.

He finished rolling his cigarette before he bothered to acknowledge her. This man was in no hurry, and his method of capture was well-tried and perfected. Every nuance, foppery and foible was practised, he knew how to make people want him. Brown ignored her quickening heartbeat, and if her loins contracted again, she'd cut the flipping things out with a blunt hunting knife.

When he did look, he made a show of being blown away. His long wolf whistle made her blush and she almost laughed at herself. If one of the guys at the station whistled at her, she'd have flipped.

'Look at you. My God. If I don't make you my wife fast, somebody else will and I'll have to kill the bastard.'

The marriage line was old already, and she'd only heard it twice. He'd spoken it to her twice, but she'd read it plenty of times in the diaries. She understood the psychology and his gameplay. It was a gamble going in hard on marriage from the first meeting. But he was no fool. A strong woman would run a mile—but he wasn't interested in them and would cut them loose before meeting them. What he targeted was the lonely woman, with low self-esteem, who just wanted a man to sweep her off her feet and carry her away on his white horse.

He probably read Mills & Boon for research into his characters. Brown was no wilting flower, but she could play the part. She'd give him just enough attitude to keep him hanging in for a payout without dying of boredom first, but an abundance of loneliness and wanting. She didn't have to try acting the last part.

He kissed her on the cheek, and he smelt good the same cologne. She left her car and they took his. As they walked into the woods, Molly kept her eyes peeled for signs of danger in case he'd laid a trap. She remembered what he'd wanted to do to Clara with a tree and a shotgun. Everything was amplified as she tuned into her senses. She heard the sound of small animals crunching on the leaves, the rustle of the wind through the branches, and the whistles and melodic sounds of birdsong.

He slipped his hand in hers and it was dry, but not hard or leathery. He had soft hands for a man who worked the land. Thornley led them deep into the woods, pointing out species of trees and shrubs along the way. She knew they weren't alone and it made her feel safe. Being here with him on her own would be terrifying. She had a job to do and relaxed. Brown listened, picking up any points of relevance, and she asked questions as they walked.

For God's sake, the man was fascinating. He talked about nature with such love and knowledge that she hung on his every word. He knew everything there was to know about the forest. He pointed out flowers and toadstools and showed her hidden aspects of nature that she'd never have known to look for. Bending down, he showed her the tracks a hedgehog made as it snuffled for grubs the night before. When Brown knelt beside him and put her head close to his, he cheekily planted a kiss on her cheek. Jesus flipping Christ, she wanted to drag him into the long grass and inflict wild sex on him.

Clara girl, I get it. I understand, she thought.

He talked about them, and how he saw their relationship. Bang. She was floored when he went straight in for the kill.

'When I wed thee, we'll open our own business. We'll raise pheasants and have a smallholding. You can have that horse you told me you've always dreamed about. Imagine it, our lass. Chickens and goats, and a couple of pigs. I might even pop thee a baby or two in there.'

'A baby, wow.'

'You want kids, don't you?'

'Of course. I love babies.' In truth, she'd never been broody, and couldn't imagine anything worse. Her greatest horror was when smug friends pushed their ugly, puckered-up babies into her arms. 'Are we having a boy or a girl?'

'One of each flavour. A boy first to look after his sister. I've seen a piece of land that's perfect for us, and I've already been thinking about how I can raise the finance. I'm going to make you so happy, lass. You wait and see.'

She noticed that he always called her lass or girl to avoid using her name. Another trick he had, was giving his victims a nickname that was easier for him to remember than their real names. He'd called Clara The Black Seal.

She was comfortable knowing she was wired, in case she needed to call for backup, but worried about him touching her and finding it. They relied on his MO.

Going by Clara's diaries, he was a gentleman and never once pushed the physical boundaries—even when she'd wanted him to. At least the wire kept her chaste. Knowing the lads were listening in, the last thing Brown wanted was to have to fight him off if he turned into an octopus. A sense of unease settled in her stomach as they got to a stunning clearing. She recognised it. This was one of the places the killer brought his other victims. It was where he'd talked to Clara about his fantasies, and sitting on the fallen tree was where they'd often kissed.

Thornley gestured to the very same tree. 'Why don't we sit down for a bit?' he said, smiling at Brown.

She hesitated, told herself not to be a pussy, and settled on the log beside him. She didn't know what she was more scared of, the fact that this beast might kiss her—or her disappointment if he didn't.

His arm came around her and he pulled her into him to rest her back against his body. It was then that she heard it – the lullaby. It was soft and haunting, barely audible over the rustling leaves, and the distant chirping of birds. But he was singing it.

Hush, little baby, don't say a word. Papa's gonna buy you a mockingbird.

And if that mockingbird won't sing, Papa's gonna buy you a diamond ring.

And if that diamond ring turns brass, Papa's gonna buy you a looking glass.

And if that looking glass gets broke, Papa's gonna buy you a billy goat.

Molly panicked, and looked around frantically, trying to pinpoint help at hand should she need it. She could have given the game away and tried to get a grip by shutting out the haunting song. Its lilt was spooky and menacing in the stillness of the woods, like a discordant nursery rhyme used in a horror movie. And, it made her think about Clara's decomposed body. It was evil. She altered her position against his chest, pretending to snuggle into him, and forced herself to be calm.

Despite the evil connotations it aroused, his voice was beautiful. He stopped singing, thank God, it was unnerving, but it served a purpose, it kept her grounded and reminded her what he was.

A shaft of sunlight broke through the trees as the weather changed, and the sky lightened. He was stroking her hair, and he turned her to face him. He was going to kiss her and she had to respond without gagging.

When it happened, she needn't have worried. Not responding wasn't an issue. When his lips came down on hers, the kiss was hard, then soft, then hard again. He skilfully parted her mouth with his but didn't ram his tongue down her throat as Phil always did. For the first few seconds, she compared her married lover's kiss to the lips of a serial killer, but before she floundered in the absurdity of that, she lost herself in the best kiss of her life.

It took everything she had to pull away. And then only because they weren't alone, and her station mates watched from the cover of the trees. She forced herself to break the seal of his mouth, and her fluster was genuine. She had to get out of there, and fast.

Molly was relieved when they walked back to his car. They were arm in arm and it was like being held by a bear. It was ridiculous feeling so protected when the arm making her feel that way was a conman's—and a killer's.

She looked at the trees overhead, feeling a sense of awe at their size and majesty. She forgot about the darkness lurking in their shadows, and the danger surrounding her because every few minutes he stopped to kiss her.

But then she heard the sound of a prey bird on the wind—a mocking prey bird. It was a mournful lament bringing her into land. As long as there were monsters like him in the world, nobody was safe.

Back at the hotel, she was greeted by a round of applause and cheers from their colleagues. She'd got him talking, and he'd spouted a lot of information. They would investigate and try to separate facts from the bulk of the fairy tales he spun. It was a moment of triumph and a march towards victory against the elusive killer.

Nash had cut Renshaw out of the field team and made sure he was left at the station. He'd made his feelings clear and lay Brown's protection solely at his boss's feet. He was still disgruntled and raged at anybody that would listen to him.

Nash was whisked away for a debriefing with the higher ranks, and Molly slipped off to drive home, her mind was racing with thoughts and new emotions.

She sank onto the bed, her heart pounding and her emotions contorted with the memory of the lullaby—and the kiss. It was a haunting melody that she'd never forget, and it chilled her to the bone—and then, as she remembered his voice, it had the opposite effect. It heated the woman in her.

She lay in the silence and realised there was something else bothering her, but she couldn't put her finger on what.

She picked up her phone and scrolled through the messages. His story didn't add up, but they knew that. She read over his excuses—the pheasant shoots, the poachers, the busy estate. They sounded plausible, but there was a hint of something else in his tone. A sense of urgency and desperation. She felt him escalating, he was narrowing his timescale. Everything he'd said to Clara the first time around was condensed. Molly felt it—Thornley was ready to kill again. There was more to him than they knew yet, and she had to find out who he was.

The next morning, she felt a tap on her shoulder. Nash was standing beside her, with a concerned look on his face.

'You did great yesterday. We're going through the transcripts now. 'Did you sleep okay?'

'Yeah, fine,' she lied.

'What's up, Molly?'

She hesitated, then confided in him. 'There's more to this Thornley guy than we already know. I can feel it,' she said.

'What do you mean?'

Molly explained her suspicions, beginning with the sense of urgency she picked up in his messages. 'I think there are more bodies out there.'

'We think so, too. But at this point it's speculation. The good news is, we've traced his phone. It signals most to a mast in a village near Milnthorpe. And guess what?'

'What?'

'You aren't going to believe this. Snow gave us the letters MIL showing the town he lived in.'

She gasped. 'Oh, my God. Yes. And we've spent all this time looking around Millom.'

'And while we pissed about wasting time in Millom, he was having a culling spree in Milnthorpe. I don't get why Snow can get half a word but not the other half, it would have saved a lot of time. But that's not all. Remember his warning about owls? And we thought it was a reference to the suspect's birds of prey?'

'Yes, he has a six-bird mews, whatever one of those is, in his garden, or something.'

'We've proven once and for all, that it's all lies. We've traced this joker from the nearest phone tower. There is no fancy estate. Guess where he lives?'

'Where?'

'He lives on a new council estate out of town. Married, as we knew, with one kid living at home, and a couple of older ones. We've looked on Google Earth, and a six-bird mews, my arse. You couldn't swing a cat in that garden.'

'You've found his actual house?'

'Yes, grotty little hole, with an unkempt garden the size of a matchbox.'

'It makes you wonder what happened to the poor Harris hawk Clara bought him.'

'He'll have had a mark to pass that onto the day he took it home but let me get to the creepy bit. Have a guess what the name of his street's called.'

'Go on?'

'Owlwing Terrace. Snow does it again. The team are getting his phone records now. We'll take a look and see what secrets they can spill.'

Molly felt a surge of gratitude towards Nash. It was good to have someone who believed in her hunches. He never dismissed her and was always ready to listen to her views. They went to the conference room, where the team were working through the information they had.

Patel was excited and shouted to them as they went in. 'Thornley's been in contact with two men and a woman recently. We're not sure who they are, yet. We only have screen names, but he's been talking to them for several months.'

'That means he'll be due to make the drop on them if his previous MO is anything to go by,' Nash said. It tallied with what Molly had told him. He went to the long table where reams of printouts were spread out, and he peered at the sheets as Patel pointed to their relevance.

Molly was satisfied at the confirmation of her suspicion. But they had to move fast before Thornley could do any more damage. Those three people were living on borrowed time. And Brown had a target above her head, too.

They spent the rest of the morning combing through the evidence and piecing together a timeline of Thornley's communications. He'd been seeing all three of them—four with Brown and discussing their plans for the future.

'With four of them on the go, that's forty K, and a whole heap of pheasant chicks,' Nash said.

It was a chilling realisation, one that made Molly feel sick. And yet, she couldn't believe the stab of jealousy she felt at the thought of Steve kissing other people. She hated herself for the attraction she felt.

Despite everything they knew, he was pulling her strings. She'd seen first-hand the darkness inside the bastard.

Chapter Twenty-Four

DCI Nash's house was resplendent, a shimmering white landmark on the seafront, overlooking the lapping waters of the ocean. The building was grand, with large windows, French doors on the ground and third floors, and an imposing oak front door. It even had a wraparound balcony under the third-floor bedrooms well away from the street noise. The house had a rounded gable-end structure at both sides giving the impression of two circular towers, and every room on the sides of the house had a circular, near-panoramic view. The walls were whitewashed to reflect the sun, and the house had a dark, slate-grey roof fitted with a block of solar panels.

As the sun set that Friday night, the lights from the house shone like beacons to welcome his guests. It was the first proper dinner party Nash had thrown in years and he was nervous. He'd told his three guests that it was a casual dinner—but Nash didn't do casual and intended to make a splash and enjoy himself.

The dining room was spacious, with high ceilings and huge windows overlooking the ocean. The walls were painted a soft shade of blue, and there was a large oak dining table at the circular end of the room. They were in the tower, surrounded by glass.

Nash had bought a beautiful centrepiece of roses and other scented summer flowers, under strict instruction to the florist that there was no honeysuckle included in the vines and foliage.

DCI Nash sat on one side of the dining table, with his new partner, Kelvin Jones by his side. Kelvin was a solicitor, and it was the first time Nash had seen him dressed in a sharp suit and tie. He had trouble taking his eyes off Kel, and it didn't go unnoticed. Kelvin was polite and well-spoken, but he had a good sense of humour and Nash had a feeling all the guests would get along.

Across from them Conrad Snow hadn't relaxed yet and looked awkward, but he seemed to like Kelvin and smiled his approval at Nash. In relation to Kelvin being the boyfriend of a very conservative Silas Nash, if he was surprised that Kel was black, he covered it well. Snow was a psychic medium known for his accuracy, especially when it came to solving crimes—but Nash bet he didn't see that.

Nash always thought of him as a tamed surfer boy. Snow was thirty-three, and tall, with too-long hair and he wore sandals made from man-made material. His floppy fringe often covered half of his face, but that night, he had it slicked back and fastened in a man bun. Nash kept looking at it as though Snow had a small furry animal stuck to the back of his head. Nash saw that he'd settled by the time he was on his second glass of wine, and any worries Nash felt that he wouldn't enjoy himself were allayed. Conrad Snow had blue eyes and a calm, soothing presence that put everyone at ease, and when he laughed, it charmed everybody.

Molly was next to Conrad and smiled a lot. She was already two glasses in and her attention focused on the discussion at hand. DS Molly Brown was the last member of the dinner party to arrive, but she'd come in with a fanfare. Out of the formal skirt and trouser suits she wore for work, she was a flamboyant dresser. She wore a stunning knee-length dress in so many colours that it was blinding. Her chestnut hair was loose because she always wore it contained for work. Nash thought it shone like a horse's flank, and when he voiced his opinion, Molly said it was a good job he was old and gay. Because if he'd ever tried that chat up line on a woman, he'd have ended up wearing his drink.

It broke the ice and after that, everybody was laughing. Brown was a young, eager detective who'd risen in rank fast to become a highly respected officer, and she was keen to leave her mark on the force. She had a sharp mind, and a quick wit, and Nash knew she'd be a lively guest. There was no rule saying officers couldn't socialise outside work, only that inter-departmental relationships were heavily frowned upon. Bronwyn and her husband Grant would have been there, too, but for a prior engagement.

Nash was fond of Molly. It was a shame she couldn't disentangle herself from Renshaw and find a nice man to have fun with. Their on-off relationship worried him, and he was sad that it would've been inappropriate to invite Renshaw to the meal.

The food was delicious. The roast beef was a tender, melt-in-the-mouth, dream, and the vegetables and mashed potatoes were cooked to perfection. They enjoyed several bottles of red wine with their meal, and the conversation was lively with everybody contributing. Nash couldn't have asked for a better night.

Dessert was a huge chocolate gateaux and cream. They laughed when Nash told the table they had Conrad to thank for chocolate over strawberry cake after he'd warned Nash in a reading that Kelvin was allergic to strawberries.

'It's true. I couldn't believe it when Si told me.' Kelvin went on. 'I've never spoken to anybody with your gift, Conrad, and I find the subject fascinating.'

'You're open-minded about it?' Conrad said.

'I can neither prove nor disprove the possibility of other-worldly things, or extra sensory perception, so I'd be a fool not to be.'

'Going on that theory, Nash was a fool for ages,' Molly said. 'Talk about Doubting Thomas, it didn't take one miracle, it took a hundred before he started listening.'

'And I still don't understand how it works. I just know that somehow it does,' Nash said.

Molly had two pinpoints of colour in her cheeks, in part from the tinge of alcohol going straight to her blood vessels and making her glow. 'Kelvin's the only one who hasn't seen you in action. Can you give him something, now, Conrad?'

'Molly.' Nash feigned shock. 'Conrad must get sick of people asking him to perform on demand. He's here to relax remember?'

'It's okay. I don't mind, occasionally. What I don't do is give unsolicited information.'

'Huh, you did with me for long enough.' Nash laughed. 'I couldn't get rid of you. And, I'm surprised Max isn't here with us tonight. It's not like him to miss a knees up.'

'He has been. And he loves this.' Conrad spread his hand around the people.

'I'm curious. Did you get anything about me?' Kelvin asked. 'Nothing deeply personal mind. I'm an open book, but even so.'

Conrad laughed, 'Okay. You asked for it.' He sat back in his chair, closed his eyes and concentrated. 'I'm seeing a building. No. It's not a building, it's more of a structure. It looks to be made out of grey marble. It has some arches at the bottom, and a long staircase rising through the middle. There are ponds in front of it, and on the other side, there's a statue of a man that looks golden.'

Kelvin's face set and his body was stiff. 'I'm not sure how to phrase this so I'm just going to ask.' Sensing a change in his demeanour, Nash put his hand over Kelvin's as he continued. 'Did you research me and my background before you came? I don't mind a bit of fun, but I'd rather not be made a fool of.'

Conrad smiled and didn't seem bothered by the accusation at all. Nash assumed that in his profession he got it all the time. 'Of course, I didn't. All I knew was that Silas was inviting a work colleague and his new partner. I didn't even know your name until we were introduced. I've never seen that building before.'

'Forgive me. I'm sorry,' Kelvin turned to Nash. 'Silas, that was very rude of me. I'm sorry. Conrad, you're so accurate that it threw me. Please forgive my scepticism. I was born and raised in Ghana, and you described the mausoleum dedicated to the first president and his wife. It's a remembrance garden of international pride for the people living in the capital, Accra. You were spot on, so I hope you can understand my momentary doubt.'

'Hey. It's okay. Occupational hazard. Let's try something more personal. As a child, you visited a village built on a lake, you had family there. Ah, your grandparents. You have three children, all grown up. Sorry, I'm being taken into your house.

Above the fireplace, you have a painting of your homeland. It was painted by somebody close to you.' Conrad gasped, clammed up, and stopped talking abruptly. 'I think that's enough for now. I don't want to hog the party. And I'm needed for a proper reading later, so I should probably rest my mind beforehand.'

Kelvin smiled at him. 'The artist was my wife.'

Conrad nodded. 'I didn't want to say or upset you.'

'She died of cancer some years ago.'

'I saw that. I'm so sorry, I'd already opened my big mouth about the painting before that information came to me.'

Molly looked thunderstruck—at least enough to stop spooning chocolate cake into her mouth for a second. 'Wow. That's amazing. A fake medium would never take a chance on saying that a gay man had been married before. Sorry about your wife, by the way. I didn't know.'

'That's okay. Nash did, and that's the main thing. It was a long time ago, and I loved her very much. Now then, enough. Is there another glass of that excellent red going? Let's bring the mood back up.'

Nash and Kelvin talked about their backgrounds and experiences, while Conrad and Molly discussed their unique talents and abilities. Nash had invited Conrad to bring a plus one and was perplexed that he still didn't know anything about the psychic, he didn't give much away but he was charming company. There was a lightness to the meal and a feeling of camaraderie and friendship that Nash hadn't felt in a long time. He was delighted when Conrad was comfortable enough to let slip that his partner was Canadian and that he had a little boy called Aether. An arty-farty name if ever he'd heard one. Nash would have laid money on Conrad being a fellow friend of Dorothy.

The serial killer they were tracking had been giving them false names and making it difficult to piece together his identity. But with Conrad's help later, they were hoping to get closer to the truth, and an air of expectancy hung over the evening.

After dinner, they adjourned to the living room where Conrad settled in a comfortable chair and closed his eyes to meditate. Kelvin excused himself and went outside. He wasn't involved in the case and didn't want to interfere with the investigation. Nash appreciated his tact and promised they wouldn't be long. Kelvin said he'd be happy letting his meal go down in the garden and was such a perfect boyfriend that he said he'd make a start on the washing up until they were done.

'Where've you been all my life?' Nash joked and kissed him.

The reading was an intense experience. But, even amid the drama, there was warmth in the room. They were in it together, working towards a common goal.

And it set the stage for the horrific events as they pursued the killer.

As Conrad opened the reading, the room was quiet. It was a still night but the curtains in both sets of windows blew into the room, and the chandelier rocked. Molly jumped from her seat and Conrad put a hand on her arm. 'It's okay, it's just Max goofing about. He wanted to bring proof to you.' A presence filled the room. The air was heavier, and they all felt it. Maxwell Jones had passed away from a brain tumour, and Nash was always delighted when he came back with a message.

'Max, is that you?' Nash was stunned.

'Yes, it's me, old man.' Conrad relayed his messages. 'I couldn't miss the chance to help you catch this killer. I think I'm getting rather good at it, don't you? I've been following him around a bit, and the killer has a tattoo of a rose on his left bicep. And, he has a scar above his kneecap, that he got from a fight when he was younger. Don't ask me how I know that, Nash. I just do.'

Conrad leaned forward. 'What about the other clues, Maxwell?'

Max's voice was cryptic as it came through the medium. 'He hides his nature, like a chameleon blending in with his surroundings. He's a fan of motor racing, and he drives a blue saloon car. A Ford Focus, I think.'

The group exchanged glances, trying to piece together the clues. DCI Nash scribbled notes in his notebook.

'Anything else, Max?' Molly asked.

Conrad's voice was serious. 'He's getting closer to his next victim. He's killed many times and there are bodies all over those woods. You need to act fast because he won't stop until he's caught. He'll kill again before the new moon.'

'When the hell is that?' Nash asked.

'Do I look like Patrick Moore? I don't know, do I? You're the detective, work it out.'

They contemplated the information as Max's voice came through again, teasing as always. 'Nash, your tie is all crooked. You're drunk. I'm liking the new man, Si, he's a keeper. And you know what they say about solicitors? Once you've had one, you never go back.' Conrad blushed and apologised for the last remark. They all watched transfixed as Nash's tie rose into the air before settling.

'I felt that. I felt him lift my tie up. And, he's as PC as he never was,' Nash said. 'See you around, my friend.'

'He says, not if he sees you first,' Conrad said.

The group laughed, grateful for the moment of levity. They felt the atmosphere change, and none of them needed to be told that Max had left the party.

The psychic reading left them all feeling shattered. It was an intense experience, filled with cryptic clues and an eerie atmosphere, and it had added new layers of mystery to the case that left the team feeling excited and uneasy. As they said their goodbyes to Max, they hoped they'd been given valuable information that would help them catch the killer.

As Conrad and Molly said goodbye, Molly pulled Nash to one side. 'What did he mean by the chameleon comment?'

'I think he means the killer is good at blending in, like a chameleon changing its colours. And whatever we think he is, it's just the coat he's choosing to wear that day.'

'I asked Thornley about tattoos, and he said he hates them and would never have one. I believed him.'

'He also said he lives on a posh estate, and his dad's Cumbria's answer to Judge Judy.'

'Good point.'

Molly said she'd work on the new clues and would try to get confirmation on their next meeting. They needed hard evidence against Thornley, that wasn't obtained by entrapment, and they wouldn't stop until he was behind bars.

Chapter Twenty-Five

Over the next few days, the team had a lot on and was split into groups. As often happened when they were on surveillance, extra bodies were drafted in. A sub-team was put on trailing Thornley to monitor his movements and build a timeline. They scoured CCTV footage, interviewed witnesses, and pored over evidence. They began to piece together a picture of the killer.

New intel came in from the phone records. They discovered that the killer's real name was Robin Hill, and he had a history of violence and abuse. He'd been using different aliases to avoid detection, but they had finally uncovered his true identity. It was a huge landmark in the case.

'He thinks we'll never make anything stick. He reckons he's too smart to get caught,' Brown said.

Nash couldn't help but feel a sense of satisfaction that they were a step closer to nailing the killer, and in part, it was thanks to the clues they'd gathered from Conrad's psychic reading. He was confident that justice would be served.

The base office was a cramped room, with papers and books stacked high on every surface. The air was thick with the musty scent of tired bodies, and the sound of rustling paper and typing filled the room. The terrible two, Bowes and Lawson, stared at the transcripts of the killer's other dates and interspersed the write-ups with watching live footage of his whereabouts on their screens.

They were the youngest members of the team and Nash had hand-picked them from a squad of rookies fresh out of the academy when he set up the team two years earlier. Bowes was the joker, and Nash had to keep him on a tight rein.

Lawson was more down-to-earth and mature. He still had Aiden living with him, due to ongoing family problems. However, his sister was ready to leave the mental health facility in a couple of weeks, and he was dreading it because Aiden was doing so well living with Paul and he didn't want to go home. Nash felt a responsibility to the troubled family.

Both officers were shaping up to be excellent cops. Bowes had a keen eye and a sharp out-of-the-box way of thinking, and Lawson was methodical. He left no stone unturned. They complimented each other's strengths and cushioned their respective weaknesses.

'I can't make head nor tail of this,' Bowes said. His sandy blonde hair smelt of apples and when Lawson ribbed him on it, he said he had a date after work.

'Me neither. But there's got to be something concrete that we can lead on here. We have to keep looking.'

'I say we sack it off and sneak to the pub.' Bowes had a mischievous glint in his eye.

Lawson rubbed his tired face. 'Aye and let me see you talk us out of that one when Nasher finds out.' The team had adopted the nickname Max had given Nash when he was alive. But only the legend that was Max, had ever dared use it to his face.

As they combed through the transcripts, they exchanged theories and conjectures, but nothing fit. None of them could get used to calling the suspect Robin Hill, it felt strange after calling him Thornley for so long. And he wasn't giving anything away. What he did say that was useful enough to investigate, turned out to be lies. His empty waffle about guns and pheasants all held up to scrutiny, but couldn't be verified, other than the fact he'd never held an arms licence. His victims were from different walks of life, with no apparent connection to one another. The only thing gluing them together, was their need to be loved, a good credit rating, and vulnerability.

'Wait a minute,' Lawson said, pointing to a passage in one of the transcripts. 'Look at this. "Yeah, I had a right go at my son's teacher. Mrs Fart-on, I call her. He's only eight, and in RE she told him that it's all right for races to mix and marry. I tell you, if I saw a ghost and an oilcan together, I'd shoot the pair of them."'

'The blatant racism makes me want to shoot him,' Bowes said. 'But he makes loads of racist comments. What's your point? If we type known racist into the database, I think we'd be checking them until our great, great, great, granddaughter lives underwater.'

'The teacher, Fart-on. What's the betting her real name is Barton? Do you reckon it's worth five minutes to check teachers called Barton in the area?'

'I think you're clutching at straws, and your brains addled, mate. But it can't hurt to look.' Bowes leaned over to read the passage. 'But even if it's right, what does that prove? We know who he is now.'

'Yes, and he made threats against her. For all we know, Mrs Barton could be lying in an unmarked grave at Foulshaw Moss.'

'Let's do it.'

As they pulled up the CCTV footage of Brown's fourth date with Hill, they saw a shadowy figure darting in and out of the camera's view in the carpark before he was due to meet Brown. It was male, but too blurry to make out any features. Whoever it was, they were up to no good.

'It's probably nothing, some scally casing the joint,' Bowes said.

'I'm writing it up in the report anyway.'

'At least we've got something to put on the table at the team meeting. A shadow figure, Mrs Farty the teacher, who may or may not be dead, and some very passionate snogging between Brown and the suspect. She takes her work seriously. I'll give her that. But, let's not get ahead of ourselves. We've still got a lot of work to do.'

As they sifted through the footage, they noticed something else. The figure was wearing a long coat, similar to the one Hill wore when he was playing his countryman game, even though it was a warm night. He wasn't due to meet Brown for another half an hour, so what was he up to? As they watched, he seemed to be jotting down licence numbers of vehicles in the carpark, and on the street outside. Some of them belonged to members of the team.

'Has he made us?' Lawson asked.

'No, he can't have. Why would he suspect anything? It's suspicious though. We'll bring it up at the meeting.'

They jotted down a dozen other things to check out, but they never got much more. The investigation was testing their skills to the limit.

DI Brown was heading three sub-teams, working on the three marks that Hill was dating. The teams of two detectives were scattered across South Cumbria; one in Kendal, one in Ulverston and the third following the man who lived in Askam.

Each team was tasked with tailing one of the three potential victims of Robin Hill. He was known to them as Mike, or sometimes Steve, Thornley, Thorn or Thornton. The detectives had been given strict orders to remain inconspicuous, to blend in and not to approach any of the suspects until further notice. They were all on high alert, and their senses sharpened by the adrenaline pumping through their veins. Their prime focus was on Cheryl Rose a thirty-eight-year-old who had already made two suspicious withdrawals from her bank account, one for four, and one for six thousand pounds. Brown thought back to Clara's diaries, ten thousand was the amount he was extorting from her before he was found out.

Team One were made up of Brown and Detective Constable Alison Jones. They were following Cheryl Rose.

She walked down the street, with her high heels clicking on the pavement as she went out to a trendy bar. Her phone was tapped, and they knew she was meeting some girlfriends, not Robin Hill on this occasion. Brown and Jones stayed a few paces behind, watching her. 'She's a Thornley type, isn't she? Slightly overweight, looking unsure of herself, but all glammed up and hoping for the real deal,' Jones said.

Brown winced, apart from the comment about the lady's weight, she was as guilty of the above. What terrified, and thrilled her, was that she thought about Renshaw less often, and when she did, it was geared to how dissatisfied she was with their relationship, and how guilty she felt. But she was thinking more about her time undercover and being seduced by Hill. She knew who and what he was, but her thoughts still strayed to those kisses. She hated herself for it.

Jones chuckled. 'Let's hope we don't lose her in the crowd. I don't fancy getting lost in this sea of chancers.' They pushed through the people standing around in groups to get to the bar. Their mark was two customers down and was being served.

Team two, made up of Detective Constables Franklin and Kumar, were following a man named Peter. They'd trailed him to Grange where he had also gone into a bar. He was in his thirties, with short brown hair and a muscular build. He walked with purpose, his eyes scanning the surroundings as if he was looking for somebody.

The detectives followed him at a safe distance, keeping their eyes peeled for any suspicious behaviour. Franklin leaned over to Kumar and whispered, 'He looks on edge. Maybe he's onto us?'

Kumar shook his head. 'No, he's just jumpy. He lives in Askam, but he's out in Grange. He doesn't look as though he knows the area well. Maybe he's being a bit cautious.' They watched as Peter sprayed his mouth with a breath freshener, smoothed his hair, and walked around the corner and into The Commodore for his date with Hill.

The final team were made up of Detective Constables Greg Mason and John Miller. They were following two women called Rachel and Sarah. The females were in their late thirties, with dark hair and tanned skin, and they linked arms as they walked, giggling, and chatting as they went into a fancy restaurant. They'd been tailing them since they got out of their taxi and walked fifty yards to the cash machine. They'd heard Rachel mention Mike's name already. They were talking about the entertainment options for her wedding. Miller and Mason were tasked with flirting with them to see if they could get any information, after sitting close to listen in.

All three teams were out for the evening and continued their surveillance, building timelines and gathering information. They knew that Hill was a dangerous and elusive killer, and they couldn't afford to slip up. As they watched the suspects from the shadows, the stakes were high, and the outcome was uncertain. But they were determined to catch him and put an end to his reign of terror. Tailing his potential victims when they weren't with him, was as valuable as when they were for gathering information. Friends talk to each other.

It was weird having a real name for their guy, and the whole team struggled with it, especially Brown after reading the diaries, and knowing him as Steve for so long, admittedly with two different surnames.

While most of the detectives were on field surveillance, DC Mo Patel was grounded at the base, but only because he was the best person for the job. His brain worked like a computer, and his expertise was working on the analytics of a case. He loved gathering intel and didn't mind. He had a cheese and onion sandwich and a cup of coffee beside him, and what more could a man ask from life?

He was looking forward to going home at the end of his shift where his wife, Judy had special plans for their Friday date night. He was at his computer, running lists and scrolling through the endless run of Blue Ford Focus cars sold in Cumbria over the last five years. His eyes were blurring, and his back ached from sitting in the same position for hours, but he was like a dog with a bone and kept adding filters to narrow his field. He rubbed his eyes and leaned back in his chair, stretching his tired muscles.

As he scrolled through the lists, he wondered if he was looking for a pig in a poke. All they had to go on was a garbled message from a supposed psychic. Mo couldn't argue with the information that had come from Snow over several high-profile cases, but he didn't hold with messing around in the occult.

Over a thousand Blue Ford Focuses had been bought in Cumbria over the last twelve months, never mind five years. On a hunch, he added a new search filter.

How many of them had been bought on a Motability scheme? He looked under Robin Hill's name and came up with nothing.

The only vehicle registered to him was his black 4x4 that they already knew about, but it didn't hurt to grab as much information as he could about that one, too.

He knew they'd be impounding it at some point. Back on the Focus, he did a random search for a 40-50-year-old man with a bad back buying a blue Ford Focus on the Motability scheme.

As he was about to give up and call it a day, he saw something that caught his eye. A green Ford Focus was sold to A Mr Harold Hill aged 78, living in a retirement bungalow in Kendal. It was Robin Hill's father, and Mo checked the notes on the case file. Green not blue, but still a Focus in the family.

He did some digging on Hill's parents and found that his Dad was called Harold, they already knew that, and he'd never been a judge in high court or otherwise. Unlike his son, he'd spent his working life in honest employment and had worked at the K-Shoes factory in the position of supervisor. He was a strong union man.

His wife, Doris, was two years younger and had worked cleaning offices until genuine back problems laid her off. He wondered if that's where Robin Hill got the idea. A bad back is an invisible condition, and he knew which hoops to jump through to satisfy the benefits agency.

Mo forgot about his own aching back and enjoyed his morning's work. He jotted down the details and typed out an email to the rest of the team, bringing them up to date on Mr Hill Junior, and his connections. As he hit send, he chuckled to himself. He'd been looking for a needle in a haystack, and if he hadn't found it, he might at least have got the thimble.

A sense of satisfaction washed over him. This was what it was all about—the thrill of the chase, and the satisfaction of putting pieces together. He knew there was a long way to go before they could conclusively prove Hill's guilt, but for now, he allowed himself a celebration. It was a good day, and his beautiful Judy was waiting for him at home.

Phil knew what Nash was doing, and he was livid. Phil Renshaw stared at the screen in front of him and didn't give a damn about work that day. He was being sidelined, and they could all go screw themselves—especially Molly. She knew what this was doing to him. He couldn't stand the thought of her cosying up to the suspect, and Nash had no right to put her in that position.

Phil was put on cold case chasing and was told to look into Megan Hartley's disappearance to see what he could dig up. She was Clara's friend when she first met Robin Hill, and the mystery surrounding her disappearance without a trace had been tasked to him to solve. Well, they could go to hell. It was a thankless job.

He went for lunch and came back in a more positive mood. Putting his bad mood aside, Phil was determined to do well, he owed that much to Hill's victims. He might be a lousy husband, but he was a good cop.

He scrolled through old police reports, searching for any clues that might lead him to Megan. It was slow going, and he was getting nowhere fast. But he refused to give up.

After the last time she was seen, she'd gone on a mystery date with an unnamed man on the night of her disappearance. If he could link Hill to her leaving, they could have the bastard for two murders.

Phil made a note of the information he had and followed up on some old and very tired leads. He called a contact who lived around Princess Street in Dalton at the time. He had informants in all three towns in the area. Phil leaned hard on his narks. He asked around, trying to find anyone who might know something about Megan Hartley, or her mysterious date. It was a long shot because she'd already moved away from Dalton years before—but she might have returned to the long-term lover she'd been seeing while she dated Simon, anything was worth a try.

She'd worked in the solicitor's office. And most of his scally narcs knew of her from their many criminal activities. She was a stick-thin, poker-faced woman, known for being stern, and brutal with her tongue. Several of the guys around town had sampled her wares, and they called her Skeletor on account of her large forehead and gaunt appearance.

The general consensus around town was good riddance to her.

After hours of phone calls and dead ends, Phil was ready to give up. But just as he was putting away his things to go home to another argument with Sal, he received a call from an old friend.

'Hey, Phil. I might have something for you.'

Phil's heart jumped with excitement. 'What is it?'

'I heard from a friend of a friend that the woman you're asking about went out with a guy named Tom around that time. Apparently, he was a ladies' man and had a reputation for being dodgy.'

Phil scribbled the name down and thanked Gary before hanging up. This was something. Maybe he could shed some light on why Meg had left town so suddenly.

As he dug deeper into Tom's background, he found a trail of lies and deceit. It looked like he might have had something to do with Meg's disappearance, after all.

But he didn't want to believe that. If there was any way of pinning another murder on Robin Hill, he would.

Chapter Twenty-Six

The small council estate where Robin Hill lived with his wife, Trisha, and son, Matt, was quiet for a change.

Two plainclothes detectives watched from an unmarked car with their eyes fixed on the door of Hill's house. They'd been there for hours, looking for any sign of unusual activity, and building a gradual timeline of the family's activities.

'He told Clara Watts that his wife was called Alice,' Patel said.

'Could be a different wife, I suppose,' Jackie Woods had been based at Barrow station for years. She was a good-natured lady nearing her fifties who was happy with her lot. She'd never climbed the ranks or wanted a higher position. She loved her job but always said she worked to live not the other way around. She'd seen what the job had done to other marriages—and other cops.

'With this joker, anything's possible, but my gut tells me he's been with the same woman all along. Unless we can add bigamy to his crimes, there are no records of any other wives dead, alive or divorced coming out of the woodwork. I've scoured the database and he's only been married once,' Patel said.

'With his philandering, it seems unlikely that his home life would have just one woman. Could be he's lived with somebody since he started conning and killing people.'

'No. I don't think he has. That's something I'm pretty confident about. He's always been a marry-them kind of man. Something in his psyche is fixated on marriage. It probably harks back to his childhood. More than once in Watt's diaries, Hill said that living in sin was wrong. 'If you bed them, you have to wed them, that kind of thing.'

'But, with respect, Mo. If you don't mind me saying, we can't forget the golden rule from the team brief meeting.'

'Go on,' Patel said, grinning at his favourite DC lecturing him in such a sweet way. They were equal in rank and worked well together. Jackie had kindness stamped into her heart.

'Don't believe a thing that comes out of this man's mouth.'

'That's a good point, and very true. But concerning his philandering, you asked why he'd keep one woman at home all these years. Don't you think that fits his personality to a T? These victims aren't people. He sees it as his job. Being a con artist is the suit he wears to go to the office. And the more people he can get on his hook at once, the more money he gets in the pot. I can't even call his victims women anymore because it turns out that anybody's fair game.'

'That came as a shock. There's even a rumour in the canteen that Nash was almost one of his victims. Hayley was cleaning outside Lewis's office and heard her on the phone to the IPCC. Poor Inspector Nash, it's a terrible to-do,' Jackie said.

'I did hear something along those lines. But let's respect the boss and keep that to ourselves. Going back to the victims, you won't believe this, but over the last two weeks, I've traced sixty-three reported incidents to the police that fit Hill's MO. They were the lucky ones who only lost money—but walked away from it with their lives. And that's just in Cumbria, I haven't strayed into the cold waters of Lancashire yet. The terrifying thing is that thirty-four of those reports were made to our station in Barrow. Can you believe that?'

'Good God, all those people. Why weren't they followed up?'

'Well, it took me a while to uncover the magnitude of his reach, because until last week I was only looking at female victims. But the reports have been followed up. Every one of them. But, just taking Barrow as an example, do you know how many reports of fraud we get every week? Just the credit card fraud, theft, phone fraud, internet, and catalogues? The reports come in, and we don't even do the initial interviews ourselves very often. If it's over a hundred quid, we pass it straight over to local fraud. They do the interviews, fill in their paperwork, and if they don't have a perp and an arrest isn't made, it goes to the national fraud squad, where it gets lost to the annals of time forever.'

'Same old story. Lack of resources,' Jackie said.

'He got away with it because of the aliases he used. And the clever git had a different set of names for every town. He's shrewd and developed a near-foolproof strategy. In Barrow, he always used a derivative of Thorn. He mainly used Thorn, Thornley and Thornton. In Kendal, it was Black. He favoured Black, Blackwell and Blackley. In Ulverston, he used Green. Green, Greenacre, and Greenwood. I've run the algorithms, and the same first response officer never dealt with a complaint with his MO more than three times and he never used the same name. With the volume of cases coming in, they never twigged on the relevance. Hill just kept getting lost in the system.'

'It's crazy,' Jackie opened a two-pack of custard slices and passed one to Patel.

'Of all the cakes you could have chosen, you get the messiest one in the world. If this squidges out of the sides and onto my good jeans, you can explain it to Judy.'

'Huh, buy your own cake next time.'

'Love it really. My favourite, thank you.'

Jackie gave him a wink. 'Damn, thought I was going to get both of them. Do you know, I've dealt with so many cases of phone and catalogue fraud, where we've even had a suspect's name. I had one last week. A woman had given up her rental and left town. A local addict saw the removal van and knew the house was empty. He jumped over her wall, in through the dog flap, and took over the house to give him an address for committing catalogue and credit card fraud.'

'It's just crazy.'

'This guy even opened the door for deliveries, bold as brass until the house was sold. He made the first few low payments until the victim's credit was increased with the company. And because he only hit every umbrella company with half a dozen frauds to different cards and catalogues, it was cheaper for the company to write it off than see it through the courts. We got as far as arresting him and had him in the cells. But the catalogue companies wouldn't press charges, and we had to let the slimeball go.'

'This is confidential, so keep it to yourself because it hasn't been released yet, but there's evidence to suggest that Hill is running the whole racket.'

'What? I don't believe it. He can't be. Are you saying that the Stuart Dimmers I arrested was working for Robin Hill? No way.'

'Yes, one and the same. And Dimmers is one of his stooges. Too stupid to have a mind of his own, but he was on the road to a life of petty crime. He takes all the risk for ten per cent of anything he brings in. It's rich pickings for Hill. He uses young lads and recruits them from local pubs to break into empty houses. They order, then sell the gear, and play the credit cards. He's running a stable of young scallies throughout Cumbria.'

'Wow, that's incredible. And we get it in the neck from the people who think they're the victim. They've been robbed and lost their credit rating for as much as fifteen years. The fraud is committed in their name— and all the thieves have to do is collect personal mail as it comes in for the previous homeowner until they hit gold and get enough personal details to ring the homeowner with account and reference numbers. Hill has an accomplice who does the books and runs the scam with him. A woman rings the previous homeowner about a bill they've received, spouts all the correct reference numbers, and Bingo. The person who has moved house spills their guts and gives out their personal details. They think they're the victim, but guess what?' Jackie takes the last bite of her custard slice and wipes her mouth before bending down for the flask of coffee she'd brought for them to share.

'What?' Patel held the plastic lid-cup steady while she poured, and he took the first sip. 'Ugh, sugar. Too sweet.'

Jackie laughed at his face. 'The tragedy is, we can't do anything for that person.'

'No. Because, legally, they aren't the victim in this at all. They might feel as though they are, but it's the card and catalogue umbrella companies that are the legal victims, not the poor woman who's had her identity stolen,' Patel said.

'I've had decent people being refused mortgages and house rentals because they have fraud attached to their credit scores when they've done nothing wrong. Do you think his wife might be his accomplice? What a wicked woman.'

'So, here's the thing. He's a busy boy just keeping his numerous dating conquest plates in the air. That's full-time work in itself, hence the reason he's so unreliable and lets his victims down all the time.'

'What a creep.'

'Yeah. I know how hard it is keeping one woman happy, never mind ten.' Patel smiled at Woods' horrified face.

'Wicked,' she repeated. 'So he runs the dating con, and his accomplice takes the reins on the fraud side of the business?'

'Looks that way. We know he's got a woman on the inside. He recruits the kids, and after that, they deal with her. They never meet her, she's just a lady on the phone. I've got half a dozen kids talking, and more coming forward, and we're interviewing all the victims of the fraud scam. It's a clever game. And, she's playing a pyramid. When the kids have progressed, and can be put in a position of trust, they run the new guys coming up through the ranks. Sooner or later, the kids always get greedy. They order more goods and credit cards than they're declaring to the boss, and she sends one of the top tiers in to give them a kicking. It keeps the lower levels honest would you believe? We're checking bank accounts and phone records. Patricia Hill's the most likely bet, and we're closing in on what could be a cosy family empire. Their grown-up children might be involved, too.'

Sitting behind the wheel of the car, Woods' eyes fixed on the Hill's front door, while Patel, rechecked his notebook filled with almost illegible scribbles, and daubs of custard slice. 'Anything interesting?' Woods asks, breaking the silence. One thing Patel loved about Jackie was that she was never quiet for long.

Mo shook his head. 'Nothing yet. As we know, she took her son to school this morning, went to work at the local supermarket, and then came home this afternoon. All regular Mumsie stuff.'

'Any sign of Hill?'

'Not since first thing. But we know he's been active. We just need to figure out if Trisha is involved, or if it's somebody else at the helm.'

Woods asked what kind of woman Trisha was. Was she an innocent victim of her husband's crimes, or was she a willing participant? They knew Trisha enjoyed the fruits of Thornley's ill-gotten gains. She drove a nice car, wore designer clothing, and dripped so much gold that it was a wonder she wasn't too heavy to walk. Woods noticed she had her nails done regularly. It was a small village and if they were lucky, she bet there wasn't more than one nail bar in town. 'You know, Mo? I think I fancy getting my nails done.'

Jackie had been on the force for twenty years and had seen all kinds of things. But the Hill case had shaken her to the core. She couldn't imagine living with someone like him. They knew from the intel they'd gleaned that as well as being racist and a homophobe, he was controlling and misogynistic. And Trisha was raising her son in that environment.

The front door opened, and Hill's wife came out. She was a slim woman with long brown hair. And she was dressed in a blouse and jeans that looked simple but probably cost as much as Jackie's old Mini. Trisha looked around, then locked the door and got in her car. Patel and Woods watched as she drove away.

Jackie started her engine, and they followed her, keeping a safe distance. Trisha drove to the supermarket where she worked as a cashier. She parked her car and went inside, and Woods parked in a corner bay, watching the entrance.

Mo's head was drooping in the afternoon sun when Jackie pointed. 'Look.' A man had walked into the store. 'Isn't that Thornley?' The team still slipped up and struggled to accept that he was called Hill.

'What's he doing here?'

'Let's find out.'

Inside, they saw him approach Trisha, who was ringing up a customer's groceries. He whispered something in her ear, then walked away. Trisha seemed worried and looked around as if she suspected someone was watching her.

Patel said they should split up. He'd stay outside and keep an eye on Hill, while Woods followed Trisha inside the store. She saw Trisha standing at her checkout counter, her hands were shaking. Something had rattled her.

'Are you okay, dear?' Woods asked.

'Yes, I'm fine. I just got distracted for a moment. That's all.'

Jackie shrugged. 'I saw that man hassling you, and you're obviously upset. Should I call security? What was he doing here?'

'No. Thank you. It's okay. The security guy is a mate of his.'

Woods made a show of looking shocked.

Trisha laughed, but it held no mirth 'Don't worry. It's my husband. He was just asking for money. Again. I'm sorry, you're here to shop. I shouldn't be telling you, my troubles. I don't know what came over me.'

'Again?' Jackie didn't let it drop. She could tell Trisha wanted to unburden herself.

'He's always asking for money. He says he needs it for his back, but I know he's lying. He never works, never helps around the house. It's all on me. And now he's involved in something else.'

Woods leaned closer, keeping her voice low. 'What is it? What's going on, love?'

Trisha tried to shrug her off and go back to work, but a tear escaped the corner of her eye and rolled down her cheek. She wiped it away and looked around to see if other customers were waiting, but it was quiet and there was nobody in the queue behind Jackie. 'It's nothing. I'm sorry. I shouldn't have bothered you. Let's get your shopping through.'

'It's clearly not nothing. You're crying, you poor thing.'

Trisha hesitated, then looked around to make sure nobody was listening. 'I don't know much, but I think Robin is involved in something. He's been acting strange, getting phone calls at odd times, and disappearing for hours on end. But he's done that for the last fifteen years. There's nothing new there. As I said, I'm just being silly. Thank you for being kind.'

Jackie had one of those sympathetic faces that people opened up to. And she looked like a frumpy housewife. It made her a good cop. 'Don't worry, naughty husbands have a habit of getting caught out dear.'

'He's always been a liar. I don't believe anything he says anymore.'

'You need to keep an eye on him. Buy him a lead and have him microchipped.'

Trisha laughed at the joke.

Jackie smiled and then jotted down her personal phone number. 'Look, if you need anything, just let me know.'

Trisha smiled. 'Thank you. But why do you want to help me?'

'I was married to an abuser too, love,' she lied. 'Ring me. Anytime, day or night.'

Tricia left the store and met up with Patel in the car. 'What did you find out?' he asked.

'Not much. But if she's in on anything dodgy, she's a bloody good actress. Trisha's scared. She thinks Hill is involved in something bad.'

'That's interesting. Did she say anything else?'

'She said he's always after money. And she doesn't believe anything he says anymore.'

'Sounds like he's up to something. He's escalating. We need to keep an eye on him. Maybe we can catch him in the act. However, I don't think your busybody act worked as well as you think. It's a good job Hill didn't see you when you came out, he was still lurking around the carpark smoking a cigarette.'

Jackie looked around in a panic.

'Don't worry he's gone. He didn't see you. But two minutes before you came out, he took a phone call. And from the way he was gesticulating, I'm guessing that when we check his phone records tonight, it'll show it was from Tricia telling him some nosey woman was asking questions about him.'

'Maybe, I did go in a bit strong.'

'I could be wrong, of course.'

'You? Never.'

They laughed about Tricia panicking about speaking out of turn to a stranger. Jackie guessed Trisha wouldn't be ringing her as she'd hoped.

They continued their surveillance over the next week on unlimited overtime, and most of the team was taking advantage of it. They watched the Hill's every move, building a timeline of their activities. Over the next seven days, Hill was busy. He met at least one of his victims every day, and that Thursday, he had no less than four dates. One of them was with a new person that they had no intel on. He must have just sourced him from the dating app. Hill looked tired. And more than once they saw him rub his stomach as he walked up a victim's path. He deserved a belly full of ulcers. His phone was tapped, and they discovered from his conversations that he always tried to arrange for the dates to be at the victim's house. He'd only go to pubs and other venues if he had no option.

They were worried about Brown. She was taking a risk with her cover story and wouldn't get away with it for long. Hill targeted people with no close family. But Brown had told him that dating at her house was difficult because she lived with an elderly aunty with dementia. A strange man in the house would confuse the old woman. She dropped hints about her aunty being wealthy and said the lady had a big house with a payday coming Molly's way any time. 'Though of course,' she said, 'I'd rather have my old aunty that I love dearly.'

Patel and Woods laughed together on their way home and stopped off for fish and chips. But they knew trouble was brewing in the form of Phil Renshaw, who was simmering under a low light ready to blow.

Chapter Twenty-Seven

The canine team had found another body at Foulshaw Moss the day before, and while Nash waited for the autopsy, he took his mind away from it with his prior appointments. He pulled up outside the whitewashed cottage where psychic Conrad Snow lived in Bouth. It was a gorgeous day, with the sun shining and a gentle breeze blowing through the trees. The chirping of birds and rustling leaves created a soothing symphony that calmed his nerves in the beautiful fell village.

The hunt for Megan Hartley had been ongoing for months, and they were no closer to finding her than on day one. Nash knew she was dead, but to add it to Hill's rap sheet, they needed a body.

As he walked down the cobbled path to the front door, he marvelled at the picturesque beauty of the place. The cottage was surrounded by lush greenery, with brightly coloured flowers blooming in every direction. It was as if he had stepped into a fairy tale.

Nash knocked, and Snow yelled at him to come in. He pushed the door open to find Conrad Snow sitting at his farmhouse kitchen table, reading a book. The psychic looked up and grinned when he saw Nash. He jumped up to shake his hand.

'There he is. The man of the hour. Come to delve into my very soul, have you?' His eyes twinkled with amusement.

'Cut the crap, and get the kettle on, Snow. Do you have anything for me?'

'Bad news first. I'm afraid not, my friend. I've been trying to get a hit, but I can't get a reading on this Megan Hartley at all. She's vanished into the ether.'

Nash let out a frustrated groan. 'Tell me about it. We've searched all her old haunts and got nothing. It's as if she never existed.'

Conrad leaned back in his chair and steepled his fingers. 'You know, sometimes the answer is right in front of you, and you just can't see it. Maybe you're looking too hard.'

'What the hell does that mean?'

Conrad shrugged. 'I don't know. It's just a feeling. Maybe it's time to take a step back and look at the bigger picture.'

'Maybe you're right. I could use a break, anyway.'

Conrad grinned. 'And now we get to the good news. I can do better than a cup of tea, how about a pint?'

'I'm driving?'

'You can have one—a shandy if you want. There's a lovely pub just down the road, and the landlady's fit. We could have a drink, clear our heads.'

Nash hesitated before nodding, he was officially on duty, but one shandy on a hot day wouldn't hurt. 'Okay, let's do it.'

Conrad's phone rang on the way to the pub. He looked at the screen before answering.

'Hello? Oh, hi. Yeah, sure, I'll be right over. Thanks for letting me know.'

He hung up and turned to Nash. 'Change of plans. There's something I've got to do. You grab a table, and I'll be right back.'

Nash nodded and went into The White Hart Inn. It was a cosy place, with low ceilings and a welcoming atmosphere. The walls were lined with old photographs and memorabilia, giving it a vintage feel. He ordered a pint of bitter and settled down at a table near the window.

Conrad came in and went to the bar where he struck up a conversation with the bartender and Nash went to join him. Conrad was giving her a reading, something, he always claimed he never did. He moved to the side to give them space.

'I can see your old Aunt Mary.'

'I never had an aunt, Mary.'

Nash smirked. It wasn't often Snow got something wrong.

'Oh. Aunt Phillis, then?'

'No. You mean my aunty Morag, who had syphilis.'

'Oh aye, that'll be the one. She had a wooden leg.'

'No. She had a glass eye, but the kitchen table has a wonky leg, will that do?'

'Yes, that must be it. Your boyfriend's very handsome?'

'Oh, is he now? On who's say so?'

'Mine,' Conrad said.

They both fell about laughing. 'For goodness sake, Con put the poor man out of his misery.'

Conrad turned to Nash who was smelling an elephant-sized rat. 'Nash, this is my girlfriend, Natasha.'

'You sods. You got me, but only until Aunt Syphilis was mentioned. Hi Natasha. Lovely to meet you. Is that a Canadian accent I detect?'

'It is. At least you didn't say American, most people do. Hi Silas. I've heard a lot about you.'

Natasha's shift was finished, and she joined them for a drink. 'Are Aether and Jonny with Mom?' she asked.

'Yeah, she's keeping them for something to eat.'

'That'll be fun for her you know how fussy Jonny is.' They shared a secret joke, and Nash was struck by what a striking couple they made.

'Jonny?' he said. 'I thought you only had Aether.'

Conrad and Natasha looked at each other. 'Jonny is a recent adoptee. A passing phase, we think. It's Aether's friend—but he's the only one that can see him, If you get my drift,' Conrad said.

Nash knew it wasn't uncommon for children to have imaginary friends, but it still seemed weird. They moved on to other subjects, and Jonny was left at the bar with their empty glasses.

When they got back to Conrad's house, Aether ran out of the house to greet them, and in a scene of total domesticity Grandma stood on the doorstep, smiling, and drying her hands on a tea towel.

'Say hello to Inspector Nash, Aether.'

'Oh please. Si will do. Hi Aether.'

The kid was like a charging angel, and he flew around the front garden chasing his football. He had a mop of the whitest hair Nash had ever seen on a child and it fell in tight Cavatappi pasta-shaped curls around his head. He smiled at Nash with the bluest cornflower eyes.

'Hi, Si,' he shouted as he ran past. 'Straighten your tie.'

'What?' Silas laughed.

'Your mum says to straighten your tie. And she says to get a nice job, like your solicitor friend. She says it's unseemly at your age, chasing after criminals who aren't nice. And she says money belongs in the bank, not stuffed in her old teapot.' Aether giggled, 'She says you're a silly sausage.'

The eight-year-old child knew details about his mother that he couldn't know. It was unsettling. And he shouldn't know a word like unseemly. His mother was always disappointed about the career he'd chosen. And everything Aether said was spot on.

Conrad Snow watched Nash. His expression was sympathetic. 'I'm sorry, my friend,' he said quietly. 'He didn't mean to upset you.'

'He didn't. I'm just amazed, that's all. How could he know all that?'

Conrad shrugged. 'Perhaps it was a lucky guess. Children have active imaginations. It's possible that Aether's just playing make-believe.'

'You don't believe that any more than I do. Is this another joke?'

'No Si. Just a case of like father like son.' Natasha said. 'Jonny was a little boy who died from tuberculosis here in 1843. See what I have to put up with from the pair of them?' Natasha linked his arm and led him into the house, 'Don't forget to let me know if you and Kelvin are free for Saturday night, it's our turn—and, Molly of course. Con says she's a livewire and I can't wait to meet her.' She turned to smile at Conrad, and Nash had never seen a more enriched family unit.

Six months earlier, he would've been envious of their love, but now he had his own relationship and didn't need to wish he had what others took for granted. And he had friends. He was looking forward to Saturday night. He shuddered as he thought about what his future could have held if he'd continued his friendship with Robin Hill.

Before he got in the car, he straightened his tie.

The next morning Nash arrived early for the team meeting. He had paperwork to write up and wanted to get a head start. All too soon the meeting crept up on him, and he had to put his work to one side.

'Listen up team.'

They stopped their conversations and turned to the front of the room. 'Renshaw, Megan Hartley. Where are we?'

Nash had spent hours combing through evidence, interviewing witnesses, and following leads, but so far, they'd come up empty-handed. It was frustrating, but he wasn't giving up. He went through all the surveillance teams in turn to get their latest intel.

'Have we got DNA results from the body they found at Foulshaw Moss, yet boss,' Brown asked. 'Is it Megan?'

'No, it's another woman. Sandra Keane. She went missing four years ago.'

A gasp went around the room, and Brown frowned. They were sure it was going to be Megan Hartley. 'That's terrible. But at least her family will have some closure.'

'They extracted enough DNA from under her teeth for identification, but her remains were too decayed to get anything on the killer, so still nothing to link her to Robin Hill. The dog team are out again today, and we expect more bodies to turn up. It's a vast area and they're leaving no stone unturned. The family say that, as far as they know, there was no man on the scene when she went missing.'

Nash couldn't shake the feeling that he was missing something important, a clue or detail that would break the case. He looked around the room, taking in the faces of his team. 'Okay, let's start with what we know.' He wrote on the whiteboard as he spoke. 'We've found a skeleton, but it's not Megan. It's Sandra Keane. And, based on what we've learnt about her, it seems that her disappearance was voluntary. She had mental health issues and may have just walked away from her life. However, she sure as hell didn't put herself in a shallow grave at Foulshaw Moss. So we can deduce that it has to be Hill. Again no hard proof.'

'So, what do we do now?' Lawson asked.

'We keep looking for Megan Hartley,' Nash replied. 'We keep searching the area, and even though the case is as cold as week-old Semolina, we keep talking to people.'

There was a murmur of agreement. Nash felt the tension building as they realised this case was far from over. The bodies were mounting up, but they still didn't have a single shred of hard evidence to link Hill to the murders.

'What about you, Conrad? Anything to add?'

He nodded at Snow who'd been invited to attend the meetings as an official on-the-books member of the team. Snow was listening and holding a photo of Megan that her daughter had provided.

He took a sip of his water and leaned forward. 'I've had something given to me while you've been talking.'

Nash threw a warning look at Bowes and was grateful that he'd got over making spooky noises every time Snow spoke.

'The message I'm getting is strong. I'm having it shouted at me. And I think there's a connection to the mining operation on Black Combe.'

'Are you sure? We've never had any suggestion that it was one of Hill's haunts?'

He regretted his bad choice of words as they cued the spooky noises from Bowes.

'Cut it out, Bowes. It's like working in a kindergarten. I swear the next time you do that I'll put you on surveillance, alone, on a night shift in Oakwood Drive cemetery. That'll give you something to ooh about.'

He turned to Snow, 'That mine was shut down years ago.'

'That's the one. I did some research and found out there were some environmental concerns. There were reports of contaminated water and soil. And rumours that the company was dumping toxic waste in the area.'

Nash frowned. 'But what's that got to do with Megan?'

'I'm not sure,' Snow said. 'But she's shouting her head off that it's where you'll find her. Maybe someone who worked at the mine knows something about her disappearance. Or maybe Hill did take a trot up there with evil on his mind, one night.'

Nash nodded. 'Okay, let's add that to our list of things to investigate. And in the meantime, we keep searching. We keep talking to people. We keep following every lead until we find her remains. I'm no psychic, but every instinct in my body is telling me that we are looking for a corpse.'

'Right team, get out and do your stuff. Let's kick a killer in the coccyx.'

Chapter Twenty-Eight

Jay Bowes and Greg Mason leaned against the peeling paintwork of the walls in the station corridor. Their hushed conversation was punctuated by bursts of laughter, and the harsh fluorescent lights gave them nowhere to be inconspicuous in their delight at sharing salacious gossip. They kept forgetting to lower their voices.

'Did you hear about the other night on Brown's sting? She was on her fourth date with, Robin Hill,' Bowes said.

'No way. What were they discussing? The weather? If he likes a nice cup of tea before he bumps some poor saddo off? I don't see why it took four dates to get information out of him.'

'Nor me, but nah mate, it was more intense than that. Brown was supposed to be getting Hill to talk, but she seemed to enjoy it a bit too much if you get my drift. He pulled her into the alley at the back of Spoons, and guess what the van caught on camera?'

'What? She didn't shag him by the bottle skips, did she? The dirty DI.'

'Not quite, but the cameras caught the passionate end of the date. I'm telling you, mate, it was like something out of a bloody soap opera, tongues, and the lot.'

The corridor filled with the sound of pounding footsteps and a noise akin to a bull elephant in full charge hit them before Renshaw did. Jay and Greg turned as Phil stormed up to them and slammed Bowes against the wall.

'Shut your damned mouths. How dare you gossip about Molly. You jumped up pair of clowns. And what do you mean four dates, I thought we were done with all that nonsense?'

Jay and Greg had the good grace to look if not ashamed, then at least caught. Renshaw's on-again, off-again affair with DI Brown had been a source of tension in the station, and it affected everybody.

'Calm down, Renshaw,' Jay said, trying to defuse the situation. 'We were just saying, that's all. No harm done.'

Renshaw's jaw clenched. 'I heard what you were just saying. You're like a pair of old women, worse, bored housewives slobbering over a fence. You're a bloody embarrassment. Haven't you got any work to do?'

The door to her office swung open, and DCS Lewis looked ready to go to town on them. 'What's going on? I heard you yelling in my office. This is a police station, not a playground.'

Renshaw straightened his posture to appear more composed. 'Apologies, ma'am. It won't happen again.'

DCS Lewis nodded, her eyes lingering on Renshaw before addressing them all. 'Good. Now, back to work, all of you. We have cases to solve. Renshaw wind your neck in, and you two fools, get to your desks. Now.'

Phil was furious. Brown's rendezvous under the guise of work, and her meetings with a serial killer were making a fool of him. He was too close to it and understood that he had no rights over Molly's conduct. He was a married man playing away. He deserved to be eaten up with jealousy—but he wasn't going to put up with it. She was providing fodder for gossip and amusement around the station, and Renshaw was sick of it. He was going to confront her after he told Nash what he thought of him.

Chapter Twenty-Nine

Later that evening, under the cover of darkness, the rain-soaked streets of the town glistened like a diamond-studded tapestry, though dotted as it was with seagull shit. The sound of rain droplets tapping against the pavement created a rhythmic symphony that played through the air.

Molly was restless and paced around her house trying to find things to do. She repeated her domestic chores and cleaned the clean worktops and cooker tops. She couldn't get Robin Hill out of her head. The man was a magnet, drawing women to him with raw, arrogant sex appeal.

He was the most dangerous person she'd ever met, and this was personal. She aligned her emotions with Clara's and knew how the dead woman must have felt. She was a professional with a job to do and having romantic feelings for a known killer—well—she thought—that just takes you right over the brink of sanity and slap bang into LaLa land. They had as much as they were going to get out of him, and Nash was on the point of pulling time on the sting. It was the right thing to do before she sank any deeper.

The bloody awful weather was affecting her mood. She went to her bedroom window and looked onto dreary Queen Street, doing its thing, with its roaming cats and emotionally over-sensitive car alarms going off in the downpour. She wanted to go off like a screaming siren, too.

The feeling wasn't improved when she saw Detective Sergeant Phillip Renshaw, marching from his car with determination. The closest parking space was five houses down, and his temper showed in his walk. Her emotions were a rocketing tempest, and he was the last person she wanted to see.

Molly's house was number twenty-five, and it was nestled on the corner of the street. The streetlamp bathed the worn brick exterior, casting long shadows that whispered her secrets to the alley cats. Seeing Phil could lead to disaster in her current mood. However, she knew that any desire to be with him had left her.

Her heart pounded in her chest as he got to the front door, and the threat of confrontation swirled in her veins. This was a long-time coming, but it wasn't going to be good.

The door opened, and without speaking she stood aside to let him in. His tight lips and drawn face told her there was no kissy-kissy greeting—and the relief she felt was overwhelming. She knew in that second, that her two-year affair with Phil was over.

She'd been in love with him for so long and didn't understand how she could fall out of love with him in the time it took her heart to beat once. And then she realised that she did know. She knew exactly why her feelings had shifted. Robin Hill had blown into her personal space like a tornado with his eyes, and his smile, and his big chest. Bastard.

Her normally vibrant eyes were clouded with melancholy, and her expression was guarded and tinged with regret. She wore a metaphorical cloak of silence, with her lips pressed together to guard her precious secret. She'd fallen for the man she was supposed to be putting away and the shame of it engulfed her.

Renshaw's voice was heavy with emotion, and it broke on his second syllable. 'We need to talk, Molly.'

She felt the weight of their fractured relationship settle on her. The walls whispered to her, and the striped paper was a witness to their anguish.

She'd lit the wood burner in the living room. And it was as much for the comfort it gave her, as the heat. The flickering flames illuminated the armchairs and her scattered photographs that were on the mantelpiece—there were none of them together, that would have been too risky. But there was one of them in uniform, standing next to each other. They had their eyes forward in the photo, all bristling business.

Renshaw sat. His posture was rigid with tension.

And Molly stood. She didn't want to sit next to him. Her gaze fixed on the dancing flames. 'What do you want, Phillip?'

She never called him Phillip, and they were both aware of it. He steadied his voice. 'I want answers. I want to know why you're still meeting Robin Hill. I thought that part of the operation was finished.'

'You know why. We have to nail him. Nash wants you to be kept well away from it in case you blow it. You know all this.'

'Me? Excuse me. In case I blow it? It seems to me that you're doing a cracking job of that without my help. What the hell are you thinking, snogging a suspect in a dirty alley? Shame on you, Molly.' The remnants of their last bitter argument lingered in her mind, and the harsh words, exchanged like blades, sliced through their fragile relationship. But he confronted her, and she let it happen to get the truth out and come to a closure.

'Enlighten me, Molly.'

God, he was a pompous arse sometimes.

'Explain why I find out from the boys at the station that you're still on surveillance with him. They were talking about you in the corridor. You're a laughingstock. How could you do that to me? They were having a good laugh and going on about how they saw the footage of you and that psychopath all over each other.'

'I was doing my job.'

'Kissing another man is part of the job now? Wow, Molly what's the going rate for a working girl in uniform?'

Her fist clenched. 'How dare you. It wasn't about intimacy. It was gaining his trust, to delve into his twisted mind, and catch him out. I was risking everything to bring him to justice. And don't you dare go there and accuse me of being with somebody else. Don't you bloody dare. I was scared, Phillip. Involving you would put you in danger, and I never wanted to hurt you.'

'But you kissed him. Why didn't you trust me enough to let me in and tell me what was going on? I know Nash said not to, but we're supposed to be partners, Molly.'

'Partners, that's a laugh.' A tear escaped her eye and glistened against her cheek. 'And what about Sal? Does your wife know you've come here playing the hurt jealous guy? You've abused me for long enough, Phil.'

He looked as though she'd slapped him. 'Abused you?'

'Yes. You're no better than Hill, preying on women and hurting them. You're abusing me, your wife, and your kids. All of us.'

He didn't reply and silence enveloped the room, the weight of their words hung in a delicate balance, waiting to tip, and they knew the tip was coming.

Phil's gaze softened and his hand cupped Molly's cheek. 'I love you, Molly. But love can't exist in the shadows of half-truths and secrets. We can't keep hurting each other like this.'

'I loved you too, but you wouldn't leave her for me.' The past tense loved wasn't lost on him. He winced. And the needle returned to the start of the song and the same tired old words trundled out of them.

'I love my family.'

'She bores you.'

'She's the sweetest, kindest, most gentle person I know.'

'Thanks.'

'She's not you, Molly. She's home, and she's comfortable, and she's the mother of my kids. You know she needs me because of Dylan. It's hard looking after a disabled child. I couldn't abandon her.' A tear rolled down his cheek. 'And no, Mol-bol, you aren't sweet. You're as hard as nails and as sexy as hell, and you consume me.'

He went over to her and put his arm around her. 'It's over, isn't it?'

'Yes.'

Renshaw's grip tightened as he absorbed her words. The storm of emotions that had torn them apart settled, leaving the aftermath, and that was only as messy as they made it. She wanted him to go.

'Molly, we can't end it like this. We've been through too much. We need to rebuild the trust. We have to face this together, as partners, as lovers, and as fighters on the streets.'

'Who do you think you are, Batman?'

The air crackled with tension. The walls seemed to shrink, suffocating the space that once held words of love, and shared laughter. It was eaten by the bitter wake of their heated argument.

The firelight cast a haunting glow, accentuating their strained expressions, and highlighting the desperation in Phil's face.

Words, as sharp as daggers, had been used between them.

'Is it him?'

'No, of course not.'

'I don't believe you, Molly. Your involvement with Robin Hill—is sick.'

It was the most honest thing said between them, and he was right. Molly's eyes flashed with defiance. 'I knew you'd react this way. I want to be free to take risks and make my own decisions. And yes, to find somebody to love who is available to love me.'

'Hill? Jesus, tell me you haven't fallen for him.'

The accusation hung like a poisonous vapour. They'd danced around their issues for months, with the tension simmering beneath the surface until it reached a boiling point brought about by his jealousy. What about hers every single time he'd gone home to make love to his wife?

'It's not about control, Molly. It's about loyalty. I can't trust you when you've been playing a dangerous game with a killer.'

A silence hit the room like a wrecking ball, broken by the soft patter of rain against the windowpane. The storm inside the house, and out of it, had broken.

Their words hung in the air, and it was a verdict that had been a long time coming. He was disregarding the part where she'd said it was over, and he was trying to make out that he was the wronged lover. For the first time, she saw him as a pathetic married man.

'If that's how you feel, and you can't see my intentions were driven by love, we're better off apart.' Molly choked back a sob. Why was he dragging this out? Her heart shattered into a thousand fractured pieces. The realisation of what they were about to lose washed over her like a tidal wave—she was filled with a feeling of loss, but what they had was nothing. She'd provided the elements of what Phil needed that were lacking at home. He did love her, but only as an extension of Sal. She was the en-suite bathroom tagged onto their bedroom. Molly Brown, strong, gobby and temperamental, making up the missing elements of Sally Renshaw—mother earth.

'I never wanted it to come to this. But it's for the best,' she said.

'Molly, please. Don't give up on us. We've faced so much together. Can't we find a way to rebuild what's broken? I need you.'

And there it was again, his need. It always came down to his feelings, and what he needed. She felt sick with guilt and self-disgust.

'Go home, Phil.'

He nodded, accepting it. 'I understand. If this is what you want, I won't stand in your way.'

Thank God, but still he wasn't done. Tears streamed down Phillip's face. His voice was choked. 'I'll never stop loving you, Molly Brown. I hope you find the happiness you deserve.' He kissed her on the cheek.

As the front door closed behind him, she felt released.

She went upstairs and splashed her face, washing Phillip Renshaw off her skin and out of her life. Then she went back to the window, making a neat bracket of before the end and after. Same window, same curtains, same man.

She thought she'd be in time to watch him drive away, but he'd already gone. She felt a fleeting moment of loss. But she was used to that. He'd driven away a hundred times before.

She traced her fingers along the glass, following the raindrops and she turned away before the man in the ankle-length deer hunter coat turned the corner. She never saw him, but he'd been watching the house in the rain for the last hour.

Outside, raindrops danced on the windowpane, mirroring the tears that welled in her eyes. She forced them down—enough crying. But she still replayed their last moments together. The scent of Phil's cologne lingered on one of his jackets hanging over the back of her chair. The ache intensified, reminding her that some loves were destined to leave an indelible mark. The void he left would make working together difficult, and she considered asking for a transfer but berated herself for being a drama queen. It would be business as usual the next day.

Even in the depths of her determination, memories of Phillip lingered like whispers in the wind. She'd miss his steady presence and the way his touch erased the world's troubles. The thought of him stirred her emotions, reminding her of the love that she'd felt—but it was gone, and the overriding feeling it left behind was relief.

She'd find solace in her journal. The ink would be a conduit for her emotions. She'd started writing it after reading the Clara Watts diaries. It was another way she had of linking to Clara. It kept the other woman current, and Molly was determined to jail her killer—if she could keep from bedding him.

The breakup was sudden and it hit hard, tearing her apart and leaving her wounded, but not by much. After two years of continual heartache, the residual hurt was minimal—that was sad. It had given her a chance to search for her own truths.

She sighed when she heard the knock at the door. Why couldn't he leave her alone?

Chapter Thirty

Molly Brown's cosy home stood in the middle of Dalton-in-Furness, surrounded by a picturesque landscape of rolling green hills. The scent of Phil's ghost mingled with the smell of brewed coffee and filled the room. When the knock came, she expected him to be on the other side of the door.

The man on the doorstep took her by surprise and rooted her to the spot. She reached for her mobile to call for help when she saw Robin Hill, holding a vibrant bouquet, and a bottle of wine.

'Hello, my little liar,' he said, but he was smiling. He didn't look angry—and that made it all the more sinister. Molly thought he looked psychotic.

Panic rushed through her, and she was terrified. How the hell did he know where she lived? She'd told him she lived in Barrow with an elderly aunt.

'What are you doing here?'

'Surprise. Yes, I'm guilty of stalking you, and I'm a very bad boy. I followed you home after our last date, but it wasn't really a date, was it, DI Brown? Well, aren't you going to invite me in?'

Before she could speak, Hill pushed her into the living room, but it wasn't aggressive—just commanding. 'Nice place.'

His gaze locked with hers. Those sodding eyes. He put the flowers and wine down on the nearest armchair, kicked the front door shut, and pushed her against the wall.

DI Brown. Oh, God. He knew who she was, where she worked and that she didn't look after her senile old aunt for a living. Perhaps he knew everything. She had a panic button direct to the station in the kitchen. All the officers had them, due to the nature of their homicide department. Molly needed to get to it.

But their lips met in a passionate kiss. The electricity of their connection pulsed through their bodies. It was a moment of undeniable chemistry and a dangerous dance between desire and suspicion. For the first three seconds, Molly's mind was focused on getting to the button, or her phone—but then her body responded to his kiss. She'd never known anybody with the power to do what he did to her—and to a lot of other people, too.

In that moment of intimacy, Molly's heart raced from the intensity of their kiss, and with the realization of her precarious position. She'd lied about everything, he had to be pissed about it. She had no idea what he'd do to her.

'It's okay, my darling. We'll talk everything through. It's all right. Just kiss me.'

She couldn't help it.

They were neck-deep in the investigation with Hill the only suspect. And here she was with him in her home, his hand exploring her breast and his lips seducing her neck and sending electric shocks through her body. She'd be struck off. They'd take her badge—and Nash would be so disappointed in her. God help her. Her fingers were inside his coat, under his shirt and raking his back. The forensic element of her brain wondered if his skin would be found under her fingernails after he'd murdered her.

This was insane. Even with that horrific thought in her head, she was excited. Her hands moved to his backside and she pulled his hips against hers –and moved. Her brain was screaming at her to stop, but her body was going all out.

'I'm sorry I lied to you.'

With her back against the wall, she leaked snippets of the truth to him, desperate to be absolved of her deception.

And, between breathless moans, she confessed her identity as a police officer investigating him. 'I've been assigned to extract information from you,' she whispered, her voice laced with elements of fear.

He laughed. He actually laughed at her. 'And how's that going for you? Getting much?'

He pulled his face away and looked at her in amusement. There was no anger in his expression. She was turned on to hell, and on the point of ripping his clothes off, and he was as cool as a salad box in the chiller.

'I've compromised everything. My career's on the line, but I have to be honest. I've developed feelings for you.'

A flicker of surprise danced in his eyes, and that bloody amusement. Damn, he looked pleased with himself. He released her from the wall, and the room was charged with tension for the second time that night. Crickey fellas, form an orderly queue and I'll get to you all eventually.

'You've caught me off guard, Molly. I'm glad that's your real name.' Rich, coming from a man of a thousand names. His voice was husky with emotion. 'I'll never hurt you. I'm innocent of the crimes you're investigating. Yes, I've had my share of dating site encounters in the past, I'm not denying that. But I've left that life behind. I want this chance at something real. And I want it to be with you, my darling.'

He'd said as much to Clara, to many others—even to Nash. Her boss, for Christ's sake, but she believed him. She believed him with her whole heart. He could tell her that Mickey Mouse was really a cat, that Madonna was a virgin, and that King Charles III was Prince Harry's dad, and she'd still have believed him. She'd believe anything he told her. At that moment, the career that was her life meant nothing. When she looked to her future, she saw her and Robin Hill—she still called him Steve—raising pheasants on a smallholding in Ulverston. They'd have a couple of pigs and some of those cute goats that leap around being adorable. And they'd live happily ever after.

His words swirled, mixing with the aroma of the bouquet he'd brought. It had some white lilies, the flowers of death, the smell was overpowering in her small living room with the fire stealing the oxygen. She was captivated by his earnestness, even as her mind warred with her, and tried to talk common sense. She couldn't trust the web he was spinning around her—but she did.

'You're asking me to believe in you, despite everything I know. I can't take that leap and trust you,' she said.

'Why not? I am after you lied to me.' Robin's gaze never wavered, his expression was open and sincere. 'I'll do anything to convince you that I'm innocent, Molly. Name it, and I'll do anything in my power to make it right. I want to be with you.'

'Promise me that you can prove your innocence, and together we'll find evidence to show them the truth.'

'I promise. I'll do whatever it takes to clear my name and show you I'm not the man they think I am. You have my word.'

She was torn between the duty of her investigation and the undeniable pull taking her to Robin. He'd lied to her about something as fundamental as his name.

Her desire for him was stronger than anything she'd ever felt. She had a panic button in the next room, it would have the police at her door in minutes, but she had no desire to press it. The thoughts running through her head were already drafting her letter of resignation. She'd have it on Nash's desk first thing. She craved this adventure and her taste of forbidden romance. Her career was over. Nash would probably accept her resignation, he was that kind of guy—but he had plenty of grounds to dismiss her on the spot for gross misconduct.

Lewis might well go over his head and fire her by eight thirty in the morning. She imagined the walk of shame with her box of belongings. The fern Nash bought her for Christmas sitting precariously on top of the box, with the photograph of her dad looking so proud. He was proud of her, and she was going to destroy him. She didn't care about any of it.

As the tension between them dropped to a manageable level, she arranged the flowers he'd bought her and got them some glasses. She could have hit that button a dozen times, but she didn't. She told Hill about it, and he smiled that same smug grin. He had her right where he wanted her and she felt his magnetism. They settled on the settee in Molly's living room. His arm was around her, and she smelled the manliness of him.

He was all man.

The bouquet was in a crystal vase, adding a burst of vibrant colours to the room, and Robin uncorked the bottle of wine, pouring two glasses as they sat on the couch, the atmosphere shifting from uncertainty to a fragile sense of connection, and of being right.

They talked, and she told him almost everything. The only thing she left out was that she knew about his involvement with Nash. She told him private details about the investigation, and that he was being investigated for the murder of Megan Hartley as well as Clara Watts. It made her an accessory after the fact and she could be arrested for leaking information. She could go to prison.

'What? I barely knew that Megan woman and I've never been near the quarry.' He said he was shaken by the news and told her he thought he was only being investigated for conning people, which he freely admitted. Until that night, he had no idea he was suspected of being a serial killer. At first, he was shocked and then he roared with laughter. 'Do I look like a serial killer?'

'As much as Connie Cross did.'

'Who?'

'Never mind.'

Humour danced around them like mischievous spirits, lightening the weight of their problems. They laughed at the irony of their situation, acknowledging the absurdity of falling for each other inside a web of lies and suspicion. The moment of laughter brought them closer. Life was playing unpredictable tricks on them, but they were going to overcome it together.

'I won't rest until I've proven my innocence. And when that day comes, I'm going to marry you. I want to show you, and the world beyond the confines of this investigation, that I love you.'

'You're still married.'

'Only on paper and the divorce is already in progress. My father's pulling strings among his judge friends to make it happen.'

'Stop it. You're lying to me. We know your father isn't a high court judge.'

The lingering doubts reminded her that there was still a lot of stuff to unravel. He had the good grace to look embarrassed in being caught out in one of his old lies.

'I want to believe you. But you have to stop lying to me. Go to the station and hand yourself in before they come for you. Cooperate with the investigation. I'll stand beside you all the way.'

'I will. I swear, I've got nothing to hide.'

'You'll do it?'

'I'll do anything for you.'

He was lying. Telling her what she wanted to hear. He had no intention of going to the station. She knew that as sure as she knew the sun would rise in the morning, but she had to give him the chance to do the right thing.

'All right. Let's face this together. We'll find out the truth and see where it leads us.'

Robin's thumb traced circles on the back of her hand which made her shiver. He pulled her into him. There was solace in his touch and a reminder that there was still a possibility for love and redemption. Until he hummed that bloody lullaby and it was like a spell being broken. She sat up and pulled away from him.

'Stop humming that.'

'What? I wasn't humming anything.'

'Jesus, you've used it on so many victims, that you don't even know when you're doing it.'

He moved and she flinched, frightened that he might hit her. But his face had the same infuriating expression of amusement.

'My darling. You have no idea, just how appealing you are, have you?'

Her blood ran cold. It was more of the stuff he'd spouted to Clara.

'You said that to Clara Watts. I've read her journals.'

'Who? Oh her. Darling, she was a long time ago. You're going to have to get over this jealous streak, you know. I'm sure you've said things to your exes that you'll say again. There are a lot of words in the English language. But I'm telling you now, in three words, I love you.'

He was so arrogant and condescending. She knew he was playing her. She'd seen the hard evidence in Clara's words, but it was as though he could hypnotise people. He spoke with such sincerity that everything he said was believable. She wanted to trust him, and her rational mind was losing. It was as though he was a mentalist who could control her thoughts.

When she handed her letter to Nash the next day, she was going to ask him to look into Hill's background and see if he'd ever taken any courses in mentalism or hypnotism. The feeling that she was being controlled was that strong. And then as fast as the thought came to her, it left. She wouldn't say a word about it to Nash or anybody else—because she believed him. He said he loved her. Just like that. After seeing her four times, her new man was in love with her, and nothing had ever felt so right.

'I love you too, Steve?'

'My name's Rob, love. It's a relief to have you use my real name when you tell me you love me.'

'I like it. And, I love you, Robin.'

The lines between right and wrong had blurred, leaving her questioning her judgment and grappling with the consequences of her choices. In her pursuit of justice, she'd unearthed truths about Robin and opened wounds in herself.

She was more of a gullible fool than Clara Watts had been. Clara knew nothing about Robin Hill—whereas Molly knew it all but couldn't stop herself. That night, she was still a police officer and was torn between her duty and her feelings for Robin. She had to remind herself of the brutal crimes he was suspected of, and the victims he'd left in his wake. When she looked into his eyes, sometimes—after the arrogance—there was a vulnerability that echoed through her. The case demanded her commitment to justice and uncovering the truth without bias or compromise. And she'd blown it.

She knew her colleagues had seen her professional carapace cracking. She was the subject of gossip at the station, and, when they weren't laughing about it, they were all concerned about her entanglement with Hill.

Nash never wanted her involved in the honeytrap—but they couldn't have predicted this. He'd warned her about the dangers of getting emotionally invested. From day one, he'd feared it would cloud her judgment, and compromise the integrity of the investigation. But Molly was stubborn and had begged him to trust her. Well, that was buggered now, too. She was throwing her life down the field and expecting Hill to be good at catching. Was he a good catch?

She didn't tell him this was her last night as a police officer. That was her business. The decision would decimate her, but she'd do it – for him.

His words resonated with a sincerity she couldn't ignore. 'I know it's hard for you. You're torn between your duty and what you feel for me. But I'll never put you in harm's way. My intentions are true, and together, we can sort this out, I promise.'

'I need you to understand the gravity of the investigation. They suspect you of the murder of at least two women. We only have circumstantial evidence so far, but they're building a strong case, and if the evidence points to your guilt, I'll do what's necessary to see you behind bars.'

'I understand that. I don't expect you to compromise your principles for me. All I ask is that you're open to the belief that I'm innocent.'

The police had uncovered connections that spanned years, revealing a complex tapestry of deceit, manipulation, and hidden agendas. There was no doubt that Robin had conned a lot of people. He lessened it and said that some gifts were given, but that he'd never illegally extorted money. Any money was given willingly.

Amid the chaos, Molly's feelings for him had deepened. She saw his vulnerability, his remorse, and his genuine desire for a fresh start. It tore her, knowing the lines he'd crossed. She was losing herself in the labyrinth they were exploring. And the reality was slipping through her fingers. Until that night, it was work, another investigation. Now getting to the truth meant as much to her as breathing.

The emotions weighed on their shoulders as they sat in the dimly lit living room watching the fire dying down. Molly stared into it, lost in her thoughts.

'I know this isn't what you imagined. You never thought you'd fall for a suspect, but it's because, deep in your subconscious, there is no doubt. You know I'm innocent. But fate was always going to bring us together, even in these circumstances. We're soulmates.'

'From anybody else that would sound like so much horseshit, but from you it sounds right. I never wanted this. I'm torn between my job and the pull I feel to you.'

'Love will creep into unexpected corners of our lives, Molly. It's a force that defies logic. And it's a choice we make. If you choose to believe in me, our love is the strongest power on earth. It can conquer the darkest shadows, and we're going to navigate the truth together.'

She was falling for his bullshit, just like Clara did—and the others. 'I want to believe you. And I know people can change. But we can't let our guard down. They're out to get you.'

'To frame me for something I didn't do. But I'll take whatever comes at me to expose the truth. And I'll do it for you, and all those innocent lives that have been affected. If we can be together, and build a future based on trust and honesty, it'll all be worth it.'

Clues would align, and maybe they'd reveal a plot that went deeper than they knew. As they pieced the puzzle together, Molly's conviction of Robin's innocence came up, and then it wavered again, when she saw Clara's words in her head. Her trust in him was tested time and again.

With each setback she threw at him, Robin laughed at her and was steadfast. He never faltered in his commitment to proving his innocence. And he had an answer for everything that made sense in the warmth of her living room. She wondered how valid it would seem under the harsh fluorescent lighting of the incident room.

'I don't know what's waiting for us, Rob. But I want you to know that I'm so happy tonight. You've shown me that sometimes you have to take that leap for what you believe in.'

She heard herself and knew that with every word she sounded more like an idiot. It was pathetic. She'd laughed with Phil about Clara's naivety and stupidity—and here she was playing Cathy to his Heathcliffe, and she was worse than Clara had ever been.

At least she hadn't bought the Lady Haversham wedding dress yet. But she bet she could pick one up cheap enough on the internet.

'Molly, you've taught me the power of trust, and the strength of the human spirit. No matter what happens, I'll cherish the time we've had together.'

Puke. Shoot me now, she thought. And then she remembered that there was a good chance that Robin has access to guns.

'Let's get out of here. I want to take you to one of my favourite places. Get some outdoor clothes on and brew a flask of coffee,' he said. It wasn't a request. It was an order.

What had Clara called him? Flaskman. 'But it's raining.'

'My darling, that's the best time, it's oppressive in here, and you have all the weight of your job on your shoulders. Let me take you to a clearing in the woods and I can virtually promise you the greatest show on earth. In one clearing, on a night like this, they'll all be out. We'll see badgers and their young, foxes, fallow deer, rabbits, and hares, pipistrels and maybe an owl or two.'

He saw the uncertainty on her face.

'You have to trust me, my darling. It's starts now. If I wanted to kill you. I could wrap my hands around your throat and do it right here. Believe me, you'd be a lot more manageable dead. I want to show you my world, and what we can have together. Do you trust me? Can you?'

He was doing it. That thing. He was taking her to the woods in the middle of the night, and every instinct screamed at her that she wouldn't come out alive. But he looked at her, and his eyes were brown, pits of coercion. She'd go to the ends of the earth for him while she was in this strange trance state, and if she didn't come out? Well, it would be worth it to see a mother badger and her young.

She was mentally going through the understairs cupboard to remember if her wellies were in there, and she had a warm hat somewhere.

'Well?'

'Yes.'

Chapter Thirty-One

Nash got home. He was in a rush, and Lola greeted him at the door, twining around his legs. His cat was indicative of home and he spoke softly to her.

'Hello, my beautiful girl. Yes, I'll feed you. You know you're the only lady for me, don't you? But your uncle Kel's coming soon, so I've got to get on.'

Kel was due in less than half an hour, but the days of Nash dropping his briefcase in the hall were long gone. Since his ex-had violated both his privacy and a high-profile case by selling stories to the press, he'd developed a new OCD ritual.

Nash unlocked his office door, and then his wall safe, and he put his briefcase inside. Before spinning the combination three times—once would never be enough. He replaced the framed yellow and green Mark Rothko print and wiped it free of his fingerprints with a soft duster and a squirt of Pledge. If the safe was touched, his prints wouldn't confuse the issue. He locked up his office in reverse.

Rushing into the kitchen, he put the kettle on. The switch flicked back up into the off position. He turned it on again, and it turned off.

'What the hell?' he said out loud.

The lights flickered. He had multi-spots all over the room, and they went insane, turning on and off in random psychedelic patterns.

His Alexa pod turned on, and its blue circular light lit up the space around it like a halo. Then the damndest thing happened. Alexa spoke to him without prompting.

'Danger. Danger. Danger. Danger. Danger.'

'Alexa. Off.'

Alexa ignored his prompt and kept screaming the word danger at him. He turned it off at the wall.

And it came back to life.

'Go. Go. Go. Go. Go. Go.'

The phone rang in the lounge, and in his frustration, he ignored it.

It rang for ages, competing with the stupid pod, and the flickering lights. He needed it to stop ringing so he could call an electrician. As he got to it, the ringing stopped. His Bang & Olufsen music centre, a hundred-flashing-light monstrosity out of the nineties, turned on. It played Bach, and the volume increased until it was at full power and deafening. It was loud, and Nash covered his ears. Lola was terrified and ran away to hide.

The phone rang, and he rushed to answer it. He shouted at the top of his voice, 'Nash speaking,' but the music had stopped making him feel foolish.

'For a clued-up police officer, you are the stupidest man I know. And that's coming from me, never mind Max's opinion of you,' Conrad Snow said.

'Excuse me?'

'Max has been trying to get your attention. He's got her. Hill's got Molly. He's at her house.'

Nash was motion.

He hung up without another word and grabbed his jacket. As he opened the front door, Kel was coming up the drive. Nash left the door open for him and shouted as he ran. 'Got to go. Help yourself.'

He got in the car and thumbed his radio.

'All units. Officer down. Repeat. Officer down. Get to Molly Brown's house. Now. Twenty-five Queen Street, Dalton. Hill's got her.'

The radio was alive with responses. Nash turned on his blues and twos and made it from Walney to Dalton in eleven minutes.

As per their training, the house was surrounded, and four officers covered the door, one held the red enforcer to break it down.

The air was electric with danger. Detective Nash ran to join his team of backup officers, their expressions were tense, and their eyes fixed on the door. They'd reached a critical juncture, and Brown's life rested on the next few minutes. The time for action had come.

Nash's voice was steady as he whispered instructions to his team.

This was his fault. He'd allowed Molly to put herself in danger. He was outwardly calm, and the guys would never know his inner turmoil and the guilt he felt. 'All right, everyone. This is it. Robin Hill is inside that house, and we're taking him down. Remember, this is a high-risk arrest. Be prepared for anything.'

'Shouldn't we wait and get the negotiator in,' Patel asked.

'No. I want Brown out of there. Now.'

The officers nodded, gripping their weapons. Their muscles were primed for action. The fear in the air was palpable. This was one of their own.

Nash gave the signal to breach the door.

Patel rammed The Enforcer against Molly Brown's dark blue front door. It crashed open, and splinters flew inwards to scatter on her lounge carpet. The team stormed the house, working on adrenaline and training. Molly was fighting her way into Wellington boots and was hopping on one leg. She sprawled against the wall as the noise from the door being rammed open startled her.

Robin Hill looked from Molly to the officers storming the small room and tackling him to the floor. 'You betrayed me?' he said to Molly. He offered no resistance as four of them pinned his limbs to prevent harm, and a fifth cuffed him with his hands behind his back.

Nash's voice blared across the room, the urgency in his tone was unmistakable. 'Robin Hill, I am arresting you on suspicion of the murder of Clara Watts, and Megan Hartley. And the kidnapping of Officer Molly Brown. You do not have to say anything, but anything you do say may be used in evidence against you in a court of law.'

Molly had screamed, but now she was furious. 'What are you doing? Let him go. Of course, he hasn't kidnapped me. Nash, for God's sake.'

'I'm innocent,' Hill said.

Nash thumbed his radio and sent word to the station to be ready. 'We have confirmation. Hill has been arrested. We're bringing him in.'

Robin's expression hardened. His gaze fixed on the officers as they dragged him to his feet, but in contradiction to that, his voice was soft as he spoke to Molly. 'Molly, listen to me, my darling. I need you to trust me. I'm innocent. Believe in me and we can find another way out of this together.'

Molly hesitated, and Nash saw the feelings she'd developed for Hill in a blaze of recognition, and his heart sank. He could see the war playing across her features as she was torn between her duty and her feelings for Robin. She knew the risks, and the consequences of harbouring a suspect, and yet she was having to be held back by two of her colleagues. 'Let him go. I'm warning you, Nash. Let him go.' The officers closed in with their weapons drawn against her and her instincts kicked in, forcing her to protect herself. 'You might as well know now, Nash. I quit. I'm giving up the force to be with Rob.'

Phil tried to push through the team to get to Hill, or Brown—or both, and he stopped dead in the middle of the small room packed with people. Officers took his arms and he fought to get out of their way. 'Molly, what are you saying? Have you gone mad? He's a killer.'

He tried to get to Hill. 'What have you done to her, you monster? Have you touched her? I'm telling you, if you've harmed one hair on her head, I'll kill you.'

'I love him, Phil. I'm sorry for hurting you.'

'Oh, you haven't hurt me, sweetheart. You disgust me.'

Renshaw dropped to his knees, defeated.

'Get him out of here. Patel, take him home.' Nash said. 'And get that bastard into the van. The show's over.'

Molly had reached for Hill, and despite relaxing their hold on her, and putting her in potential danger again, her friends let her hold his hand. The moment hung in the air, teetering on the edge of a precipice. Then, with determination and anguish, Molly came to a decision. Despite it not being her place she took control and released her grip on Robin's hand. She raised her hands in surrender.

'I'm a police officer,' she called out, her voice carrying the weight of her decision. 'At least for tonight, I am. You can stand down and release me. Rob's under arrest, and you can take him away.'

Nash and his team moved fast, their movements calculated and precise as they took Hill outside.

Robin's eyes locked with Molly's, and Nash was glad to see the expression of betrayal cross his face. Hill nodded, accepting the inevitable. He relaxed against the handcuffs, sealing his fate. And he was meek as the officers led him away. Nash was sad for Brown. She'd fallen for a monster and believed in him. But when the chips were down, despite her talk of resigning, she was an officer first. And she was the final instrument of his capture. Nash had never admired her more or felt as much pride in her.

'I know this wasn't easy for you. But you did the right thing. We'll take it from here.'

'I wanted to believe in him. I thought he was innocent.'

'He isn't, Molly. Sometimes, people surprise us. But our duty is to justice, and to protect the innocent. To protect you. He's dangerous, sweetheart. You made the right decision and did what you had to.'

As the officers left with Hill in custody, Molly stood with Nash. It was over, they had him, and her heart was broken.

'My resignation stands, Nash. I'll have the letter on your desk in the morning. I did my duty and I'm finished. I did what I had to—but that doesn't mean I won't stand by him. I love him, Si.'

Nash couldn't believe how it could happen so fast. Brown was the most down-to-earth officer he had. How the hell had Hill got under her skin?—And so thoroughly, it was frightening.

He thought back to his online dating experience with the killer and conman and gave thanks that Snow had warned him off.

Molly was in her winter coat, with one wellie on, the fire was in the grate and still burning, though it had died down to embers. The room was stifling—but Molly was trembling.

'Come on DI Brown. You're coming home with me.'

'No, Nash. I want to be alone.'

He put a pair of shoes in front of her. 'No, you don't. Come on.'

He led her out to his car among the staring neighbours, and Molly crumpled against him, letting herself be led.

At the house, Kelvin met them in the hall. He wore Nash's frilly pinny—a gift from the team's Secret Santa last year. Kelvin kissed him on the cheek. Without saying anything, he took Molly's other arm and helped lead her into the lounge.

'Another one for dinner, then. Good job I made plenty. Cottage pie, just the thing for putting things right.'

Molly snorted, and Nash mouthed in a stage whisper over her head, 'She's had a bit of an upset.'

'Good job I did dessert, as well, then.'

'I am here, you know,' Molly said.

Days turned into weeks, and the investigation pressed forward. The evidence against Hill mounted, connecting him to a web of criminal activities and fraud that went far deeper than anyone had imagined. The revelations were both shocking and heart-breaking, shaking Molly's faith in her judgment.

Brown had bypassed Nash and put her letter of resignation on Lewis' desk the day after Hill's arrest.

'Nash warned me this was coming,' Lewis said. Bronwyn couldn't do this sitting down it needed the brevity of being stood up. She picked up the envelope as Brown shuffled her feet, and she tore it into little pieces and threw them in the air. 'I don't accept that Brown. I'm not losing one of my best officers. And I'm especially not losing one of my best officers to a mere man.'

'You can't say that ma'am. It's discriminatory.'

'And there she is. There's our Brown.'

'I'm leaving the force, ma'am.'

'No, you aren't. All joking aside now though. Obviously, you're off the case. That goes without saying. You will have no contact with Hill. He's being held on remand, and you will not be granted visiting or even mailing rights. Due to the sensitivity of your involvement, we are denying him phone and internet privileges.'

'You can't do that.' Two pinpoints of colour flared in Brown's cheeks as the indignation rose.

'Oh, believe me, I can. If I have to tie you up, to stop you seeing that monster, I will.'

'He's not a monster. We're going to get married.'

'Oh, Molly. Love. He's guilty. We have a pile of evidence as long as your arm, and people coming forward all the time. Yesterday we spoke to a young man who has been on anti-depressants for six years because Hill took his life apart. He was only twenty-eight, that's how powerful this man's reach is. That young man had his whole life ahead of him and has never got over being robbed of his life savings—and his love. We have enough evidence and hard witnesses to do him and his wife for the credit card scams and leading the fraud ring. But, that's not all honey.' She put her arms around Brown and pulled her into her bosom. 'Yesterday they found three more bodies at the nature reserve. He's evil Molly. You'll see that in time.'

'You've got him all wrong.'

'No, Brown. Get a grip. You've got him wrong. Look, I'm putting you on the desk for a few weeks. Don't see it as a punishment—it's not, it's healing. And, this is non-negotiable, you are seeing a counsellor, starting today. If you need garden leave, I'll arrange it, and there will be a psyche evaluation at regular intervals.'

'No. That's not fair.'

'Molly, we care about you. I promise you, every single officer in this building has your back. We're going to get you through this. I'm no shrink, but you're suffering a form of Stockholm Syndrome and brainwashing. You need de-programming. That's going to take time—but you know what? We've got you. Now go and talk to your friends. They're waiting for you.'

As she opened the door, the corridor was lined with her colleagues. They chanted her name, slapped her on the back, and gave her a round of applause for no reason, other than she was one of their own. When they were done, Nash was waiting for her. He opened his arms and she ran into them.

'It's going to be all right, Molly.'

Chapter Thirty-Two

Over the next few weeks, Brown threw herself into work, determined to find closure. The days were long and filled with interviews, forensic analysis, and the unyielding pursuit of the truth in other cases. But amidst the chaos, there was a void and a lingering ache for the man who'd taken her for a fool and deceived her.

They found a loaded rifle in the boot of his car, rope, gaffer tape, chloroform, cable ties, and a shovel. If she'd gone with him that night, Molly was never coming out of that wood. The knowledge of that sobered her and brought her to her senses. Hill's semen was found in one of the more recent male corpses, and other DNA from a bite mark tied him to one of the others.

Days turned into weeks, and the investigation intensified. The evidence against Hill was irrefutable, linking him to a string of crimes that had plagued the vulnerable for years.

Molly's heart was heavy with the weight of the truth. The man she'd fallen in love with was a dangerous criminal. He was going to kill her that night after he'd found out she was a police officer, but as the case unfolded, she couldn't shake the lingering affection she'd had for him. The love was gone—she hated him, just like Clara. But the memory of the feelings still burned inside her and made her ache.

One evening, as the sun descended, casting an amber glow over the town, Molly sat alone. The living room was dimly lit, with shadows dancing on the walls, and mirroring the uncertainty filling her mind.

A knock at the door shattered her thoughts, jolting her back to reality. Her heart skipped a beat as she hesitated, not knowing who it was. After that night, she never opened the door without fear crawling up her back. Could it be Hill, escaped, desperate, and seeking refuge—or revenge?

'Who is it?' She called through the wood of her new front door. It was Phil Renshaw. He held a bouquet of flowers, and a bottle of wine, just as he had on their previous encounter.

'Can I come in? Please. It's okay Molly. It isn't what you think. But we do need to clear the air. I've left it until now to let you—you know.'

'Phil, what do you want?'

'I want to know that you're okay.'

Molly's voice quivered. 'I never meant to hurt you.'

'I know. I care about you, and I'll always love you, Molly, whatever happened. I'm here to tell you that I'll be there for you, no matter what.'

'Thanks, Phil. That means a lot after everything, but I'm sensing a, but.'

'Look, can I come in? We've been through too much to have a conversation like this on the doorstep. I have things to tell you, and I want you to hear them from me.'

'A conversation like this? What things?' She opened the door, and they went into the living room.

'Can I get us a drink?' Phil asked.

She nodded and as he had a hundred times before, he went to the correct drawer and got the corkscrew. He took their usual wine glasses from the cupboard on the left. The bog-standard ones, not the good ones. It crossed her mind that she was due a cupboard reshuffle. He handed her a glass and looked awkward. Molly raised an eyebrow. She didn't have the energy left to tell him to spit it out.

'I didn't want you to hear this from somebody else.'

'Right. You've already said that.'

'Sal's pregnant.'

Molly gasped, but only because she wasn't expecting it. It didn't cut her.

'We've... well... things have been better lately. We're going on a second honeymoon.'

Molly stood up, she was going to hug him, but didn't and stood with her arms out. She put them down before he moved. She was pleased for them. The old stabbing agonising jealousy was gone. So was her love for Philip Renshaw. But she did care about him, and she wanted him to be happy. 'Phil.' She choked back the tears. 'I'm happy for you.'

He pulled her into his arms and stroked her hair. 'Molly, I want us to be friends. After what we've been through together, our bond is so strong and I still need you in my life—just not like that. I've told Sal everything.'

'And she's forgiven you? I wouldn't.'

'No, you wouldn't. You'd have removed my balls with a serrated knife while I slept.'

'I want us to be friends too, Phil. But that's not fair on Sal?'

'She understands. She's pretty incredible, you know. It was her that told me to come and talk to you tonight.'

'She's the strong, silent type. You look after her from now on, or you'll have me to answer to.'

'Hypocrite.'

'Too much?'

'Yeah.'

'Sorry.'

'Brown you're a nightmare, but I love you.'

'No, Renshaw. You like me. And I like you. Today is a new start and everything behind us is in the past.'

'I'll drink to that. Sal says she misses you, and now that it's all over, and she understands why you distanced yourself, she'd like to come and see you, to clear the air—she said to tell you there'll be a lot of wine involved, and maybe even the good rum.'

Tears welled up in her eyes. 'That's kind of her. I don't deserve it. We need to make things right, Phil.'

'We do. Too much has happened, but I can't believe you fell for his lies, Molly. You of all people. Don't worry, we'll bring Hill to justice. We've got him down for a long, long stretch.'

When Phil left, Molly felt a deep sense of loss, knowing that her actions had cost her relationship with Phil, but also part of herself. It had all worked out for the best. In a strange way, Hill had freed her. But she still had demons to fight. It felt as though the walls were closing in. The hollow knowledge that the man she'd fallen for was in the crosshairs of justice shamed her as she'd never felt shame before. This was worse than her affair with Phil.

The therapy was helping her redress the lack of balance in her life. Her therapist asked that Molly be allowed back on the case, but very much in the background. She said Molly needed to see how evil Hill was, to help in reprogramming her. And it was crucial that she was involved in the case when he was put away for several life sentences.

Molly was better—not well yet— but improving every day. She had been given restricted access to certain aspects of the case. But only as a backseat observer and under strict supervision, due to her personal involvement. But as a kindness, Bronwyn got permission to let her have copies of the transcripts of the Clara Watts diaries. Brown still felt a close affinity to the murdered woman and was sorry for letting her down. She knew that Clara would have understood.

She threw herself into her work with renewed determination. Every lead was pursued, and every connection unravelled. As the evidence came together, a dark and intricate tapestry of deceit and corruption emerged, intertwining Hill's name with scallies all over Cumbria who had eluded justice for far too long.

With a shared understanding, Brown and Nash embarked on the final phase of the operation. They were both giving evidence at the trial. Everything was meticulously laid out, and the tension in the air was thick with anticipation.

Brown would look him in the eye as she gave her evidence. Anything received during the honeytrap was inadmissible, but the fact that she'd been brainwashed by Hill during it, wasn't.

Brown was going to confront the man who had entangled her in his web of deception. He'd shattered her trust and tested her loyalty to the people that mattered to her.

She was sworn in and spoke in a calm and dispassionate voice, giving the facts as they'd happened. It was nine months since the night at her house when he was arrested and, with the help of a deprogramming course, normally kept for victims of cults, kidnapping and terrorism, her feelings had changed. She didn't love him or despise him. She wanted to fully hate him, but she wasn't there yet. And she still remembered the feel of his arms around her, and the overwhelming safety she'd felt in the monster's embrace. She forced her mind back to the photograph she'd been shown of the boot of his car that night. He looked at her with love—but had chloroform for her in his boot.

At first, Hill simpered and blasted her with his trademark goo-goo eyes. But as she gave evidence against him and thoroughly condemned him, his expression changed. His eyes hardened and he lost his veneer of control.

'You stupid bitch. Do you think I ever wanted you? You're pathetic with your need, and your grabbing hands fawning all over me. You tramp. I despise you. You were weak, just like all the others. No better than a street walker, and so bloody stupid. God, I hate stupid people. You make me sick. I should have killed you when I had the chance.'

'Silence in court,' the judge said.

'I'll get out. And when I do, you'd better watch your back Molly Brown because I'm coming for you.'

'Silence.'

'See me in your dreams, Brown. Because I'm your worst nightmare. I'll get you. I have contacts.'

'Control yourself, Mr Hill, or I'll have you removed from my courtroom,' the judge said.

'You're a sociopath,' Molly told him.

'Oh, at the very least, my darling. Didn't you know?'

'DI Brown, restrict yourself to answering the questions asked by counsel.'

Molly stood in the witness box, and her voice was steady as she recounted her involvement and the profound impact it had on her life.

After she'd given evidence, and read her Victim Impact Statement, Nash, gave her arm a reassuring squeeze. 'You're not alone in this, Molly. We've all got our mistakes to reckon with. What matters now is getting this bastard put away. All this shows is that you're human like the rest of us, and you make mistakes. One day, I expect you're going to step into my shoes, and you'll be fabulous. There's nobody I'd rather hand over to.'

Molly appreciated Nash's words. They were a glimmer of hope piercing her darkness. Most officers had at least one nervous breakdown behind them by the time they made chief, and after this, she was no exception. She had to make amends for the trust she'd misplaced.

Chapter Thirty-Three

Hi Clara, it's me again, Molly.

I hope the sun's shining wherever you are, girl, because it's a good day here. We got the bastard, Clara. Eighty years. He's never going to hurt anybody again. His wife got three, and his two eldest kids got eighteen months apiece. I'd say that was a pretty good result.

They found your friend, Megan, she was in the quarry, just as Conrad Snow predicted. Hill's DNA was all over her. Hey, if you get the chance, you should see if you can give Snow a poke, or whatever it is you guys do to get attention.

It's a comfort writing this diary to you because I know you get me. We're a right pair of idiots, aren't we? It would be good to know you're there, looking down on me. And if you could send a lightning bolt next time I get mixed up with a no-good bastard, it would be appreciated. You were as daft as me, but I trust your judgement and think of you as my guardian angel.

If I think about you before jumping headfirst into something dumb, it'll jolt me to my senses—maybe. That's you being an angel, isn't it?

Did I tell you, I'm an only child? I always wanted a sister, and this may sound stupid, but I think of you as the sister I never had. Your words touched me even before I met our mutual dickhead. I wish I'd known you, and I wish I'd been there to save you, I'm sorry for that.

Anyway. I've to go, I've got a date tonight. Now, don't go yelling at me, you'll damage your voice for all that angelic singing and stuff, and you don't want to dislodge your halo. I didn't meet him on a dating site. He was in the Fish & Chip shop. He recommended the curry sauce. He seems okay. I'm being very sensible and taking it easy.

He's called Danny, and tonight he's taking me bowling. Can you imagine? I'd rather poke my eyes out—but I'm trying new things. He's cute and looks like a rock star, with hair down to his waist and a lot of ink. I think you'd like him. Nash will be mortified. Speaking of which, Hill did have a rose tattoo on his left bicep. God, he had me fooled with all his lies.

I'll write to you again tomorrow and let you know how it went. Who knows, one day I might take Danny to Nash's for one of our dinner nights. Can you imagine?

You can sleep now, Clara, It's over.

Yours united,

Molly.

~~~

DI Molly Brown shut down the computer, applied her red lipstick, and grabbed her coat.

Nobody was going to make her feel worthless again.

'This bitch has balls—and access to the police weaponry,' she said into the streetlights and early evening drizzle.

Printed in Great Britain
by Amazon